THE SHADOWS KNOW

Don Marsh

KDP

CONTENTS

CAST OF CHARACTERS

Hank Tollar--Stars and Stripes reporter
Willi Berkfeldt--Tollar's Frankfurt Assistant
Lieutenant Kurt Wunderlich--Army CID
Marcus M. Marcus--Stars & Stripes Editor
Gene Talbot--RFE News Chief
Tivador "Ted" Domjan--Hank's Munich Assistant
Ilse Stengel--RFE Archivist
Tom Morrow--AFN Reporter
Matthieu "Lucky" Manon--Race Car Driver
Col. Antoine Argoud--Member OAS Leadership
Albert LeClerc--Anti-Gaullist
Pierre Blanchet--Member LeClerc's Cell
Marcel Blanchet--Pierre's brother
J. Harding Bell--Consulate Press Officer
Charles Howell--Consulate Cultural Attaché
Lt. Hans Erbach--Munich Police Department
Captain Dieter Krausweg--Bavarian State Police.
Major Todd Zwilling--Army Criminal Investigation Division (CID).

Guy Dupuis--French Consular Officer
Kay Montgomery--Aspiring Journalist
Istvan--Hungarian refugee
Anton Vesely & Hynek Svoboda--Czech refugees
StB--Czech Secret Police
Fr. Gabriel--Priest
Ross Thomas--Journalist
Nipsy Delgado--Helicopter crewman
Sunny Day--Singer

FOREWORD

I thought I knew what everyone was
doing. But I couldn't see what they were doing.
I was in the light, but they
were in the shadows.
Is clarity possible where there is no
light and only the shadows know?
And, when there is light, does it
illuminate, or does it create more shadows?
It's complicated.
It began sixty years ago in a nervous
and troubled part of the world.
H.T.

PREFACE

West Germany in the early 1960s was a study in contrasts. There remained significant visible damage left over from the war. Pockets of rubble, neatly placed by the fastidiously industrious population, were still visible within sight of modern city buildings, roads and bridges...daily reminders of the consequences of war...and peace. The economic miracle, the "Wirtschaftswunder," had taken a firm grasp on the country's way of life. But even a miracle can only move so quickly.

In the countryside, it was not rubble reminding a sullen population of the bad old days. The memories there were in bountiful remembrance of lost fathers, sons and neighbors.

In the early part of the decade announcers on a daily radio broadcast were still reciting the names of missing soldiers in the long faded hope someone might offer some sort of closure.

It was just another reminder of the Nazi era. The nation's guilt was intensified early in the

decade when the engineer who drove the Holo-
caust train was seized by Israeli agents. Adolph
Eichmann's capture and subsequent hanging was
the subject of an emotional debate when young
Germans born after the war wondered why they
should be made to suffer the nation's humiliation
for crimes committed before they were born?

And there was continued division on a much
broader scale. The old Germany had been quar-
tered then halved by post war agreements. The
eastern half, the German Democratic Republic,
the GDR, was overseen by German communist
puppets whose strings were being pulled from
Moscow

The new Federal Republic of Germany was
presided over from a village in the middle of the
Western Zone by an old man. *Der Alte*, Konrad
Adenauer, paid close attention to American, British and French friends who gave up their occu-
pational control to stage-manage creation of the
new Germany.

Americans were everywhere. Tens of thousands of GIs, diplomats, bureaucrats and many of
their families settled throughout the country in
what promised to be a permanent presence. They
were entertained and informed by the American
Forces Network, the U.S. government radio network manned by GIs and civilian broadcasters.
Also by the Stars and Stripes, a military newspaper, formatted for military men and women

and their dependents. A little touch of home.

But, all eyes were on the eastern border, where the big guns on Russian tanks pointed west, an omnipresent threat to rumble to the English Channel. The Americans, with tanks pointed east, were the stop sign.

Berlin, the former capital, was a de facto island in the Eastern Zone. The island was divided into four sectors, the American, British, French and Russian. In August of 1961, the German Democratic Republic (GDR), tired of throngs of its citizens choosing the allied hospitality and opportunities in West Berlin, began construction of a wall to keep them "home." It was a ninety-six mile barrier that so closely followed the sector border that in places it was literally constructed through the middle of homes . It was at the Berlin Wall that John Kennedy declared himself a "Berliner." He went home, The Wall stayed, and he was assassinated before the year 1963 was out.

This was the Germany of the 1960s. It was a country trying to pull itself together in so many ways. On the one hand, it was a thriving new nation taking a more and more prominent place on the world stage. On the other, it was a paranoid puppet state that posed the threat of disruption, and even war, every single day. It was a place of frustration, deceit and espionage, and a literary cornucopia for the likes of John le Carré, Len

Deighton and others.

It was just part of the world tumult of the time. Colonialism was coming to a bloody end in Africa. France was reeling in the violence and torture that was an overture to Algerian independence. The country was wounded by loyalists supporting de Gaulle, and anti-Gaullists longing for a return to Algerian subjugation. The French leader survived some thirty assassination attempts.

In the background, although it would not be known until years later, the US and France were at odds over American intelligence information from a purported Soviet defector saying the French government and military were riddled with Russian agents. De Gaulle did not believe the Americans. The very existence of the NATO Alliance was threatened.

The Brits were struggling with de Gaulle's France on Common Market membership.

Vietnam was pinging on America's radar.

But the biggest world threat was the prospect of nuclear confrontation between the United States and the Soviet Union. And, the world worried that if it came, the trigger would be Germany, and especially Berlin.

Yes, Germany in the early sixties was a cauldron: a grab bag of conflicting ambitions, intrigue and loyalties that touched every part of Germany and beyond.

PART ONE

CHAPTER 1

Hank Tollar was a young journalist who would be recording "the first draft" of modern German history as a fledgling reporter with the Stars and Stripes, the military newspaper for members of the armed services and dependents. He was excited and enthusiastic to immerse himself in the country's history...past, present and future when he arrived in Frankfurt am Main at the beginning of the decade of the sixties. He did not know he would be a part of that history.

It was not an auspicious start. He was the new kid in town and got the newbie assignments. His days were filled with military news conferences, military ceremony and military wives' garden clubs. But Hank made friends easily. He was good looking, gregarious, had a good sense of humor and didn't complain. His co-workers liked him from the start and helped him get the lay of the land, both professionally and socially. He was smart enough to know that sooner rather than later he would transition from "newbie" assignments and put his journalistic talent and passable German to a more professionally satisfying use.

And, he was available when a small military plane went down a few miles east of the Frankfurt suburb of Hanau. It had been on a routine reconnaissance flight along the East German border. Such flights were commonplace, a means of tracking Soviet and East German communications along the border, as well as eyeballing any significant troop or armor movements. The plane, manned by a crew of three, had exploded in the air and crashed into a mound of flame in a sparsely wooded area.

When Hank and his German photographer Willi Berkfeldt arrived, Army teams were on the scene as well as several curious area resident onlookers. The military's biggest concern was not the obvious lost cause of the plane and crew, but rather in gathering various manuals and schematics related to the plane's sophisticated technology always carried on board. The plane's explosion had unleashed a snowstorm of small and large pieces of classified confetti blowing in the wind for hundreds of yards around the crash site. It was important that none of it fall into the wrong hands. Willi, an old hand on the post war beat, reminded Hank that both the Russians and

East Germans would highly value such a techno-logical trove.

"Believe me," said Willi nodding toward a group of some thirty to forty Germans, "more than one of the local folks would be more than happy to sell that paperwork. It would not be difficult to find a buyer. There are agents and sympathizers all over the country." He watched the group closely.

Hank looked at him incredulously. "What? It's hard to believe anyone in this part of Germany would want to do business with anyone in the East."

"Number one," answered Willi, "there are a lot of Germans in the West who have relatives on the other side. They might hope to strike a bar-gain to bring them over here. Number two, a lot of these people hate Americans."

"You're kidding."

"They blame them for destruction, the death of loved ones, and for their occupation of Germany."

"Occupation?" asked Hank. "Who would look at it that way. I think most people would consider the Americans the guys who are keeping the Russkis from taking over the whole place and who are helping to rebuild."

"Most people would," said Willi pointing his camera toward the small crowd. "but some don't." He snapped several pictures.

4

"Why are you taking pictures of them?" asked Hank.

"See that lieutenant over there?" Willi asked pointing with his chin toward an officer with two soldiers several yards away.

Hank nodded.

"He's an intelligence officer. I know him. And, it's only a matter of time before he asks me to take a picture. I'll give it to him, and he and his crew will check out who's here, and who perhaps should not be."

Hank shook his head. "Wait a minute. Are you working for the lieutenant or for the paper?" He put his hands on his hips. "There's an issue here. Journalists are supposed to be on the outside looking in...not working and cooperating with people we're covering. We work just one side of the street." Hank was getting hot. What was happening was an uncomfortable, ethical concession to him.

Willi looked at Hank through eyes that had narrowed. It was not a friendly look and it was not lost on Hank.

"I don't see any streets here," said Willi..." just a burning plane probably with three or four bodies inside. I see a crowd of people who may just be a group of bystanders. Maybe one or two are more interested in what's going on than the others...more interested than they should be. If there are...I want to know about it, and I want that lieutenant to know about it too and do something about it if it comes to that." He put hand on Hank's shoulder. His expression had softened. "Keep in mind that the *street* in this case is in Germany...my Germany. I don't want it to be what it was a few years ago, and I sure don't want it to be what it's like on the other side of the border." He paused. "Journalistic ethics can be different here. They have to be."

"Do they?" said Hank. "Start making concessions, even small ones and you're right back where you don't want to be. Seems to me that's how the whole mess got started here thirty years ago."

"Hank...you are a young man. When you're older, you'll learn a lot more about concessions...and perhaps even ethics. But I would...respectfully...suggest that you not lecture me...or anyone who lived through those years."

Hank stared at the older man and nodded his head slowly, not sure if Willi would interpret it as agreement, or understanding, or both. He wasn't sure himself. Willi was a middle aged German, old enough to have memories of the War, and perhaps old enough to have fought in it. Hank, who had only worked with Willi on a few previous occasions, had not yet felt comfortable enough to have asked. But he knew in that moment that he would...that he had to.

"They've got something over there," said

Willi looking at a pair of GIs gesturing near a smoldering tree fifty feet away. They were calling for a sergeant who had been collecting documents found scattered around the countryside by teams of two. The photographer and the reporter walked slowly over to the two GIs who were staring at the nearby tree.

As they neared it, they were aware of an unusual smoking lump in the middle of the trunk. Hank looked at it closely. What eventually came into focus made his stomach churn. He took a few steps away and threw up as Willi's camera recorded the scene. What had come into focus in both Hank's eyes and Willi's Leica was a smoldering rib cage; a human torso. It had been one of the plane's occupants, apparently blown from the craft when it had exploded. There was nothing more than the torso. Hank threw up again when he realized the rest of the body was undoubtedly scattered in pieces around the area.

The lieutenant came over a few minutes later and shook his head as he absorbed what was still smoldering on the tree. He turned away without speaking and sidled up to Willi. He gestured toward the small crowd of Germans who had been drawn to the crash site and looked toward Willi, lifting his eyes. It was a question. Willi nodded once in response. "I'll get a print to you as soon as I get back," he said.

"What do you know about this?" Hank

asked the lieutenant.

He offered a tired smile. "About as much as you do," he said. "We've got a reconnaissance plane down. Three aboard. All dead." He looked at the tree. "Two are still aboard, but this poor motherfucker was apparently blown out. We know, according to witnesses, it exploded at about two hundred feet. What we don't know is whether it was a malfunction or sabotage. What we do know is that we've got to find any and all technological information that didn't burn up, and any bits and pieces of the sensitive equipment scattered around...before anyone else does." He looked closely at Hank. "Now that I've told you that, forget it. Your story is a small military plane has crashed, three are dead, the military is investigating. The rest of it is not for publication."

"Can you tell me anything about the reconnaissance flights?" Hank asked timidly.

"No!" barked the officer.

"Picture?" asked Hank.

"Me?"

Hank nodded.

"No way."

"What's your name?" asked Hank.

"Lieutenant Kurt Wunderlich...not for publication."

He paused and took one step toward Hank and put a single finger on his chest. "Got all that?"

Hank swallowed hard. "Got it," he said

8

softly, realizing that journalism in this time and place, was going to be a lot different from what he'd learned in J-school.

The lieutenant glared at Hank. "Good," he said. "Just remember we both work for the same company." He then extended his hand. "What's your name?" his tone more friendly.

Hank shook the officer's hand. "Hank...Hank Tollar."

"Nice to meet you. I'll look forward to reading your story tomorrow" he said as he turned and walked away. To Hank he still sounded friendly but he also took the comment as a warning.

"See," said Willi, "same company. We're all on the same side of that street you mentioned."

"I'm going to talk to some of those people," said Hank gesturing toward the onlookers. "Come on over. You can get some close ups."

Hank was feeling a lot better about his story after talking to some of the Germans who had seen the plane go down. They gave him enough material to flush out details of the story that Wunderlich had insisted be edited. Or as Hank called it, "censored."

"What do you know about Lt. Wunderlich?" he asked Willi as the older man drove them back to the office. "With a name like Kurt Wunderlich he sounds more German than the people I just interviewed."

"Not quite," said Willi, "but close." He hit the horn to chase a wagon drawn by an ox to the side of the road. "He was born in Germany but left with his parents as a small child in the early thirties. They got out before it really got nasty and made it to the United States...Milwaukee I think. His family spoke German at home. He's fluent. They loved that when he joined the Army just as Korea was winding down, and it was a natural that he found himself in the Army CID...Criminal Investigation Division. It was just as natural that he wound up here." He turned to Hank. "He's a good guy, but he goes by the book and won't take any crap."

Hank thought about the officer's demeanor during their brief conversation.

"I've known him for a long time," said Willi. "He can be intimidating, but he's a good guy. If you play your cards right and play nice with him, he might even become a source some day."

"He loosened up a little at one point," said Hank, "but I don't think he's going to be reading my story tomorrow as a friend."

"You're right. But if you do right by him, he'll begin to trust you. It will take time, but that's the way it worked with me."

"How did you meet him?"

"On a story. Like you. He asked me to take some pictures at a rape-murder scene. He would have gotten them from his own people eventually, but I was there before they were and he was impatient. The pictures turned out to be helpful." He looked at Hank. "Those photos would never have made the paper in case you're having another case of ethical heartburn. Too brutal for most readers. Editors would never have signed on. So I was not playing on the *other side of the street*." He looked at Hank expecting a reaction.

"Okay...okay...I get it," said Hank, embarrassed.

They drove on for a few minutes. "Your story like his?"

"No. I left Germany in the forties. I also went to America. As a guest of the United States Army. I was in the Wehrmacht. Not by choice. I was captured, thank God, at Anzio. Do you know anything about Anzio?" he asked Hank.

"I know it was a big deal and one of the war's major battles."

"It was indeed. It lasted for six months... back and forth. Bloody. I was thrilled to be captured. And while it went back and forth, I was held behind the lines, I think for twenty days. Then it was over...for me. I was put on a plane, then a boat, and then shipped off with other prisoners. I wound up in a POW camp in Belleville, Illinois.

"Belleville, Illinois?"

"Pretty good spot...unless you wanted to escape. It was a long way back to Germany. Trust me, nobody I knew there wanted to escape. The food was good. It was easy work. We helped make K-rations for the Army. We had plenty of time to study. They even had classes. They were happy to teach us English. Typically American. They taught us English so they didn't have to learn German. We practiced on the guards and on the local kids who came up to the wire on their bicycles to gawk at *the Nazis*."

"Sounds like a country club."

"It wasn't bad. I was a good student and was recruited when the war ended to work for the Army at Nuremberg during the trials. Translator. I didn't like the Nazis before and during the war, and liked them even less when I met the defendants in Nuremberg and learned what they had been up to while I was shitting in my pants in combat. If we had known at Anzio, I guarantee we all would have been waiting with open arms when the Allies hit the beaches in '44. Anyway I made it to Nuremberg and have been working for the Americans ever since."

"Wow, that's one helluva story," said Hank shaking his head. "It's a book." He looked closely at Willi, seeing him differently than he had earlier. "Any family?"

"Everybody died in the war. Dresden. What's left of the city is in the East now. I never married. Came close once, but that's another story," he said as he parked the car at the Stars and Stripes building. Hank thought to himself that was a story he wanted to hear, but it would have to wait.

CHAPTER 2

Military Plane Down Near Hanau...3 Dead
Hank Tollar

Military authorities are investigating the explosion/crash of a modified Grumman Mohawk border reconnaissance aircraft near the town of Hanau. All three crewmen aboard the aircraft were killed. They have not been identified pending notification of kin.

Investigators are unable to explain why the plane exploded and are not commenting on its mission described only as a routine reconnaissance flight.

Startled residents who converged on the scene moments after the plane went down say the aircraft exploded in the air some two hundred feet off the ground while en route to the Frankfurt airport.

Guenther Gronau, a local farmer said he heard the first explosion and saw the fiery aircraft plummet into the field a few hundred yards behind his barn. He told the Stars and Stripes that there was a secondary explosion and fire when the plane hit the ground.

Residents who lived nearby quickly converged on the crash site but were unable to approach the wreckage or attempt possible rescue because of the heat and flames.

The wreckage was still burning when Army investigators arrived on the scene. The site has been sealed for half a mile around the crash scene while the investigation continues. Local farmers have complained because they are unable to get to their fields. An Army spokesman said the wreckage will be removed as soon as possible and the site will then be reopened to local land owners.

Hank's story in the following day's paper was short, factual, and in Hank's mind full of holes he wanted to fill. He had had a long talk about it with his editor who subscribed to the Wunderlich version. "Think of it this way," he said. "We always know more than we can put in a story. We're in the business of informing GIs, their wives and kids...not the Commies. We have to keep that in mind. We are at war. They call it a *Cold War* but it's still a war."

So that's the way it's going to be thought

Hank. He wondered if correspondents for the New York Times, the Tribune, Time Magazine and other premier publications were playing by the same rules. Some of the biggest names in journalism were in Germany, primarily Bonn and Berlin. "Are they restricted in what they report?" asked Hank.

"Only if they want to stay in country," answered the editor. "Most of them are savvy enough to know when they're getting close to the line. They know the Embassy keeps a close eye on their stuff."

He could see disappointment in Hank's expression. "Think about it Hank. In the last war military censors had control over press dispatches, photographs, letters from GIs. It was heavy duty censorship.

"There was also an official Office of Censorship. A lot of big stories didn't get told until much later. The Manhattan Project for instance. Censors scoured everything to keep that quiet and even worked with papers and radio stations to make sure nothing leaked that might be helpful to the enemy. And, it worked until the lid was lifted after Hiroshima and Nagasaki."

He folded his hands and leaned toward Hank. "Like I say Hank. We're at war now...a different kind of war...but we've got to be realistic and think about what some words would or could mean to our friends over there," he said pointing his thumb toward the border. The Censorship Office is long gone. Now we self-police."

"What about that plane going down would jeopardize anything?" asked Hank petulantly. "The Russians know we fly up and down the border and that we watch and listen."

"But they don't know exactly what kind of equipment we're using, and what we have available that's new. They would love to pick apart that plane...or what's left of it...to learn more. They'd like to know who's leading the investigation. Maybe it's someone they could compromise. They might like to know the surveillance schedule so they can mind themselves during an overflight.

"Intelligence doesn't come in one pretty package tied up with a nice bow. It comes in bits and pieces and is put together like a jigsaw puzzle until, voila, there's a clear picture. Two pages of a hundred page technical manual blowing around in that farmer's field could be a last piece. That's why we don't need to tell them the CID is scrambling to corral everything it can."

Hank sat silently absorbing what he had just heard. "Okay boss, I get it," he finally said. He stood and managed a smile. "I guess I'll have to put my Pulitzer on hold. For a while." He chuckled.

The editor smiled. "I was one of those guys in the war who had a lot of my stuff killed. It hurts. I don't know how many of my Pulitzers went down the drain." He had a funny, high pitched laugh. Hank wasn't sure whether he was kidding or not.

"I'm very careful about my friends...or I should say about the people I choose as friends." It was Willi lifting a one liter mug of beer at a local tavern, or *Gasthaus* as the Germans called their neighborhood drinking establishments. He was talking to Hank as they had stopped for lunch after an assignment.

"That came out of nowhere," said Hank as he lifted his own mug. "Why do you make that point?" He took a deep swallow.

"I know you've been making German friends. And, that's great. But as this whole Eichmann business shows us more than ever, this is a divided country. The commies want to turn this country upside down and take it over. There are plenty of Nazis still around and they have their own agenda. The point is you've got to learn whom to trust. For the most part, I don't trust anyone I don't really know. Sometimes even the ones I do know."

"Whoa...whoa," said Hank running the back of his hand across his mouth after a generous swallow. "You're going too fast for me. Communists? Nazis? Eichmann? He's on trial. The Nazis are done. And...everyone knows about the commies."

"The Nazis aren't done. They're just dormant. There are still plenty of them around. They've taken off their armbands and uniforms and meet by themselves to remember the 'good old days.' And, a lot of them are people in high places. That's why Adenauer has been so concerned about the Eichmann trial. He's scared to death Eichmann might start naming names and that some of those names might be people in the Chancellery, the Foreign Service, the Federal Intelligence Service...BND...and municipal governments around the country. A lot of the Nazi functionaries were trained bureaucrats, just right to step in when a new Germany was being built. There was a lot of looking the other way. I'm sure you've been reading that our friends in the East were eager to fund Eichmann's defense hoping to learn things that could be used to embarrass Bonn."

"Yeah, I've read some of it," said Hank. "But even with the Eichmann trial, most Americans consider Nazis old news."

"Well, they're not," said Willi slamming his big glass mug loudly on the wooden table for emphasis. "You haven't been here all that long. As you get to know more and more people, you won't find any who will admit to any Nazi connection...family...friends. They don't even admit having fought against the Allies. Everyone I talk to fought against the Russians on the Eastern

Front. I guarantee you the people in the East are saying they fought against the Allies." He took another swallow of beer. "Just so you know, they're out there and looking for an opportunity to have another chance at raising the flag of National Socialism. If they can use you, they will. So...just keep that in mind."

"Well as a matter of fact I know a girl from Mönchengladbach and she told me her father was a card carrying Nazi. So there," teased Hank.

"Then I'll bet the father's dead," said Willi raising his eyebrows. "Mom probably was too. Otherwise she wouldn't be talking. And," he raised his finger, "remember the apple doesn't fall far from the tree."

"I don't think so. She was all pissed off about the Eichmann trial and the feeling that she's being blamed for the sins of the past. She was five years old when the war ended." He paused. "Dad is dead, by the way, killed in a bombing."

Willi pursed his lips, remembering the terrible bombing of Dresden in which his family was killed. He looked at Hank. "Who did the bombing...Americans? Brits?"

Hank shrugged his shoulders.

"If it was the Americans, she may resent it. Her mother undoubtedly does if she's still alive. That's what I mean. Just be careful around her. Get to know her before you feel you *really* know her."

"Okay, now that you have me totally paranoid about Nazis in the woodpile, what about my other friends. Are those who aren't Nazi sympathizers, commies?"

Willi laughed. "I don't want to make you paranoid...just careful and alert. This country is crawling with people with communist sympathies...for all sorts of reasons. They like the system, or hate the West...or have friends or relatives trapped on the other side of the curtain. They'd deal to help them. Or they have no allegiance. They just sell what they know. Their currency is information. They have their eyes open for anything they can use or sell." He finished his beer. "Believe me, they're all over the place. Just be careful of people asking a lot of questions." He put down his mug.

"Ready to go?"

Hank took a final swallow. "Yeah...I'm ready to go...ready to go to a cave with a good book, and wait for the world to straighten itself out."

"When you find that cave," said Willi standing, "let me know. I'll join you."

The world was nowhere near to being straightened out. Neither Hank nor Willi would have a chance to find that cave. No one knew what lay ahead, or what fuses were being lit. The Bay of Pigs, Russian missiles in Cuba, an ugly wall, assassinations, and jungles beckoning half a world away. When Hank arrived in Germany, the world was restless and dangerous and simmering. And, when the thermometer rose, the temperature was always highest in Europe. Especially Germany.

Hank Tollar's world was about to change. His days of attending garden parties and change of command ceremonies were largely over. He was becoming a familiar byline in the Stars and Stripes. It was a busy, exciting and fulfilling professional life. He was barely twenty-five and was...if not exactly in the middle of...certainly on the fringes of major events in the history of the second half of the 20th century. He felt he was on his way.

And he was. To Munich. It was not the assignment he wanted, but it was the assignment he got.

"I'm disappointed," he told his editor. "I was hoping for Berlin. That's where the action is."

His editor was an old timer. Old school. Suspenders. A stained and wrinkled shirt that looked as if a basketball were stuffed into it just above the belt. Tufts of Brillo lined the sides of his otherwise bald pate. His nose was lined with purple veins leading to staffers' correct assumption that there was a bottle stashed in his desk.

Just to complete the picture, a brass spittoon was placed strategically at the back corner of his desk. He was right out of *Front Page* minus a fedora with a card reading "press" tucked into the hatband. His name was Marcus M. Marcus and he had long since grown tired of people making fun of his name. He was, of course, called Marcus.

"Any way the assignment can be changed Marcus?" asked Hank. "Munich doesn't sound very exciting. Seems like I'm being sent farther away from the story."

"Look Hank, I think you'll be pleasantly surprised. Munich's a great city. Bavaria's a great state. Good beer." He laughed and coughed loudly like the veteran smoker he was. Hank shrugged.

"Fact is you're pretty new to this game. I respect your wanting Berlin. But the fact is I've got some veteran guys up there. You need to cut your teeth a little more. Get a little time in grade in Munich, and Berlin...or Bonn...is the likely next stop."

Hank didn't like what he was hearing and it was clear he was not going to change Marcus's, or anyone's mind. He stared blankly ahead.

"The military's all over Bavaria," said Marcus. "Plenty of news. You'll have a keyhole into Eastern Europe through Radio Free Europe. It's headquartered there and produces a lot of information you'll be able to use. Munich's got lots of cultural stuff and lots of history...Nazi history...good feature material."

"I don't want to do features," interrupted Hank. "I feel like it's a step backwards. I thought I was through with that kind of reporting."

"I get it," said Marcus. "I respect the way you think. Fact is this is the way it has to be. Be patient your time will come. This is not a demotion and doesn't indicate we don't think highly of your abilities. It just means that we've got an opening we have to fill in an important part of the country." He paused, observing Hank closely. "If you want to do news...find news. But you're going to have to find it in one of the best places to live in Germany. I promise I'll be keeping you in mind as openings develop."

Hank slapped his thighs. "Okay. That's that I guess. Marcus...thanks for being upfront. I'm going to hold you to thinking of me when the next assignment opens. If you don't, I'm going to start calling you Mark."

Marcus lobbed a load of phlegm into the spittoon. "A one way ticket to oblivion if you do," he said wiping his mouth with his sleeve.

Hank laughed. "It's been a pleasure working with you." He stood and reached across the desk to shake hands.

He's a good kid, thought Marcus. If he holds his own in Munich he's going to be okay...unless Time or the Trib grabs him away from us.

It was Munich that grabbed him. While

significant wartime damage remained, Hank was immediately taken by the medieval city. Amid the scars of war was surviving architecture dating back hundreds of years. Framed by the Alps to the south, and the industrialized north, it was the capital of Bavaria, and an arts and cultural center. Its citizens were a cheerful rosy-cheeked population who dressed in lederhosen and dirndls, the leather shorts and colorful ruffled apron dresses, distinctive to Bavaria for generations.

While many parts of Germany were populated by citizens described as sullen, dour and humorless, Bavaria and Munich broke the mold. The population loved to play and party and Bavarians seemed an outwardly happier kind of German. They welcomed the world to their biggest party, the Oktoberfest, to Fasching, the annual Lenten carnival, and to numerous other festivals that crowded the city's calendar.

They welcomed anyone anytime to visit any of the city's numerous beer halls, as well as its art galleries and museums. They shared long strolls and picnics in the famed Englisher Garten. They drank locally brewed beer a liter at a time, and debated anything debatable, or not, in outdoor cafes in the student and Bohemian district of Schwabing.

While its history was rich, and culture robust, it had been severely sullied after World War One, when the seeds of National Socialism were sown and a young Adolph Hitler harvested the crop. It was in Munich that Nazism was born and flourished. And, where just few miles beyond the city proper, one of Nazism's darkest places...the Dachau concentration camp...was established. It was a prototype for other malevolent places like Auschwitz, Bergen Belsen and Buchenwald.

Hank had visited the Oktoberfest while working out of Frankfurt and that had been his only previous exposure to Munich. He'd been too busy drinking beer to take in much else. But he was a quick study and when he arrived for his new work assignment, he immersed himself in all that the city had to offer. As a young man in a vibrant community with a large population of contemporaries, students who seemed to be everywhere, Hank felt very much at home. It was not long before he lost any sense of resentment for having been given the Munich assignment. Berlin could wait, he thought, as he went about enjoying where he was and all that it had to offer.

The Army was a prominent presence in and around Munich and was a source for much of his day to day writing. Pieces on change of command, maneuvers, accidents and visiting officials from Washington or Bonn, who usually found a way to spend some time in the city, were a staple. To that end, reporting in Munich was a lot like Frankfurt. But there was a lot more to focus on in his new environment.

He found himself writing less hard news in Munich, but developed a taste for, and a flair for, writing features. He mined the region's rich and sometimes sordid history, along with its plethora of available arts and cultural material.

A movie studio, Bavaria Film at nearby Geiselgasteig, provided story after story opportunities as European and American filmmakers utilized the famed historic production facilities. Hank was happy to come to know numerous film stars he had admired for years and watch them perform in person. He was reluctant to admit to friends that he was not immune to being star struck. But he was. It was all fun.

The fun was set aside when he visited the former concentration camp at Dachau. His story was to acknowledge the sixtieth anniversary of the camp's establishment. It was the first of Hitler's concentration camps established shortly after he came to power.

As he drove to the site, Hank was struck by the quaintness of the village which proved to be in such sharp contrast to the camp itself. He was reminded that when the camp was liberated villagers had claimed to have been unaware of the gruesome activity inside. Even those who had been employed there in various capacities played dumb to the horrors. It was hard for him to believe the villagers never questioned he greasy smoke from the crematorium that must

have hung like a shroud over the village on wind-
less days. They could not deny the reality when
the camp was liberated. The American liberators
forced the villagers to bury the dead. Bodies were
everywhere...in barracks and in sealed railroad
cars.

The real surprise for Hank came inside the
camp itself. He was stunned to find that sixteen
years after the camp had been liberated, people
who had been imprisoned there were still there
and living on the site. Several families lived in
the remaining buildings that had once housed
prisoners. Women hung wash on improvised
clotheslines. Children played in the dusty streets.
He learned they were largely Eastern Euro-
peans, many gypsies and Sudeten Germans from
Czechoslovakia. They refused to return to their
former homes when the war ended because of
communist authoritarianism was no better than
Nazi totalitarianism. They were afraid and chose
instead to remain in a place where they had been
cruelly suppressed.

There was one shock there after another
for Hank. The walls of the gas chamber, that had
been the model for others that followed in other
infamous places, were covered with graffiti from
visitors from all over the world. For Hank, it was a
sacrilege that those walls where so many died had
been defaced by insensitive tourists.

Hank was dumbstruck by a structure just

outside the camp itself. It was a place for those same tourists to relax before or after their visit. It bore a huge sign..."Gasthaus am Krematorium"...an easy translation that Hank found profane, offensive, and blasphemous.

His story startled Stars and Stripes readers who found it difficult to comprehend that a place of such historic significance could have been so indecently slandered.

For the rest of his life Hank would take pride in feeling that his Dachau story may have contributed to the camp's finding its rightful place in post-war history. With the help of former prisoners and the Bavarian government the site was eventually designated a national memorial and a fitting tribute to those tens of thousands who had lived and died there.

Hank became increasingly involved in a different world of refugees from Eastern Europe through Radio Free Europe which was headquartered in Munich. The complex was located amid the thousand acres of the Englischer Garten, the lush public park near the center of Munich. RFE, as it was known, was a post war creation designed to broadcast information about the free world by targeting Soviet Satellite states, broadcasting in the native languages of the targeted nations. At the same time, it was also gathering information. In effect it was recreating those captive nations on paper.

The staff was primarily comprised of exiles, refugees, defectors and other emigrés from the satellite nations. Using information gathered from people who had fled the captive nations, monitoring publications and broadcasts from them, they meticulously compiled the comings and goings of communist functionaries at every level, national to local.

They catalogued trends, power shifts and all the relevant information they could glean about day to day life in Czechoslovakia, Rumania, Poland, Albania and other nations. This enabled solid analysis about what was actually going on, and why, in those nations. This enabled analysts to project future changes in power structure and policy. The analysts at RFE often knew about changes at all levels of government in those satellite nations before their citizens did.

The information that came into RFE every day also went out...to a selective audience. The data was compiled and printed in what was called the "daily budget." It contained a detailed synopsis from monitors and analysts and was eagerly awaited by editors on the separate editorial desks responsible for each targeted satellite nation.

Among those with interest in the daily budget was Hank Tollar. He had a "secret" government security clearance which gave him access to mid-level intelligence data. He visited RFE daily to pick up the hefty packet of material, some of which was sensitive. It was a frequent source of information he could report. In a sense he was an Eastern European correspondent even though he was not able to actually travel in those satellite nations.

Even more detailed information, compiled, analyzed and annotated at RFE was also digested with interest by the western intelligence community, especially the Central Intelligence Agency, a largely silent RFE partner. It was out of Hank's reach.

"Is RFE a CIA operation?" Hank put the question to Gene Talbot, a pipe smoking veteran journalist who oversaw the collection of data and presided over what was called "the newsroom." It was where the budget was edited by English speaking journalists from half a dozen countries.

Hank and Talbot, a prodigious pipe smoker, had struck an early friendship largely because Hank supplied him with American tobacco. Tobacco was expensive on the German market, and according to most Americans not very good. Hank had access to the military PX, or Post Exchange, which was off limits to civilians not working for the military. Hank kept his new friend plentifully supplied with inexpensive one pound cans of Prince Albert pipe tobacco.

They joshed a lot with lots of friendly banter. Talbot's background was impressive and included a wartime stint with the New York Times foreign desk. He had become an expat when the war ended. His visage was that of a stern professional who had seen too much. Which he had. The memories of which were in a mental lockbox behind bushy brows, a long sharp nose and tobacco stained teeth. Hank was delighted and surprised to learn that he had a sense of humor that contradicted first, and even second impressions.

"You keep wondering about that, don't you?" laughed Talbot. "Thanks for the tobacco, by the way. I appreciate it, but you can't seduce me with it."

Hank was aware of all the rumors that the Central Intelligence Agency was more than close to RFE. It was after all the brainchild of Allen Dulles, the long time Director of Central Intelligence whom John Kennedy fired after the Bay of Pigs fiasco. It was an open secret that the CIA and RFE slept in the same bed, but the Soviets were the only ones speaking about it out loud. And often. Hank wondered that if he ever had proof of the extent of the relationship whether he would write about it. Or could? He remembered that conversation with his editor in Frankfurt.

"You're a smart kid," said Talbot. "You really wouldn't want to get into the CIA's crosshairs by writing a story would you?" he asked raising bushy brows.

"I think you just answered my question,"

answered Hank. "Why would they care if it's not true?" He tried to hold a smile as he spoke and Talbot was stuffing tobacco into his pipe.

Talbot took his time. "Because," he said, interrupting himself to light the pipe, "the boys at the CIA don't like to read about themselves in the newspaper and I assume would be most unhappy to do so in a quasi-government publication like yours." He took a deep drag.

"Ah, I'm no threat. They don't even know I'm alive," Hank joked. "Small fish."

"You'd be surprised," Talbot said through a cloud of smoke. "You'd be surprised," he repeated, leaning back. A favorite pose. "What are you working on now?" he asked, changing the subject. For a moment the two sat staring at each other listening to the clack-clacking of typewriters and wire machines. Newsrooms were noisy places.

"Ilse," Hank finally said.

"Ilse?"

"Yeah...Ilse Stengel,"

"Who's she?"

"Go down to the Archives sometime and find out."

"Ah. The blonde."

"Uh huh...see you later."

A slow smile softened Talbot's face as he thought to himself that if Hank wanted to know more about the CIA, Ilse Stengel might be a good one to ask. Ask yes, but don't expect an answer.

CHAPTER 3

I n the Soviet orbit, RFE was not only a nuisance, it was a threat. Moscow's almost constant jamming of its signal testified to that. And it was also a target as the Soviets were desperate to learn as much as they could about how much RFE knew and how it knew it. With that information, it was only a short step to manipulating that information to its own advantage. Needless to say RFE was on constant high alert for those inside the organization who might work...not for it...but against it.

Hank had a luxury in Munich he didn't have in Frankfurt. It was a small bureau and came with a personal assistant to help him with language, as needed, and help him navigate the new turf. He was a Hungarian-born refugee. His name was Ted Domjan. Hank assumed it was a simplified version of a complicated Hungarian given name. Ted was himself complicated, but competent. He would say only of his wartime experience, and Hungary's juggling of loyalties, that he got out before the Russians came in.

He was tall and lean and reminded Hank of the actor Basil Rathbone. All that was missing was a deerstalker hat. His large nose dominated his features. The rest of his face was all angles covered by tightly stretched skin. His jawline was sharp. His lips thin. His cheekbones were high and well defined. His clothes were second or third generation second hand shop. Nonetheless, he carried himself like the aristocrat he sometimes hinted he once was. He was bright and perceptive, and knew his politics on both sides of the Iron Curtain. He was perfect for his position with Hank, as he had been with Hank's predecessors. He knew it and Hank did too.

"Do you think the CIA runs RFE?" Hank asked him during the first days of his new assignment.

"Yes," answered Ted simply.

"What makes you think so?" asked Hank.

"Because the CIA is involved in everything in this part of the world." He paused, adding, "And other parts."

"Isn't it a story?"

Ted looked at him warily. "Sure it's a story, but not one for you to tell...unless you want a one way ticket back to Baltimore."

"How did you know I'm from Baltimore?" asked the surprised young reporter.

"Because the CIA told me," said Ted laughing. "Let the Times, Trib or DER SPIEGEL worry about the CIA. Then you can spend more time with Ilse Stengel."

Stunned, Hank's jaw dropped. "How did you know about..."

"The CIA told me," interjected Ted laughing so hard his eyebrows bounced.

"Seriously. I've only known her for a short time. We've only said hello."

It took a moment for Ted's laughter to fade. "I know her," he said. "I've known her since she was a little girl. I helped her get her job."

"You are full of surprises," said Hank. "Put in a good word will you. I like her."

"I will," said Ted picking up one of the newspapers on his desk. "Just treat her right," adding, "I'll be watching." He said it as a joke but Hank also interpreted it as much more than a suggestion.

Hank didn't need Ted's help for a big story that came out of nowhere on the streets of Munich. It was on Leopoldstrasse in the heart of the student district. A seemingly innocent moment degenerated quickly into a full-fledged confrontation between students and police. Three young people were playing guitars for fellow students, tourists and other passers-by across from a line of restaurants serving diners and drinkers. A crowd gathered around the musicians, then a larger crowd, making it difficult for pedestrians, and then automobiles, to move through the area. Police arrived to disperse the crowd. The young people did not respond. They dug in.

"Jesus Christ," said Hank as he and Ted were nursing beers and watched police move in on the musicians. They had been sitting in a café across the street and had been only slightly aware of the musicians a hundred feet away. "Where did the cops come from?" he asked as they watched the crowd begin to build. "And why?"

"German police don't like crowds," said Ted as the two watched the situation develop.

"But they're creating the crowd. We've got a ringside seat," said Hank pulling out his skinny reporter's notebook. He watched and scribbled as police night sticks came out and were put to use bloodying many shouting students and some passersby caught in the middle. The outnumbered police were pushed around by the angry students as the confrontation grew ugly quickly. The sound of grunts and groans and yelps of pain carried across the street.

"This is turning into a very bad situation," said Hank as he, Ted and others in the café watched the ebb and flow of humanity edging ever closer to where they were sitting.

"Look over there," said Ted pointing down the long avenue. "Reinforcements."

A broad line of officers on horseback came into focus quickly as they neared the melee. The big animals moved shoulder to shoulder, a wall of horseflesh, squeezed tightly from one side of the street to the other.

The officers on foot, and on horseback, offered a menacing, and to some, an all too familiar image. In the ambient, dwindling light their uniforms seemed even darker. Their high peaked caps and polished boots, reflecting dim light from the streetlamps, were an eerie reminder of the not too distant past.

"Not a good look," said Ted. "Déjà vu."

"But effective," said Hank as he watched the line of uniformed humans and snorting equines slowly and effectively clear the chanting and obstinate crowd. The students eventually dispersed down side streets. Police, on and off horses, remained until well after midnight to ensure they did not return.

The next day was quiet, but when the sun went down, the musicians were back. They had added to their number and a crowd of mostly students built very quickly, more of them than the night before. They were clearly ready for another encounter.

Hank and Ted had been talking to students during the day and were on the scene long before it got dark. Everyone was expecting an encore that night, and wondering if the police would ratchet down their response, or whether the young crowd would ramp up theirs? Or vice versa.

"I don't think the German psyche works that way," said Ted. "Not with the police. When there is resistance to compliance...defiance...the first impulse is to strike back...overreact. Orders are meant to be obeyed."

"You know them better than I do," said Hank, "but I thought the criticism over their tactics last night might dampen the response." He shook his head. "All they were doing was playing music...isn't that supposed to be part of the charm of the district."

"Only until it's not," said Ted. "We'll see."

Hank looked at his notes. "Twenty arrests last night. Dozens of injured that I could see. Blood on the streets. Literally. The press in the East must be having a field day with it." He paused, "I wonder why they didn't use tear gas. That would have moved things along more quickly."

"The horses," answered Ted. "Tear gas and horses don't get along very well. The horses introduce an element of fear. Besides the local police seem to prefer banging heads."

"Imagine what the pictures would look like. German police using gas...any kind of gas. I'll have to ask Talbot how this story is playing on his beat."

The mounted patrol was back as dusk turned to darkness, accompanied by other officers on foot who were followed by a phalanx of police cars, their annoying sirens an unpleasant accompaniment. Red lights flashed ominously. Students shouted defiantly. Their numbers and the accompanying noise added an additional element of chaos.

The officers had less patience than the night before and dozens in the crowd were badly beaten. Police were impatient to get it over with. Several protestors were arrested quickly It took two hours, but the crowd was finally forced off the main street and stumbled down smaller side streets. Again, when Leopoldstrasse was cleared, the officers on horseback and on foot remained to ensure that order was restored and remained so. Eventually, finally, unimpeded, late evening pedestrian and auto traffic slowly returned. The curious came back cautiously as outdoor cafés slowly reopened to resume service outdoors.

"You were right," said Hank as they found a table. "Police were more impatient tonight," he said as they sat and ordered beers. Tables that had been cleared earlier as the clash seemed inevitable began to refill. "Just standing on the edge of the crowd made me nervous."

"Don't get in the way. A press card won't help," said Ted. "Tomorrow will be worse."

Authorities issued warnings throughout the following day promising less patience and more arrests if the protestors defied orders not to congregate again. U.S. Military personnel were told to avoid the area until further notice. The warnings were to go unheeded, at least among young Germans and some tourists.

Hank ran into a civilian AFN reporter during the afternoon. He was surprised to see two distinctive lumps on his cheek.

"What happened to you?" He asked feeling that he already knew the answer.

"They beat the crap out of me last night," said the young man. His name was Tom Morrow. He was about Hank's age and the two had crossed paths on various assignments. The closing line to his reports..."Listen tomorrow to Morrow"...always made Hank chuckle.

"Where did this happen?" asked Hank. "You didn't mix it up on the street did you."

"Hell no. I was a block away doing some interviews with students and these two cops came by and started wailing on me shouting 'no interviews...no interviews.' Then they just started hitting me with their nightsticks. A couple of times on the head, but mostly my back and shoulder. I've got some major league welts. I pointed to my recorder with the big AFN logo but they just laughed."

"What the hell are you doing back out here? You probably shouldn't be."

"The bosses won't let our GI reporters anywhere near here. The military's afraid there could be an incident. It was an order from on high. So, I don't have a choice."

"I'm going to do a story on it," said Hank. "Have you got a few minutes"

Morrow nodded. "Just go easy on it. Don't make me sound like a whiner. The powers that be are scared to death of an incident that'll embarrass the Germans. Just play it straight, okay?"

"Sure. But I think the Germans already have plenty to be embarrassed about." The two chatted with Hank rapidly scribbling notes. They shook hands when the conversation ended. "Keep your distance tonight Tom," said Hank. "These clowns seem to be enjoying what they're doing."

On the third night there were more musicians and a larger crowd than during the previous nights, as more students, more civilians and even tourists joined the protest. And there were more police. They had recruited reinforcements from towns as far thirty miles away. Their mood was even darker and their patience more limited. Their batons flailed at protestors. Horses snorted and whinnied amid the chaos. Wounded protestors screamed and shouted, whistles blew, and officers cursed. It was another evening of mayhem that otherwise followed the script of previous nights.

It provoked an incident that brought about exactly the kind of publicity that neither the Germans nor the Americans wanted.

An American movie star, making a movie at the Geiselgasteig studios, had been drawn to the protest by the media publicity. He told AFN's Tom Morrow that what he saw reminded him of what it must have been like in the Nazi era with Brownshirts beating Jews.

The interview was broadcast the following day and did not play well among Bavarian or Federal government officials who demanded apologies from the actor who said it and the reporter who broadcast it. Officials threatened to toss both out of the country if that apology were not forthcoming.

To make matters more complicated, the U.S. military was drawn into it because the actor had been a wartime member of the Army's fabled 24th Infantry Division headquartered thirty miles down the road from Munich.

The actor's comment embarrassed the highly sensitive U.S. Army, the U.S. Embassy, as well as the German and Bavarian governments. It was a diplomatic mess only resolved when the actor, with an unfinished movie to complete, grudgingly apologized. It was sufficient balm to the wound to keep James Garner in Germany to finish his work on The Great Escape. Everybody apparently forgot about Tom Morrow.

Meantime, the protest had run out of steam and on the next night, the streets were quiet. Students were left licking their wounds, and those who had witnessed what almost everyone felt was a police overreaction, wondered if the Garner hadn't gotten it right. How far had Germany come in three decades?

"I guess Morrow's off the hook," said Hank a few day later as he and Ted sat in the office. "He's still here after Garner's mea culpa."

"He was small fry in this," answered Ted. "I do think they would have kicked Garner out if he hadn't apologized. If they had, your friend would have been gone too."

"Can you imagine what that would have looked like?" asked Hank. "You've got what amounts to a police riot. It's criticized by a celebrity and it's all reported. And everybody's got their feelings hurt."

"Believe it or not, all the interested parties...aside from Garner and Morrow...are still feeling their way. It wasn't all that long ago that the Germans and the U.S. were at each other's throats. Now they're trying to find a way to get along, as you say in America, without 'rocking the boat.' The stakes are high, but the scars are deep. Europe's still a tinderbox. Nobody wants any sparks.

"You see what Moscow did with those demonstrations, saying it looked like the Nazis were back. You can bet some of the Kremlin's friends were encouraging the students. Every minute of every day the Kremlin is looking for ways to bring the Alliance down. Dissention here is success there. There's nothing they'd like more than to drive a wedge between the U.S. and Germany.

"Don't forget it doesn't hurt their cause when a famous American movie star is saying the same thing as Pravda and Izvestia."

"It's complicated," said Hank.

Ted looked at him sternly. "Yes," he said, "and Tom Morrow's a very small cog in a very big wheel." He took a deep breath. "Most of us are."

"So, how are our friends in the East handling the protests over the past couple of days?" Hank was delivering another pound of Prince Albert to Gene Talbot in the RFE newsroom the day after the final street confrontation.

"Thanks," said Talbot holding the can as if it were the Stanley Cup. "I was just about out." He set the tin gingerly on his desk.

"Well, you can probably guess the reaction. It's unanimous. Everything from the rebirth of Nazism to an attempted putsch. They criticize the kids...the cops, and are praising Jim Garner. They don't miss a trick." He paused. "You were out there. What was it like for you?"

"It was pretty brutal. Worse each night than the night before. Ted and I had a ringside seat but we made sure we had an escape route."

"I understand they were beating people a block or two away on the side streets. Some of my people here couldn't get home until two or three in the morning."

"Tom Morrow of AFN was one of those beaten. I have a piece in today's paper. He's worried that his bosses won't be happy. Everyone's concerned the Germans will be offended...that they're more concerned about negative publicity than they are about a bunch of cops out for blood."

"I'll look for your piece. I haven't gotten your paper yet." Talbot scraped ashes from the bowl of his pipe. As he began to reload, he said, "Anybody talking about some of our friends out there revving up the crowd?"

"Not that I've seen but Ted seemed pretty certain that some of them would be...on both sides working up both the cops and kids."

"Hank, I'm sure you've already figured it out, but our friends from the other side have lots of buddies over here. That's the way they work. You can't trust anybody. Christ, they're in government, law enforcement, journalism. Take my advice and keep your eyes, ears and instincts wide open."

"I'm not sure I know what to look or listen for."

"Everything," responded Talbot softly. "Everything."

"How do you vet the people you have here?" asked Hank. "They're all from the Eastern bloc. Refugees, exiles, defectors. I don't imagine they all have papers. You pretty much have to take their word for who and what they are, don't you?"

"We put them through a pretty rigorous process. We have our own sources. You'd be surprised at information we have in our archives from our target countries. Often our own people can vouch for them."

There was a knock on the door. Talbot shouted a "come in" and the door was opened instantly. In stepped an ad for the Bavarian Department of Tourism. Blonde hair, blue eyes set far apart, a colorful dirndl. The traditional dress was pinched at the waste with a crisp white blouse showing a generous amount of cleavage. The only thing whiter than the blouse were her teeth most of which were on full display thanks to a wide smile.

"Right on cue," said Talbot. Here's one of our archivists now," he said smiling and turning to Hank. "You know Ilse Stengel?"

"Not as well as I'd like to," said Hank blushing.

"Hello Hank," she said laughing. "I don't

know if what you say is nice...or naughty." She turned to Talbot. "Here are those files you asked for. She handed them to him, turned with a swish of her aproned skirt and headed back to the door, where she said over her shoulder, smiling, "Nice to see you Hank." She pulled the door closed behind her.

"I had forgotten you said you knew our lovely Ilse," said Talbot. He lit his pipe and between puffs teased, "Do you blush like that with all the girls?"

"Was I blushing?" asked Hank, embarrassed.

"She is lovely," said Talbot. "If I were only forty years younger."

"That would make you my age," said Hank. "If you were, what would you do?"

"Probably nothing. I was as shy then as you apparently are now."

"Think she'd go out with me?"

"Not if you don't ask." He picked up the file Ilse had brought in. "Now get out of here. And thanks again for the tobacco."

CHAPTER 4

"**H**ave you been waiting for me?" asked a surprised and delighted Hank when he found her lingering down the hall from Talbot's office.

"As a matter of fact I was," she smiled. "I wanted to talk to you about the demonstrations on Leopoldstrasse. I saw you there the other night."

Hank was taken aback. "You were there? Why?"

"I was recording some sound for the news-room. I would like to be a reporter some day and I thought I could be helpful...that maybe one day they'd take a chance on a female reporter."

Women in journalism was not unknown, but it certainly was not commonplace. Certainly not in Europe. Back home they were few and far between, thought Hank, and usually relegated to covering garden clubs and New Year births. They would never have been assigned to cover a riot. Maybe that's why she did it, he thought.

"It was a pretty dangerous place," he said. "I hope you didn't get too close. You could have been run over by a horse or been beaten...or both."

"I wasn't too worried about that," she smiled coquettishly. "I was close enough to smell the horses..."

"And wink at the police I'll bet."

"I can do that," she said, her smile widened.

I'll bet you can he thought, admiring the sparkle in her blue eyes. The perfect Aryan he thought. "Did Talbot know you were there...with an expensive recorder?"

Her smile faded. "No. He hardly knows I'm alive. No one knew. They never would have allowed it. I was going to surprise them." She shrugged. "But the surprise was on me. When I got back I discovered that I hadn't put the tape in correctly. I had no recording. Nichts! All for nothing."

"Well, I'm glad you didn't get hurt. You could have."

The smile was back. "I wanted to talk to you about it. Maybe you could give me some advice."

Hank was more than pleasantly surprised at this opportunity. This very pretty German girl had caught his eye during his very first visits to RFE. He hadn't been sure how to approach her, but her willingness to talk with him now, moments after his conversation with Talbot emboldened, him. "I'd be happy to."

He invited her for a beer at one of his favorite cafes and she seemed happy to accept.

"The Gasthaus Leopold at five?" he asked. "On the Leopoldstrasse. If you feel comfortable there," he teased, "when there is no chaos."

"Ah, the scene of my crime," she giggled. "I will see you there at five."

It was a lovely evening, traffic was light, and there had been no threat of further clashes on the street. He arrived first and sat nursing a beer, hoping she had not forgotten. He sensed she was coming when some of the male students at adjoining sidewalk tables all seemed to turn their heads in one direction at the same time. And there she was, smiling at the young men as she passed and finally at him as she sat down.

Ilse was in her early twenties. While she must have been aware of her attractiveness, and the reaction of men to her, she did not carry herself with off-putting self-awareness. Self-confidence yes, but not in a way that suggested vanity or narcissism. Quite a package he thought as he stood while she sat. Her smile was hypnotic. The early evening sun both complimented and competed with her golden hair.

She nodded as he stood thinking that here was an American who was polite and who was not undressing her with his eyes. I could like him she thought, unless he lectures or drinks too much.

He ordered a second beer and she a Riesling. While they waited they chatted about the contrast in the neighborhood that evening compared to the chaos of recent nights.

When their drinks arrived, he reminded her that she had said she wanted his "advice."

"About what?" he asked. "I don't think I'd be much help in loading tape in your recorder." He chuckled hoping she would understand that he was joking.

"Oh, I've figured that out," she said. "It was my mistake. Stupid. It won't happen again." She said it with a conviction that assured him that indeed it would not.

"My only other advice," he added, "would be to be very, very careful when working around a mob like the other night. Tom Morrow of AFN...do you know him?" She nodded yes. "Well they beat the crap out of him. His recorder didn't help him." She rolled her eyes. "In fact it might have been what prompted the attack."

"I know about Tom. I saw your story." Hank nodded his appreciation. "But," she went on, "isn't that part of the job? Taking risks to get the story? I saw him at RFE. He didn't look too bad."

"Yeah, it's part of the job. But you have to be careful. Assess the risk. It's not good journalism if you wind up in the hospital before you file the story. And...Tom took some lumps, but a lot of those kids challenging the cops really took a beating. The police have their adrenaline going in situations like the other night. They're not able to determine who's who, and how hard to smack someone in the middle of something that's out of control." He reached across and took her hand. "And, they're not always able to differentiate between a man or a woman. And, given what I saw the other night, they didn't seem to care much. And," he added with emphasis, "they seemed to enjoy it."

She looked at his hand on hers and pulled her own away. "Are you saying that it's no place for a women? That women can't handle it...or handle themselves? Because if that's what you're saying I resent it. I can handle it. Probably better than a lot of men."

"Whew," he said, startled by how defensive she seemed. "I touched a nerve, but didn't mean too. All I'm saying is you've got to be very careful and know what you're doing. Always have an escape route. Just be careful and don't take unnecessary chances."

"I understand. I'm sorry. I can get pretty defensive when I think men don't think women can do what they do."

"I noticed.

"I appreciate your advice." Her smile was

not convincing, but it was still a smile.

"I like it better when you smile, by the way."

"I do too," she replied.

They sat silently for a few minutes. She checked her watch and he hoped she wasn't getting ready to leave.

"How about another glass of wine?" he asked hopefully. "I'd like to get to know you better...get to know more about you."

"Just one more," she said softly, her smile back. "I don't want to get tipsy."

He signaled the waiter who promptly brought them their order.

"One of the things I've been curious about," said Hank, "is how you know My Man Friday, Ted Domjan. He said he helped you get your job at RFE."

"My man Friday? I don't understand."

"It means a helper. It's from a book."

"Hah," she said pausing. "So Ted's been talking about me, eh? I'm surprised. He's not much of a talker."

"You can say that again. But when he does talk, he usually has something to say. But he didn't tell me much about you. Your secrets are safe with him."

Ilse got a funny, quizzical expression on her face. "Secrets? Well I guess we all have secrets. I have my share. Life is full of complications." She took a sip of wine.

"Complications? Anything I could, eh, un-complicate?"

"You're sweet," she said. "I don't think there's anything I can't handle."

She changed the subject. "Speaking of secrets and Ted... he has one. His real name is Tivadar...Tivadar Domjan. He changed it to Ted. He thought it would be easier for Americans.

"I've known him most of my life...since before my mother, sister and I arrived in Munich from Czechoslovakia...I was very young."

"You're from Czechoslovakia? I thought you were German."

"I am, thanks to Herr Hitler. I'm Sudeten German. When he overran the country to *liberate* us, he granted us all German citizenship. That's why so many left and went to Germany when the war was over. Especially when the Russians moved in and established a friendly government. My mother, sister and I were among those who left. I was barely five. My sister was seven. The three of us walked from just north of Prague."

"Walked?"

"Only way. It was difficult. I don't know how my mother did it. It was a journey of about five hundred kilometers...three hundred miles. Rain...snow...mud...ugly men. She never wanted to leave. She wanted to stay and try and reclaim property the government seized."

"No father?"

"He was drafted in 1940. We did not see him or hear from him until late summer of 1945. Our house had been seized but he found us at our new home just before we left. He had walked from France where he'd been captured by the Americans. They sent him home with his backpack and a few marks. He too had to walk. He refused to leave Czechoslovakia with us. So he stayed. I heard from him a few times but now don't know for certain whether he's dead or alive." She stared at the wine glass cupped in her hands before adding, "He made his choice."

"Your mother? Sister?"

"Dead. My sister was run over by a drunk GI shortly after we arrived.

My mother, I think, died of a broken heart after that. She never felt like she fit in in Munich. She was furious over the reparations fight about the property she'd lost when the Czech government was restored. It wasn't much, but she always felt someone...Germans or the Czechs...owed her for what she had to leave behind when we were essentially kicked out of Czechoslovakia." Her eyes grew moist. Hank thought she was going to break down.

"What a story," he said, hoping she would hold it together. "Where does Ted fit in?"

"You mean Tivador?" She tried to smile but her lips just quivered. "I'm not sure. He just appeared one day. I was still a little girl. I'm not sure how they met. He won't talk about it. But he was very kind to her and to me. I think he had a soft spot for refugees. He'd been one at one time. I don't know if he and my mother were lovers." She looked hard into Hank's eyes. "I hope they were for both of their sakes. He took risks for her and even went to Prague to try and get her some satisfaction for her confiscated property."

"Any luck?"

"No, he was there for months as they strung him along. He said he felt like a prisoner." She looked absently at passing pedestrians. "Anyway, when I was a little older and he'd come back from Prague he stayed with us only a short time. He then left again and told us he and was going to work with the Americans. He was gone for a year or two. When he returned he helped send me to a good school, a gymnasium we call it, where I qualified for university. He helped finance my studies at Heidelberg University."

"He did all this out of the goodness of his heart?" asked Hank. "He's quite a guy."

She leaned toward him and put a finger to her lips, glancing from side to side, pretending she was looking for eavesdroppers. "I think he was in love with my mother at one time and helped me because of her." She leaned back. "I want to think that." She closed her eyes and nodded, recalling a fond memory.

"When I came back and was looking for a

job, he introduced me to some people at RFE and they hired me because of my language skills. I do a little freelance work with the U.S. Consulate. I also speak French, Czech, and a little Russian." Her smile was back. "End of story."

""Some story it is. You're a walking Tower of Babel," he said. "Where did you learn English? You've got the American idiom down pat."

"Languages always came easy to me. I've worked with and around Americans for a long time...the PX...the Consulate...RFE. I had English at university. Ted's been a big help. My French is also pretty good. I love the language...and France." She interlaced her hands in her lap. "I've always had to work. Fortunately, most of the time it was around Amis as we call you. And, AFN. Lots of Germans learn English...American English...through AFN." She chortled, "Do you know what we call AFN?"

Hank shook his head.

"AFN-sender."

AFN-sender?" He pronounced it as he heard it. "Afn as in monkey? Monkey radio?"

She nodded.

"Not very flattering. Sounds insulting in fact."

"It's a joke," she said grinning. "Just a play on words. I have to say though that some Germans say it with disrespect."

"But not you?"

"Hah. Never."

"After a not great start with the war and all," he said after a moment, changing the subject, "it sounds like you've been able to put things together and put the past behind you."

She looked at him reflectively for a moment. "Many have had it worse," she said, her tone now serious. "I could be in Prague right now wondering how to get out."

Hank wanted the lighthearted Ilse back, so he changed the subject asking, "Do you see Ted much."

"From time to time. He's busy. I'm busy. He's like my uncle. I love him. I owe him so much." She pointed a finger at Hank. "And, he's told me a lot about you," she said playfully.

"Such as?"

"He says you're a good guy. A good journalist and you have a good education."

"Sounds pretty lame next to your story."

"Sounds pretty good to me." She looked around. The sun was going down. Her blonde hair was on its own, but Hank noted it didn't need any help from the fading sun. She touched his hand and it made his heart skip. "Everyone's eating," she said. "Aren't you going to buy me dinner?"

They spent the next two hours making small talk and filling in the gaps in their stories. She laughed easily and he became more enchanted as they got to know more and more about each other. When it came time to leave he asked to drive her home.

"Of course. I want to thank you for dinner. But I must tell you that driving me home is as far as it goes. I like you, but I have a," she hesitated..."a friend."

"A boyfriend?"

"A friend. He sometimes stays with me."

Hank's knees felt rubbery. It was the last thing he wanted to hear. He had not expected she would invite him in for the night, although the thought had crossed his mind. He was crestfallen when she revealed that she was seeing someone. She had alternately joked, laughed, and, he thought, at times flirted with him during the past few hours. Was he surprised she had a "relationship?" Of course not. He might be more surprised to learn that she only had one.

"Who's the lucky guy?" he stammered.

"He's a race car driver. He races all over Europe."

"What's his name?"

"You wouldn't know him. His name is Matthieu Manon. His nickname is Lucky...Lucky Manon.

"Is he any good?"

"He's a champion. He's won many regional races. He won last year at Nürburgring. That was big for him."

Great, thought Hank. I'm in competition with a champion whose name is Lucky.

"What do you know about Lucky?" he asked Ted as they sat in their joint office the next morning. "Ted slowly put down one of the several newspapers he read every day looking for news that Hank could use as leads for stories of his own. His lips stretched slightly in what Hank thought might have been a suppressed smile. It was hard to tell with Ted who was not celebrated for his sense of humor.

"So, you've had that beer with Ilse and she's already keeping you at arms length. Not surprised. She's a very careful young lady.

"He's Alsatian," he continued. "French name and German sensibilities. Most people who come from that region are confused. They don't know whether they're French or German." Hank vaguely remembered history lessons telling of how this real estate in France, only a few minutes from Germany had been juggled by both countries for centuries. Germany won the toss in World War Two. No wonder, he thought, people who lived there might be confused.

"Well, she indicated that Lucky was special to her."

"He's French...Alsatian French, and she likes all things French. Lucky is special only to himself. His success has gone to his head."

"Well, I guess I'm glad to hear you say that. It looks like she likes him more than you do."

"I don't totally dislike him. He just seems to think the world...especially Ilse...owes him a living since his accident."

"What accident?"

"He crashed a few years ago at Monaco. It was bad. They didn't think he would live. He did and came back in almost a full body cast. And with the nickname 'Lucky' which I guess he was. Ilse met him on a trip."

"Serious?"

"I don't know. I guess only time will tell. He's away a lot."

That's good to know mused Hank thinking it might give him an opportunity.

Ted took a phone call, interrupting their conversation, and Hank busied himself with the day's routine...mostly phone calls to contacts and sources. It was little more than busy work and provided only a few uninspiring news releases about daily life in a military world, comings and goings, promotions. Very dull stuff for a young reporter who wanted to get his professional teeth into something more interesting and challenging.

"Anything we can follow up on in the papers?" he asked Ted who, with scissors snapping, was busying himself by cutting out interesting stories from the papers.

Without looking up, Ted muttered, "Nothing I can see."

Hank leaned back in his chair. "You know, there's something I've wondered about."

Ted raised his eyebrows.

"Where did you learn your English?" asked Hank, surprised that he had never asked before.

"Well, I studied it in school for a bit. I watched a lot of American movies after the war. I've been working for you Americans for a long time. And Ilse's a natural. We always speak English."

"She told me quite a bit about you and her family. You've really been very good to all of them. Especially Ilse."

Ted looked at him suspiciously. "I hope she didn't talk too much. To be honest I think my life is my business. I don't like to think of people talking about me when I'm not present." Hank could see than Ted was borderline angry. He spoke very deliberately but with an intensity that was a give-away.

"No gossip Ted. She just told me how kind you've always been and how you helped her get an education. How you tried to help her mother in her reparations claim."

Ted relaxed a little as Hank spoke. "I wasn't much help there. But I did want to help Ilse." He examined his hands for a moment, then said sadly, "I always thought of her as a daughter I never had." He pulled out a handkerchief and noisily blew his nose.

"Tell me to stop asking if it makes you uncomfortable," said Hank earnestly, hoping he sounded compassionate. "Were you ever married?"

There was a long pause as Ted thought, not about the question, but about whether he wanted to answer it: whether he wanted to open a page in a painful chapter in his life. None of his business he thought. But I work with this young man. If he is curious, and he's obviously interested, he reasoned, perhaps he should know the story, not all of it. Just some of it.

He took a deep breath and said, "I was born to a very good family in Hungary. Before the war we had it much better than most of my countrymen. So many of us became more and more alarmed as the government became cozy with Hitler and joined forces against Yugoslavia and Russia. Because I was from a family with rank, I was a junior officer in the Army. I had married a beautiful woman." His expression turned wistful.

"I became involved in a minor way in quiet peace negotiations between Budapest, Washington and London. I was away a lot.

"The Nazis got wind of these talks and invaded Hungary. Their collaborators suspected my family's...basically my...involvement in the negotiations. They were taken from our home in the middle of the night. My wife was raped. My parents brutalized. My siblings shot. Everyone was killed. When I heard what had happened and confirmed it...I was devastated. I took off my uniform, dressed like a farmer and left my country in a honey wagon. Do you know what that is?"

"It's how raw, human sewage is collected," answered Hank who was spellbound by Ted's story.

"Yes, a wagon filled with shit and piss. I was able to cross into Czechoslovakia."

"Out of the frying pan and into the fire," said Hank solemnly.

"Exactly."

"And?"

"You can probably guess the rest. I was able to make contact with people in the Czech underground. They put me in touch with a family who would hide me."

"Ilse's family?"

"Yes. At great risk to her mother. Ilse was too young to remember. I was with them for months. I was desperate to leave them. Every day I spent with them was a huge risk. Eventually I made my way to the West and turned myself in to American intelligence where I could tell them what I knew. I may or may not have been helpful."

"I'm having trouble absorbing all of this," said Hank. "I've heard so many incredible stories.

How did you wind up here with the paper after all of that?"

"I wanted to work for the Americans.   I did some work with U.S. Intelligence. I was sent to Monterey, California to teach language for a while, and to improve my English. I became homesick for Europe. But, I didn't want anything political. So, they arranged for me to join the Stars and Stripes." He put his hands flat on his desk. "So here I am."

PART TWO

CHAPTER 5

France had its hands full in the early sixties. Former war hero Charles de Gaulle was at the helm, but his ship of state was sailing in choppy waters. All because of a North African nation France had colonized a hundred and thirty years earlier: Algeria. It had been an uncomfortable, often bloody, relationship from the start fueled by the arrival early on of French and other European settlers who, despite their minority population status, forcefully and cruelly elbowed their way into economic and political domination. Unrelenting antipathy for the French festered until it was unleashed in rebellion among native Algerians seeking independence and self-determination from the French. In the mid-twentieth century the inevitable war erupted, led in Algeria by the National Liberation Front (FLN). The conflict was brutally waged, during which French forces were accused of barbaric repression which included especially hideous torture of captured rebels.

In the late fifties, with both eyes on much of the world's condemnation of the war, and the United Nations' backing of independence for Algeria, de Gaulle negotiated a settlement with the FLN. French citizens, tired of the conflict, voted overwhelmingly for independence. But de Gaulle's effort was strongly challenged by a secret organization. It was comprised of members of a variety of fascist organizations, but primarily by many high-ranking officers of the French military who steadfastly opposed Algerian independence and were committed to a French Algeria. It was known as the Secret Army Organization (OAS). The right wing extremist organization was responsible for repeated but unsuccessful assassination attempts against de Gaulle and for numerous deadly terrorist bombings in Algeria and France.

Independence resulted in a flood of European Algerian refugees from the North African nation to Europe. There was a price on the head of members of the organization, including members of the French military who were affiliated with the OAS. Many of them returned to Europe as well. Some of the best known went underground outside of France. Several went incognito in Munich.

They included a former officer named

Albert LeClerc. He had at one time been a de Gaulle staff associate, but the two had a falling-out over the President's policies on Algeria. Le-Clerc, a passionate ideologue, was an early supporter of the OAS and had helped plan at least two assassination plots against his former military colleague, now President, de Gaulle. Disgraced, in exile with a small band of radicals, he remained in contact with some of his extremist former OAS colleagues around Europe. They plotted yet another attempt on the French president's life. Their objective included plans to take over the government in Paris and ultimately re-subjugate Algeria.

LeClerc was on the French government's most wanted list. He lived a cautious life in Munich and often moved about the city in disguise. Otherwise, he would have been easy to spot. He was unusually handsome with dark black hair, matched by hypnotic black eyes. His skin was deeply tanned by years in the desert sun. He was well over six feet tall. And while none of these features made him unique and easily recognizable, one feature set him apart from most. He had only one arm, having lost his left arm in an abortive OAS terrorist bombing attempt in Algeria. It left him with his right limb, and with a bitterness that was all-consuming, and infectious to his small cadre of accomplices in Munich.

He and his band were well-known to Antoine Argoud, the former Army colonel who was active, and a leader, within the OAS organization. While on the run, Argoud had been sentenced to death in absentia for his activities. He was also living incognito in Munich trying to revive his cause among supporters in French Army units stationed in Germany.

Argoud would have nothing to do with Le-Clerc. He considered him dangerously overzealous and unpredictable. Each was aware of the other's presence in the Bavarian capital but they remained at arm's length forging independent plans for the future of de Gaulle and Algeria.

LeClerc outlasted Argoud. The disgraced colonel was abducted in Munich and spirited to Paris in the trunk of a car. After a shaky border crossing, the car and its passenger were abandoned conspicuously in mid-town. An anonymous phone call alerted authorities to his whereabouts. He was arrested and faced a long trial and an ultimate sentence of life imprisonment. Neither his abductors nor the anonymous caller were ever identified.

The entire episode was received with mixed feelings by LeClerc. He understood that Argoud must have been the victim of treachery. The two men promoted conflicting strategies to effect the same outcome. He was at once relieved that his rival was out of the picture, but became increasingly fearful and paranoid that he could suffer the same fate. The more edgy he became, the more careful. He called his small group of cohorts together as soon as the word of Argoud's capture was announced.

They met in his dingy apartment near the historic Odeonsplatz, a public square closely linked to early Nazi history. The men were all dressed as common day workers. They arrived one by one. Their darting eyes and fidgety gestures betrayed their nervousness. The Argoud abduction left them feeling vulnerable and uneasy with the feeling of betrayal.

LeClerc stood before the tiny group, a band of sunlight shone on half his body drawing attention to the empty sleeve of his denim shirt. He got right to the point. "Someone betrayed Argoud," said LeClerc to all six of his stone-faced compatriots. "I need to know who it was and whoever it was has to be eliminated." He paused and looked closely at each of the men in the dusky room. "I must ask each of you if you have any idea who might have betrayed him. I need to be convinced that it was not one of you."

The men were startled at his accusatory bluntness. The only sound was that of the noisy traffic in the street below. LeClerc turned to each man and asked directly how they would answer either question. He watched each one of them closely as he asked and waited for their answer. He was intimidating. He used his dark eyes as weapons, piercing, questioning as if they would enable him to see through a lie.

"I want each of you, on your honor, to swear to me and before God right now that you had nothing to do with this betrayal." He put his hand on his hip. "Yes or no?"

One by one they nervously answered by shaking their head or with almost unintelligible responses of "non."

When each man had responded, LeClerc remained silent, staring at his colleagues as if he could elicit further information through silence. Those who stood shifted from one foot to the other. Those who sat were equally restless. Was it a natural reaction thought LeClerc as he studied each man? Or was it a guilty reaction? He could not tell. Yet. He longed for the days in Algeria where, if his officers needed information from FLN prisoners, he could employ knives, needles and electrodes to acquire it for them, sometimes just before the captives passed out, or sometimes died.

He reasoned that he would have to find a way to be certain that he could trust his own cohort. He knew that the worst possible position for a leader...aside from defeat...was not being able to trust his own men. They knew too much. They knew his plans. They knew where he was. It would take only one of them to destroy everything.

There were only a few French civilians scattered throughout the Munich area. Ever mindful of their need for security LeClerc and Argoud had both determined to their satisfaction through discreet questioning, investigation or intimidation, or all three, that none had any apparent inclination toward political activity. Through their independent vetting techniques, each man became convinced that the French ex-pats posed no risk, had no knowledge of their activities, and therefore there was no likelihood of treachery or active opposition.

But they were not the only Frenchmen in the region. There was a post- occupation French military presence in West Germany stationed in Baden Baden almost two hundred miles from Munich. The military was another question. The OAS was comprised of many embittered military men, though primarily in Algeria. Some of that bitterness had spread to ranks within the entire military establishment. However, it was hardly unanimous. There was an enormous contingent of loyalist support within the military. It was to this fact that LeClerc turned his attention.

One of his men, he knew, had a brother stationed in Baden Baden. The siblings met from time to time in small towns between the two cities. LeClerc had been assured again and again that their meetings were solely to catch up on family news and other personal business. After all they were brothers. But, he thought, brothers sometimes told secrets to brothers.

"I need to talk to you," he said trying to sound friendly a few days after the apartment meeting. Pierre Blanchet, a former corporal in the Army responded to what he interpreted as a friendly request. Meetings with LeClerc were not unusual.

Blanchet was a young man who had fallen under the spell of disenchantment with his government while serving in Oran. He felt betrayed by de Gaulle and ultimately by his fellow countrymen who had voted so overwhelmingly in favor of Algerian independence. Shortly after refusing reenlistment he followed LeClerc to Munich.

"Of course," he responded easily to LeClerc's request. "Do you have something for me to do?"

"No, I want to talk to you about your brother and your conversations with him."

Blanchet was bewildered and swallowed hard. He sensed an ominous undercurrent. He was now finding the tone less friendly. "What about him?" He added defensively, "He is a good man. A good soldier." He wished he had not added those last words. They could be misunderstood by the often paranoid LeClerc.

LeClerc seized on them. "A good soldier and a good man. Should I conclude from that that he's loyal to de Gaulle?" His almost hypnotic black eyes burrowed into Blanchet. "Yes or no?"

Blanchet was feeling more uncomfortable with an early flush of fear. "I...I don't know. We never talk about such things. Our conversations center on home...our parents...women...our memories of our childhood. Innocent stuff. What else do brothers talk about?"

"You tell me. I find it hard to believe that two Frenchmen...military men...would not talk about the capture of Colonel Argoud."

"I have not seen my brother since the colonel's abduction. I'm sure we'll talk about it when we next meet."

LeClerc stood and moved closer to the younger man. "I'm not talking about a discussion after he was taken. I'm talking about before," he said emphatically, "before he was abducted and captured. I'm wondering if you might have said anything about Argoud's or our presence here. Our strategies."

Blanchet twisted in his chair with discomfort. It was clear that LeClerc suspected he, his brother, or both might somehow be connected to the Argoud matter. His discomfort was not only the result of LeClerc's interrogation.

"Of course not," he said uneasily, almost whispering. He knew that he had indeed talked to his brother in very general terms about the rival subversive cells in Munich. He had once mentioned Argoud. His brother, Marcel Blanchet, an army sergeant, had reacted with interest, but he had not overreacted although he did raise his eyebrows at the mention of Antoine Argoud.

Pierre knew Marcel was loyal to the government, and they had argued about Pierre's opposition. But their discussions were primarily philosophic and not focused on personalities. Marcel knew Pierre was in contact with members of the OAS but Pierre had not revealed the extent of his involvement nor who was involved. Nonetheless, Marcel had warned Pierre to "be careful" on more than one occasion.

Is it possible wondered Blanchet, as LeClerc paced silently around the room, that his brother was somehow involved in the Argoud abduction and arrest? Is it possible their discussions led to that? If so, it was a betrayal of himself as well?

"I need to talk to your brother," LeClerc said, suddenly turning toward the increasingly jittery Blanchet. "Can you arrange a meeting? Here...or in Baden Baden. I have to know what he knows."

Blanchet's eyes widened. "I've told you he knows nothing about any of us." His heart rate accelerated with the lie. He knew that LeClerc, a former military interrogator, was not insensitive to deception or signs of it.

But where do his sympathies lie?" asked LeClerc leaning in close to Blanchet.

"I don't know," was his response. "We don't talk politics."

"You mean to say that in today's world you two sit down and only talk about Mama and nieces and cousins? I find that hard to believe." He clasped his hands behind his back. "Set up a meeting," he snapped. "I want to meet your brother. I need to be sure I can trust him...and you."

"I will try," answered Blanchet softly. He hoped he was convincing. He could not look Le-Clerc in the eye, something that did not escape the older man's notice. "But it may be difficult. He is in the army after all. He cannot come and go as he chooses. My brother is not political," he added. "He may suspect that I'm anti-Gaullist, but he could care less."

"Do it!" said LeClerc gruffly. "You recognize how important it is for you. Make him understand that, and he will find a way to get some time off."

Blanchet stood, hoping that the alarm he was feeling did not show. Given the way LeClerc stared at him with those piercing eyes he wondered if it were possible it did not. "I will do my best," he said weakly as he walked toward the door. He could feel heat on his back, knowing LeClerc's eyes were on him as he opened the door and closed it softly behind him.

Pierre Blanchet was not a man of the world. He was in his mid-twenties, had not been an exceptional student, and was ordinary in every respect. He left his primary education at seventeen to join the military. He rose only to the rank of corporal. It was during the time he was stationed in Algeria that he became an outspoken opponent of Algerian independence and an admirer of the military officers, and the rank and file who were affiliated with the Secret Army Organization. He joined his colleagues in strikes against the National Liberation Front and on more than one occasion participated in the torture of captured rebels.

While he was considered a competent soldier he was not perceived by his superiors or fellow soldiers as particularly bright. However, he was military-trained and was welcomed by the LeClerc faction when he quit the army and found his way to Munich.

It was his military training, and instincts honed against the FLN that put him on special alert after his conversation with LeClerc. Those instincts that had wakened in the North African desert were working on the streets of Munich. It was like an itch he could not scratch.

Blanchet was desperate to contact his brother and warn him of LeClerc's wish to meet with him. He needed to explain to him the importance of assuaging LeClerc's suspicions; however, within hours after his meeting with LeClerc, he had sensed rather than detected that he was being watched.

He never saw anyone specifically following him or surveilling him. But he felt it. He felt eyes on him rather than saw the eyes. There were a few occasions in which he saw someone on the other side of the street whom he thought he had seen someplace else the day before, who then later appeared sitting a few tables away at a café. He was certain that his modest room had been searched, only comforted in the knowledge that there was nothing there to be found. Nothing incriminating. The itch he could not scratch, to his mind, did not mean there was no itch. He became increasingly nervous and it showed. And his nervous demeanor was reported to LeClerc.

Blanchet was in a dilemma. LeClerc wanted him to arrange a meeting, but that was easier said than done. It's not always easy to contact active military personnel. When the brothers wanted to get together, as they did a few times a year, they usually made the arrangements by mail. Letters, some of which Pierre had saved, were likely read by those who went through his room. There was nothing political in the notes. Just times and places to meet. Complicating the situation at the moment was the fact that his brother's unit was currently on maneuvers, making contact all but impossible until the exercises had been completed.

LeClerc became increasingly impatient

after he received the news. The delay in arranging a meeting with Marcel Blanchet accelerated his suspicions and paranoia. His ordered surveillance of Pierre Blanchet had produced nothing to indicate that he was less committed to the cause than he had indicated. Strangely it only intensified LeClerc's concerns. Was it possible, he wondered, that Blanchet had no apparent flaws in his loyalty? He may have been one hundred percent committed to LeClerc, but that did not dilute his filial loyalties. Equal and total commitment to either man was not out of the question reasoned LeClerc, but could he command a greater loyalty from Blanchet than was available to his own flesh and blood? To himself? Of course not he finally rationalized. And if his brother were in any way connected to the abduction of Argoud, it would then follow, reasoned LeClerc, that Pierre Blanchet would protect his brother while also protecting himself if he'd had loose lips.

At the end of a week with Pierre having been unable to contact his brother, LeClerc's impatience overtook him. Through a daedalean series of communications with former military and OAS colleagues he managed to track down a member of his old unit in Algeria stationed at the French base in Baden Baden.

The process had taken several days at the end of which he learned that all recent maneuvers on the platoon, company or higher level had been completed within the past week. That meant that Pierre Blanchet had been lying both about his brother having been unreachable and about the difficulty of contacting base personnel. If Le-Clerc had been able to contact a stranger in a few days, should Pierre not have been able to reach a brother?

The disturbing revelation unsettled LeClerc and set him on an irreversible path for which many consequences were possible if not probable.

"Have you contacted your brother?" He asked Pierre sternly during a meeting in his room. "Maneuvers, I have learned, have been completed. I need to talk to him."

Blanchet had spent nervous days wondering and worrying about next steps since his earlier meeting with LeClerc. He had sent a letter to his brother when he learned of the field exercise and assumed that Marcel would contact him after reading it. He had been afraid of putting specifics in writing, but had made it clear that he urgently needed to talk to him. There had been no response. Now LeClerc was telling him that Marcel was back in Baden Baden. He was also telling him more by revealing that he apparently had a contact at the French base who could provide him with information.

"I have not heard from him," he said as calmly as he could. "He may be on leave. He has a girlfriend in Stuttgart.'

"You said you wrote to him. Would he have ignored your letter?"

Blanchet tried to smile. "You are French. What are your priorities after ten days in the field...your brother or a beautiful woman?"

LeClerc stared at him silently contemplating both the question and the man who had asked it. Finally he said, "I cannot overstate this. It is imperative that I speak with your brother without further delay. I don't know how you can make that happen, but you must. That's all there is to it. Do you understand? If you have to go to Stuttgart and drag him to Munich...do it! I have run out of patience."

"I have no idea where she is in Stuttgart, but I will try my best to find him," said Blanchet, feeling the new pressure intensely. "I'm not even sure he is with her."

"Get on it," said LeClerc with a dismissive wave of his only hand.

For the first time in days Blanchet felt a measure of relief later that same day. He had been worrying about his next steps when he answered a knock at the door to his modest room. When he opened it, he reacted with shock and disbelief to find his brother standing before him, tall and erect and handsome in his uniform. Instinctively, he said his name, then wrapped his arms around him in a tight hug. "You have no idea how glad

I am to see you," he said emotionally, stepping aside to let Marcel into the room.

He was unable to see the look of distaste on his brother's face as he scanned Pierre's modest accommodations. A sink with a single spigot stood against one wall, adjacent to a small bed with a ratty blanket cover. There was a single upholstered chair. His dirty jacket hung over the back of a lone wooden chair next to a small table containing a tiny lamp. The only other light in the room came from whatever could force its way in through a grimy window.

"I thought my room at the base was bad," said Marcel, "but this is a dump."

"Yes, it is," agreed Pierre. "I have very little money. But that's beside the point. We have to talk."

"That's why I'm here," said Marcel. "I just read your letter yesterday. It sounded urgent and I've had some leave time." He looked around the room again shaking his head. "Let's get out of here. I'll buy you a beer and we can talk."

Pierre led him to a nearby Gasthaus. He began his story as an overweight waiter limped away to fill their order. Pierre recited the situation in detail and answered Marcel's questions honestly. Marcel left no doubt about his displeasure over LeClerc's fraternity with radicals, their OAS connections, and his brother's involvement with them.

"I cannot believe that you think that you can change the world," he said as he slowly shook his head from side to side. "Kill de Gaulle?" he whispered. "Are you crazy? Trained assassins have not even gotten close and could not. Look what happened to Argoud. They found him. Here of all places. He's as good as dead." He hung his shaking head. "And...restore French rule in Algeria? That song has been sung," he said, "and the musicians have left." He grabbed his brother's hands. "What are you thinking?"

Pierre could not answer. His brother was older and they had always been close. He respected him and his every critical word was like the cut from a knife.

They sat silently, unaware of an unshaven man in workers' clothes nursing a beer and watching their emotional conversation from a few tables away. Not close enough to hear, but close enough to observe the younger brother stifling tears while the older brother patted his hands.

Pierre sniffled. "I have to know," he said looking at his brother intently. "Is it possible you repeated to anyone that I'd mentioned to you that Argoud was in Munich, or that there were anti-Gaullists active here?"

Marcel slowly pulled away from his brother's hands. He wrinkled his brow thinking as he took a swallow of beer. "It's possible," he said. "But I don't know. Perhaps while drinking with my friends..." His voice dropped off. "I just don't know."

"Your friends? I assume your friends are your friends because they are like you...think like you...and therefore are 'friends' who are loyal to de Gaulle?"

"We don't talk much politics. But you are right. I know we think alike. You pick up on things like that. But again, we talk about other things...women...football." He chuckled. "Mostly women." He smiled.

Pierre looked at him seriously. "Would you meet with LeClerc and tell him that. Swear that I never talked politics with you, that you knew nothing about Argoud in Munich and therefore could not have mentioned it to anyone."

"This is very serious for you isn't it?"

"It could be a matter of life or death. For me," and he added grimly, "and for you."

CHAPTER 6

The brothers met with LeClerc late the following morning. Pierre was somewhat more comfortable with LeClerc than he had been in their most recent meetings because his brother was with him and because he and Marcel had had a chance to talk. LeClerc asked questions about "political" conversations between the brothers. Marcel conceded that he was aware of Pierre's opposition to the de Gaulle government, but made it clear that it was not a subject they had talked about much less argued about.

The conversation proved testy when LeClerc asked pointed questions to Marcel about his own beliefs. Marcel, a seasoned military man, was no shrinking violet and made it clear that his beliefs about politics or anything else were none of LeClerc's business. As a former officer, LeClerc seethed that Marcel, a sergeant, was impertinent enough to treat and address him disrespectfully. He summoned all the self-control he could muster, knowing that it would be counterproductive to end the conversation with Marcel leaving, carrying with him a feeling of rancor that had not existed earlier. It could be dangerous for him, a man wanted by the government Marcel supported.

"Well, I thank you and your brother for coming," LeClerc said abruptly. "I hope you have not been offended. I trust we can end this conversation with an agreement to live and let live."

Much to Pierre's relief, Marcel nodded. It was without enthusiasm, which was duly noted by LeClerc who was increasingly uneasy. Nonetheless, he managed a slight smile and said, "Good. Again, thanks for seeing me. I hope we have an understanding. Now you can get back to your woman friend in Stuttgart."

Pierre felt himself shudder slightly, realizing this was something he had told LeClerc but had not mentioned to his brother.

Marcel looked quizzically at LeClerc. "Woman in Stuttgart. I have no woman in Stuttgart." He stood to leave. "I don't know what you're talking about."

"Oh. I guess I was misinformed. Sorry."

Pierre stood and moved to his brother. He was inwardly alarmed. A contradiction. What he had told LeClerc in trying to cover his inability to reach his brother a few days earlier could prove dangerous. An expressionless LeClerc looked at the two. He was difficult to read. But Pierre, who knew him well, realized this was a foreboding moment.

"Sorry. This guy," he said patting his brother's arm, "has women all over Germany...and France. Who knows where they all are." He turned fully to Marcel who was looking at him questioningly. "Ready Marcel?" he said quickly. "Let's go."

They left with no goodbyes. LeClerc watched the door shut behind them and stood staring at it for moments afterward.

"That was a mistake," said Pierre as they walked away from LeClerc's building.

"What was?" asked Marcel. "Meeting him?"

"No. When he wanted to meet with you and I couldn't track you down, I was looking for excuses, I said you might be with a girlfriend in Stuttgart. I didn't mention it to you. Forgot." He pounded one fist into the palm of his other hand. "I know him. I saw his face. He picked up on it. He was pretty good at that sort of thing in Algeria."

"I think he's convinced we had nothing to do with the Argoud matter."

"I hope you're right. God...I hope you're right." They walked a few paces and Pierre added, "But I wouldn't count on it." Marcel looked at his brother, wondering if he was overreacting to the situation in general and to LeClerc in particular. One look at Pierre's pinched expression told him that while he thought that might be the case, Pierre obviously did not.

They walked to the main train station and had lunch and a beer at a nearby beer garden. There was a nice breeze and a mixture of people who wore expressions showing sadness over imminent departure, or delight over recent reunion.

It was a largely silent hour as Marcel waited for a mid-afternoon train back to Baden Baden. At the appointed hour, the two men walked to track number six, dodging people who were coming and going. As the train whistled an all-aboard, Pierre hugged his brother. Standing with his hands on Marcel's shoulders he said quickly, "If anything happens to me it will be LeClerc's doing." He took a deep breath. "And mine," he added.

A speechless Marcel tried to find something to say, but could not find the words before the train began to move, making him run to get aboard before it was out of reach. Pierre watched him grab the iron handrail next to an open door and swing himself aboard. He wondered if he'd ever see his brother again.

At that very moment, LeClerc was meeting

with one of his men. The meeting with the two brothers did not entirely convince him that the two were totally trustworthy. The man with him was the same man who had been assigned to keep an eye on Blanchet, and later, his brother. He was an older man, with a shock of gray hair, and wrinkled face of leather cured by a lifetime outdoors, making him appear older than he was. His dialect was from southern France. He reported their emotional discussion the evening before at the local Gasthaus. While he could not hear what was being said, he reported that it was very intense. He did not know what to make of it other than to report that it seemed to him an unusual reunion.

LeClerc listened with his elbow on the small table before him. A finger on his only hand rested on his lips as he were trying to shush a child. When the other man had finished, LeClerc told him of the woman in Stuttgart that Blanchet had mentioned as a possible reason he could not track down his brother.

"The brother told me a few minutes ago that he knew nothing of a 'woman in Stuttgart' and had not been there." He jabbed at the table with his stubby finger. "What would you make of that?" he asked.

The other man's eyes brightened an otherwise cheerless expression. He looked like someone sensing that a long sermon was coming to an end.

"I would have to conclude that he was lying. At least about the woman. Then," he added, "I would have to ask why? And then I would wonder that if he would lie about one thing," he shrugged, "why wouldn't he lie about another. Once you know a person is capable of evasion, can deception or even betrayal be far behind?"

LeClerc sat silently flexing his jaw muscles. "Indeed," he said. "Indeed."

Two days later, LeClerc called his Munich associates to his office. Blanchet was relieved to see the other men and that he was not again alone with LeClerc. As was always the case when summoned by LeClerc, all of the men in the room showed some evidence of nervousness. None had any idea why they had been called together, and they were surprised when LeClerc entered the room smiling and in unusually good spirits. That made some of them even more jittery. They knew that the things that made LeClerc happy were often the things that made others sad. They wondered what he might be up to.

"For the first time since we've all been in Munich," he said, "we have what I consider to be a meaningful assignment. We have been asked by some of our opposition friends in France to strike at a target here."

The men looked at each other as if the details would come from one of them rather than LeClerc.

"De Gaulle, as you may know, has a small economic liaison office here in Munich. It's designed to work on shared Common Market interests. That's the official version. I suspect he wants to keep a close eye on the Germans. He's never trusted them. My guess is that some of his economic *specialists* have other talents. I suspect some of the members of the Trade Mission are security agents watching the Germans. And," he paused, "more important from our point of view, are also looking for people like us. They may have even been involved in the Argoud abduction. Our friends obviously want to disrupt any momentum along these lines."

One of the men shouted, "How?"

LeClerc was obviously enjoying the moment and the promise of action. He was also a man who, during his military career, had taken more orders that he had given. He relished his role as the leader, even though he led only a small band of acolytes.

"Simple," he said. "We are going to bomb it...bomb the Trade Mission."

There was a buzz of excitement and anticipation in the room as the men reacted.

"It's going to happen tomorrow night," said LeClerc picking up on the excitement in the room. "One of you will be assigned to this...mission. It is simple. We will toss a bomb through the window of these offices. It will be powerful enough to shut down the operation and send a message to those who need to hear it. We're doing it at night. It's not that we don't want blood on our hands. It will just make escape easier."

The men nodded approvingly.

"Obviously, we must keep this to ourselves. I am hopeful we'll have more assignments in the weeks and months ahead. It is critical that this mission be a success." He looked around the room. "Not all of you have military experience. Some who do have not had much of it. For this first assignment, I need a veteran army man." He turned to Pierre Blanchet.

"Blanchet," he said moving to him, "you have the honor to strike this blow."

Pierre lost his breath over the shock of his selection. He was nonplused. It was entirely unexpected and somewhat unwelcome. His selection after the recent tension with LeClerc was not entirely without suspicion. On the other hand, he thought he could also interpret his selection as a vote of confidence: a signal that he was trusted. Nonetheless, he felt his throat dry as LeClerc dismissed the men while asking him to stay. The group broke with his colleagues patting him on the back and shoulder as they filed out of the room.

When all the men were gone LeClerc said,

"You look surprised. Or am I misreading you?" Perhaps you are disappointed or unwilling to carry out this task?"

"I am surprised, but only at the suddenness of learning of the mission. It came out of the blue. I'm pleased that you have confidence in me being able to carry it out."

"It makes sense. You have had missions like this in North Africa. We want someone with experience and nerves to carry it out. You are the best man."

"Okay then. What do I need to know."

"Here's the address," LeClerc said handing him a piece of paper. "I think you should go by and take a look at the target. See what you're getting into and what the best approach will be."

"Makes sense."

"The bomb will be very simple. A timed device. You push a button and walk away. A minute later it blows. It's not a busy street. At a late hour, no one is likely to see you coming or going." He put out his hand. Blanchet responded. As they shook hands, LeClerc said, "Congratulations. You are going to make history for a new France."

"Thank you," said Blanchet, still debating to himself whether he was encountering sincerity or seduction.

Blanchet left the meeting convincing himself that he had been reinstated in LeClerc's good graces. The meeting between him, Michel and LeClerc had apparently gone better than he had feared. He was energized by his selection and by the prospect of contributing to the cause and proving his loyalty. He felt the mission made obvious sense. Certainly, any French security or intelligence personnel in the Trade Mission's orbit represented a threat. Discovery would not be met with handshakes and pats on the back.

He wanted to inspect his target immediately. It was only a mile or two away from Le-Clerc's apartment. He decided to walk and take advantage of a nice day and bask in his reestablished status. Over a period of several blocks, he moved through dingy residential neighborhoods with old stone houses that included many still in need of repair from wartime damage. The people he saw there looked just as sullen and gloomy as the neighborhoods themselves. How un-Bavarian, he thought.

The apparent mood of passersby changed for the better the closer he got to the commercial quarter. Shops occupied street level space in buildings that dated from the past century and beyond. The sound of traffic was pleasing. He was chased by splashes of sun reflecting from shop windows winking at him as he passed.

As he neared the French Trade Mission, he crossed the street so he could observe the target less conspicuously. He saw no risk in standing for a few moments observing the target while hurried shoppers, and an occasional trolley, moved by. It would be an easy assignment. The office was on ground level near an intersection that would give him the option of any one of four directions to leave the scene. While it was busy now in the middle of the commercial day, shops would be closed late at night. As promised, foot traffic would be all but non-existent. There were no eating or drinking establishments in the immediate area which would further reduce traffic.

He saw that he had an option of placing the bomb near the entrance door which was recessed in a small alcove a few feet from the sidewalk. Or, he could, as LeClerc had suggested simply toss it through the large window that faced the street. He decided on the alcove. Less noisy and therefore less conspicuous he thought. Yes, it would be easy, and it would solidify evidence of his commitment to LeClerc's fledgling organization.

After the best night's sleep he had had in recent weeks, he reported his findings to LeClerc the following morning. LeClerc seemed satisfied with his plan and told Pierre he was convinced he had made the right decision in choosing him for the assignment.

A man Blanchet had never seen before arrived as he and LeClerc talked. He was introduced to Blanchet simply as the bomb maker. He nodded without speaking as he pulled a dark, metallic device from a gunny sack he had carried in with him. He handled it gingerly and advised Blanchet to do the same as he placed it carefully on a table.

"Keep it someplace safe, quiet, and away from anyone who is especially curious" he warned. "It is safe, but not for the curious to examine. It's no toy." It was a caution Blanchet knew was directed at him.

"Until Blanchet plays with it tonight," said LeClerc with uncharacteristic humor. The other man laughed. Blanchet did not. The device was about the size of a car battery and looked innocent enough. It was square and innocuous with no visible telltale wires or gauges. But the man explained that it contained enough explosives to do serious damage to the small office.

"How about the rest of the building?" asked Pierre.

"There will be some peripheral damage." He pointed to a small mark on the side of the case. "Point this toward the door and the blast will be directed primarily in that direction." He then moved his finger slowly toward a small switch on the top of the device.

"Here is the trigger," he said quietly. "Just flick this switch and the bomb is activated. It cannot be turned off once it's turned on. It's set on a delayed action and will detonate approximately forty five seconds after you turn it on."

"Approximately?" asked Blanchet.

"Yes, a few seconds variation one way or the other, but you will have plenty of time to get beyond the force of the blast."

"Lift it," ordered LeClerc. "Make sure it is not too heavy for you."

Pierre could not tell if it was another attempt at humor. He picked up the device. Instinctively, LeClerc took a step backward.

The bomb maker held his hand in the air. "Handle it as little as possible between now and tonight," he said. "It is quite stable, but there's no point in tempting fate." A slight smile was not reassuring.

Blanchet lifted the bomb gingerly. It was heavier than he thought. He held it for a moment, returned it to the table, and gently set it down.

"If I were you," said the bomb maker, "I would not take the trolley to the site. The device does not like a lot of vibration."

"So how do I get it there?" said Pierre alarmed.

"Carry it in this sack. It will be all right. I carried it here." He thought for a moment, adding, "Think of as carrying a bucket of beer that you don't want to spill."

"Just don't bump into anything," said LeClerc laughing, again uncharacteristically.

Blanchet looked at him and the other man, who was not laughing. At that moment he wished he had not been given the assignment. "Seems simple enough. I'll just take it home now and wait for the sun to go down. And hope I don't blow myself into smithereens in the meantime," he said sarcastically. He was indeed eager for the moment when the assignment was completed and he could get as far away from the deadly device as possible.

His room was not far away, a walk of about fifteen minutes. His fear subsided as he carried the sack and managed to easily maintain balance and stability. Nonetheless he was relieved to park it in a corner of his room and await the coming night. He was confident that the device would be secure until then, and that he could manage it on the walk to ground zero. Relieved, he took a fitful nap and dreamed of noisy, fiery combat against FLN forces in Algeria.

The hours passed slowly after he woke. He couldn't eat. He was more nervous than he thought he would be. His stomach was queasy. He checked his clock to make sure it was still working. He stood over the bomb several times and just stared at it as if it would talk to him and reassure him that everything was all right.

Finally, the self appointed hour for beginning his adventure arrived. Blanchet carefully lifted the canvas sack, took a deep breath, and nervously left his room for the targeted site. He hoped the walk would be uneventful. A trolley on the route he knew would have taken him to his destination screeched past him and he wished he could have been on it. The sack became heavier and heavier as he plodded along a route he'd selected to ensure limited contact.

It was moments before midnight when he arrived at the French Trade Mission. All was quiet. There were no vehicles and no pedestrian traffic. The trolleys were now on a reduced overnight schedule. It was exactly as he had hoped and planned. At the intersection he looked in all directions to reaffirm his solitude and departure route.

He crossed the street and walked toward the entrance to the office. He was about ten feet away from the entrance alcove when he heard a noise behind him. He turned quickly, and as he did, the canvas bag clunked against the sidewalk. Blanchet froze. His heart raced. Across the street, a man was walking unsteadily toward the intersection, coughing loudly, like a chronic smoker. Apparently oblivious to Blanchet, he stopped and leaned toward the curb and vomited fiercely into the street. When he had finished, he looked up, saw Pierre, waved as if he were an old acquaintance, and moved on.

Blanchet had been holding his breath. It was only fully restored when the other man turned a corner and was out of sight. Blanchet turned to the entrance to the office. He was breathing hard now. The moment was close at hand.

Step by step, his temples throbbing, he made his way closer and closer to the door where he would place the bomb. He arrived, stood there for a moment, and gently placed his device against the door, checking to make sure the mark that would ensure proper deployment of the payload was properly aimed. He stood for a moment, then bent to flip the switch that would trigger the device. He counted to three and activated the bomb.

It blew. Immediately.

The door in front of Pierre and the device was disintegrated and the room beyond was shattered. The ceiling and walls smashed into the room sending shards of concrete, wood and glass in all directions. Sections of the building above split and cracked and fell in a cloud of dust and ear splitting noise, obliterating screams from residents above.

Pierre Blanchet never heard any of it. His body had been ripped apart within a millisecond of touching that switch.

More than a hundred yards away, around the corner from the blast site, a young drunk who had, seconds before, been retching across the street from the damaged building, was thrown to the ground, wondering what the hell had happened?

It was a question Pierre Marcel would never have a chance to ask.

CHAPTER 7

There was still evidence of smoke and dust eight hours later when Ted and Hank stood outside the badly damaged building. Bits and pieces of glass, wood and concrete littered the sidewalk and street. Indistinguishable from the other debris were parts of Pierre Blanchet's body. His other remains had been removed. The area had been closed off as German technicians systematically collected samples for analysis in and around the rubble.

A portion of the front of the building had been sheered away and was part of the litter on the street. A few civilians, some in nightclothes, stood off to the side still in shock over the explosion that had rocked the building and destroyed some of their apartments as they slept. The building had been ordered evacuated. Inspectors moved carefully inside the structure to determine if any of the building was still habitable.

The French Trade Mission was in complete shambles. Two men were inside trying to salvage whatever was intact and might be of further use to them. They eventually came outside carrying some papers and folders which they placed in a car just outside the line of police tape. They were in and out half a dozen times before they emerged for the final time and stood before the wreckage shaking their heads.

Hank and Ted joined other journalists, some of whom had been gathering since dawn. Eventually the two Frenchmen agreed to the journalists' demands for answers to their questions. They were asked and answered in German but provided little in the way of useful information.

The two Frenchmen could offer nothing in the way of an explanation for what happened beyond confirming what everyone already knew, that this had been no accident: that a bomb had been intentionally detonated, directed apparently at the French Trade Mission. And that a man...they thought it was a man...the suspected bomber, had been killed in the bombing. The Frenchmen looked tired. One wore a black turtleneck sweater that was dusty from his time in the damaged office. He had been doing most of the talking. His colleague was more formally dressed in a dirt-smudged white shirt with no tie, and blue trousers.

"Why do you think the office was attacked?" asked Hank.

The man in the sweater shook his head. "I can only assume," he said. "I have no knowledge. But attacks against French property have not been uncommon before or since the Algerian settlement at Evian. Remnants of the OAS are all over Europe...including Munich. Remember that Argoud had established himself here. This may have been a response to his capture." His colleague rubbed his chin at the mention of Argoud's name.

"So, you're guessing it's the OAS," said Hank. "Do you have any idea about OAS cells in Munich? Germany?"

"They are like ants," said the Frenchman. "You have no idea who they are, where they are, or how many there are until you open the cupboard and they are all over the bread." He rolled his eyes.

The other man suddenly spoke up. His German was not as good as his colleagues. His face reddened as he spoke. "We are always on the alert for them," he said. "We have people in Germany who are very much on the lookout for them."

His colleague put his hand on the other man's arm, a clear signal for him to stop speaking. "That's enough," he admonished sharply.

"In Munich?" asked Hank.

"What?" said the man in the sweater.

"He said you have people in Germany looking for these terrorist types. In Munich?" he repeated.

"As I said, Argoud was here. What do you think?" He looked closely at Hank. "We have to go." He nodded to his partner and they walked briskly to their car. The man in the sweater seemed to be speaking angrily to the other Frenchman as they walked.

Hank and Ted backed away from the half dozen other journalists, some of whom were still making notes from the short conversation with the two Frenchmen. As they reached the other side of the street, Hank turned toward their car just as the Frenchmen were slamming its doors. He couldn't believe what he saw as the window rolled down on the driver's side and the man in the turtleneck was engaged in animated conversation with a very pretty young woman. It was Ilse Stengel.

I have a little French Hank remembered her telling him once.

The conversation went on for several minutes as Ted and Hank watched. Hank's surprised expression did not change as he observed the conversation at the car. He could see Ilse's reflection on the shiny vehicle. Ted watched with a slight smile on his face. A passerby might have compared it to that of a proud and pleased parent. They waited in place until the conversation was over and the car backed away from the police lines protecting the site. Ilse stood and watched them leave.

She turned and looked surprised as if she were noticing Hank and Ted for the first time. She waved and smiled just as she might when coming across friends in the park. She continued waving as she walked toward them. She gave Ted a big hug and they spoke rapidly in words Hank could not understand. When they finished, she extended her hand to Hank.

"He gets the hug, and I get a handshake. What's wrong with this picture?" asked Hank. Ted laughed out loud.

"Why nothing," said Ilse playfully. "I just don't know you as well as I do Ted." Hank thought that that was something he'd like to correct as he bowed slightly and said nothing in response.

There was another flurry of the common language between Ilse and Ted. *Didn't Ted say they always spoke English wondered Hank.* When there was a pause, Hank said to Ilse, "I'm surprised to see you here. It's a long way from the RFE archives."

"I thought I might stop by on my way to work and that perhaps I could learn something I could pass along to the newsroom. Always trying to get on their good side."

"I think you're covered. Your guy Dieter was here with the other press. He had his recorder," Hank said, unable to resist being just a little sarcastic.

"Yes," she said, "but Dieter did not have a private interview with Monsieur Garnier." She lifted her brows. "For that matter, neither did you," she said grinning. "I've got to go," she added. "I'm late for work."

Ted chortled, "You've got your hands full with that one," he said. "She's sharp, and can give it as well as she takes it. And, take it from me, she's not going to take a back seat to anybody when it comes to getting what she wants."

"Point taken," Hank said as he watched Ilse walk quickly out of sight. "Let's go to the office," he said starting to walk the other way. "I think we've got a story here, he said to Ted." He stopped suddenly and turned to his companion. "You know what really pisses me off?" he said without waiting for an answer. "I never got the French-man's name."

"I'll get it," said Ted. "And don't worry, I won't ask her for it."

"Much appreciated," said Hank, trying not to sound deflated.

One Dead in Munich French Trade Mission Bombing
By Hank Tollar

Munich---A powerful bomb ex-ploded early yesterday at the small French Trade Mission office in down-town Munich. One person was killed in the blast. Damage was extensive to the office and to the building which houses several apartments on the upper floors.

While no one was injured inside the building in the overnight bombing, the badly mangled human remains of one person were found outside the office. It's believed they are those of the bomber, or perhaps a passerby. German police are investigating. They say it will take some time to identify the remains.

A Mission staff member said at the scene that it is possible that the bombing was connected to recent attacks in Europe and elsewhere carried out by the Secret Army Organization, the paramilitary organization opposed to Algerian independence. The OAS has targeted French officials and property in Europe and Algeria.

The spokesman, Antoine Garnier, cited the abduction in Munich of Colonel Antoine Argoud, a leading member of the anti-Gaullist opposition, a month ago. He was later captured and arrested in Paris. It was suggested the bombing attack might have been in retaliation for the Argoud abduction.

Another Mission staffer, Julien Raphael, said, "We have people in Germany who are very much on the lookout for them." He refused to elaborate.

There is no information available on the extent of the anti-Gaullist opposition in Germany or in Munich specifically.

Neither the U.S. Embassy in Bonn nor the Consulate in Munich is commenting.

Eight families living in the bombed building have been displaced. None are American. German engineers say it will take several days before it can be determined whether the damaged building is fully habitable.

"What can you tell me about the Munich bombing," asked Hank. He was sitting at the desk of consular press officer J. Harding Bell. Hank thought the name fit the job, but Bell was not blessed with Hollywood's version of members of the diplomatic corps. He had a mild lisp, wore an uneven mustache and had large ears that hovered over jowls hanging like pouches from his cheeks. But, he was friendly, forthcoming, and had a sense of humor that Hank had come to enjoy.

"I can't tell you squat about it other than that the French are freaking out. The quote you have in your story is an understatement. Off the record here...they have teams of agents from the French Special Intelligence Service, to the National police, the Sûreté nationale, here and else-where. They're all over the place and have been for a while...even before the bombing. They got Argoud. Apparently with a little help from a friend...whoever that might have been." He pulled a pack of cigarettes from his breast pocket and took a minute to light one.

"There's a rumor de Gaulle may be coming to Germany in a couple of weeks to talk trade."

"I've heard that," said Hank. "We're waiting to hear. Could be dangerous for him."

"Understatement."

"Yeah, the OAS has tried to get him more than once."

"He was in Bonn last year. He had so many security people jammed so tightly around him he was like a cigarette in a pack. Someone said he could have been shot and not fallen to the ground."

"Jeez."

"You can use this from an informed source," said Bell abruptly changing the subject. "We have offered to bring in some FBI analysts to help with the bombing. The offer was to the Germans. They're good with it. The Frenchies will be sending in their own bomb experts. They'll be falling all over each other."

"What about the body?"

"This is just me talking. No attribution." He waited for Hank to signal he understood. "There's pretty much a consensus that it's the bomber. It's not a resident. No one's been reported missing. German forensics types are on it. Not much to work with. We do have a hand, so fingerprints are a possibility. But...there are burns. So, that may not work." After a deep breath he said, "It's a mess. A real mess."

Hank slapped his notebook shut and thanked Bell. He hadn't given him much, but he knew he could get a few graphs out of it, advance the story and keep it alive. The two men chatted for a few more moments before Hank left to go back to the office.

He had just reached the front door when he heard his named called from behind. He turned quickly and found himself facing Ilse Stengel, almost jogging to catch up with him. She was dressed in tailored ski pants, favorite attire for young German women when the weather was turning cool. A light parka had her looking like a commercial for winter Alpine vacations in Bavaria. She also wore the now famous and always charming Stengel smile. It made Hank smile too.

She was slightly out of breath when she caught up to him. "You're everywhere," she said pleasantly.

"I could say the same about you. Don't you ever spend any time at your office at RFE?"

"Too much time," she answered. "The archive offices are in the basement. It's dark and chilly.

I like to get out once in a while."

"Yeah, like to bomb scenes and student demonstrations," he said in mock reproach. "Did you just decide to wander over to the U.S. Consulate?"

"I'm over here a lot. They help us out when there are new employees we have to vet. We can do it with our people but we always run it by the Amis...excuse me...the Americans. They have the best intelligence from the East."

"Better than the refugees?

"Oh yes. They have people on the ground there. These regimes in the East are always trying to slip one of their own, a ringer you call it, into our operation. You can't be too careful. Mr. Howell has identified several over time."

"A ringer? Where did you learn that one?"

"Hank, I watch American movies. It's the best way to learn English."

After a moment Hank asked, "Who do you work with here?" He asked matter-of-factly. He was going into reporter mode. He sensed he was learning something that could be useful to him... something that maybe he shouldn't otherwise be allowed to know.

"The Cultural Attaché," she answered breezily. "Charles Howell."

Cultural Attaché thought Hank. He wondered what a consular officer responsible for promoting the cultural attributes of his own country would be doing vetting refugees, emigrés and political dissidents from the communist East. Hank made a mental note to look up Charles Howell the next time he was in the consulate and see if he could confirm what he was thinking. Howell sounded more to him more like a CIA operative than someone whose job it was to arrange speaking tours for artists and poets.

He remembered an early conversation with Gene Talbot when he questioned the connection between RFE and the Central Intelligence Agency. Talbot had avoided the question. But now it seemed to make sense. If Radio Free Europe was as closely aligned with the CIA as many people thought, it would make perfect sense to use the agency to help cross check the backgrounds of RFE employees...old and new.

He was preoccupied with these thoughts when Ilse asked, "Where did you go? I just asked if you wanted to have lunch. You looked like you were a million miles away."

"No, I'm right here at one of my favorite places. Next to you." She blushed, something he had never seen her do before. It surprised him and, at the same time, delighted him. Could it be that she'd forgotten Lucky for a moment, and perhaps for an afternoon?

"I'd love to," he said. "I know a nice little place just a few minutes from here." He reached for her hand and was surprised when she took it. She looked up at him grinning like a little girl. In those moments he forgot about the CIA, or Lucky Manon or anything other than the beautiful young lady who held his hand willingly and tightly as they walked to a tiny café at the edge of the park.

They ordered lunch and made small talk. She questioned him about his work and about the kinds of things she would have to learn to be a good reporter. He asked her more about her relationship with Ted, and even ventured a question about Lucky. He wanted to see what her reaction would be.

"Lucky's in France," she said. "He'll be in town in a couple of days." Hank's heart fell. "He wants to race in the US and is trying to set up something at a place I think is called Watkins Glen. I never heard of it."

"It's a very famous track and has been around for a while. I don't know much about racing but I know Watkins Glen is a big deal and that the really, really good...the best drivers...compete there."

"Well, I know he wants to race there. He wants to meet with folks at the consulate to see if they can help him. He needs US sponsors. Can't race without them."

"Howell?"

"I don't know. We'll see," she said as their lunch arrived. The waiter held two large plates covered with open-faced sandwiches. Generous slices of ham and cheese rested on crusty rye bread placed before them.

"That's some sandwich," she said. "I hope you can eat some of mine."

"That's not a sandwich," he said laughing. "A sandwich is two slices of bread with the ham and cheese in between. Something I've noticed. Every German worker I see, whether they work in an office, on a streetcar, or anywhere, carries a briefcase to work and it invariably contains a sandwich...something between two slices of bread. And yet you can't order a sandwich as a sandwich in a restaurant. Do the Germans even have a word for it?"

'No," she shook her head. "But I think the word would be understood. Even most German waiters speak some English."

"Well what do they call it...what's the word...when a husband tells his wife to make him a...whatever...to take to work?"

"Whoa," she said, dabbing the corner of her mouth with her napkin. "If you want a sandwich in a restaurant and the waiter doesn't understand what you want, all you have to do is describe it. Literally. Say you'd like ham and cheese put together between two slices of bread. Or, if you want to really get daring," she said teasingly "cut what you have in front of you in half, clap it together, and voila, you have a sandwich.

"As for the husband telling his wife to make one for him, I think the proper response is to tell him to make it himself. There!" She put her hands on her hips pretending to look angry. But it only made Hank laugh.

"Wow. I touched a button didn't I? You win. I'll just order soup from now on. It's a lot less complicated."

Ilse raised both arms in the air like an Olympic gold medalist. "I consider the great sandwich debate over." She watched as he cut the bread on his plate and made a sandwich, smiling like a little boy.

It was one of those days. Cotton balls drifted in the deep blue sky, nudged by a comfortable breeze. Passersby seemed in less of a hurry than on another day. No rush to get back to work. People were smiling. That kind of a day. Hank watched Ilse, wondering what it was going to take to get to know her better. He enjoyed being with her and enjoyed their conversations although it seemed he had to work harder at drawing her out than she did with him. Maybe it's just shyness on her part, he thought.

"I'd like to meet Lucky," he said as they were finishing coffee.

She looked surprised, then questioningly, wondering why Hank might think that would be a good idea. "Why?" she said without enthusiasm.

"He's a friend of yours number one. He has

an interesting career, and I'd like to learn more about him. Maybe I can do a story." He didn't say what he really wanted was to see what Ilse might see in him, as well as get some notion as to how he felt about her.

"He might like that." Hank could not escape the feeling that she seemed guarded, even cautious, though he couldn't begin to imagine why. "I can ask him when he gets in."

"I would think someone who does what he does might like the publicity. By the way, when is he getting in?"

She put her elbows on the table, brought her hands together, and played with her fingers. She looked at him in a circumspect way. Finally, she said, "He gets in tomorrow morning sometime. I'll see him after work."

"Where does he stay when he's in town?"

Again, she fidgeted with her fingers until she reached across the table and cupped one of his hands in hers. "He stays with me. When he's in town he always stays with me." She tried to smile as if her words were inconsequential. But they were anything but that to Hank, who felt as if his breath had just been taken away.

"Oh," he said meekly. "I see." He was struggling to find appropriate words as well as to breathe. For a moment he thought he would not manage either.

She continued to hold his hand. "I'm sorry

Hank. That's just the way it is. I feel I've hurt you. That's the last thing I would want. I'm very fond of you, but as I say...that's just the way it is." Her attempt at a reassuring smile was unconvincing.

"I'm your friend," he finally said, "and I want to keep it that way. I'm not a judge." He put his other hand on hers. "But I do reserve the right to be disappointed. Will you give me that?"

"Of course. You flatter me. And I want to be your friend too." Their hands remained clasped for a moment until she pulled hers away.

"I have to go. Believe it or not I do sometimes go to the office and I'm sure they're eager to hear what information I have to give them from Mr. Howell."

He looked at her, wishing the earlier part of the conversation had never taken place. He was hurting.

Hank called for the check and as they stood he saw Ted crossing the street. He looked like he was in a hurry. Hank and Ilse both waved to get his attention.

He gave Ilse a hug. "I'm glad I ran into you. I thought you might still be at the consulate," he said turning to Hank. "Bell's secretary called. He has some information he thinks you would want. He'll be there at two." He looked at his watch. "Twenty minutes from now."

They said their goodbyes to Ilse and headed for the consulate speculating on what J. Harding

Bell might have to tell them though neither had a clue. They walked in silence. Hank was morose.

The consular official was waiting in his office. Tom Morrow was there when the two arrived. They nodded hello.

"Okay fellas," said Bell. "I thought you might be interested in this." He turned to the AFN reporter. "Tom, sorry no recording. What I have to say did not come from US sources. It's just for background. You can follow up with the Germans or French." He leaned back in his chair. "Ted, I'm afraid I'm going to have to ask you to leave. Sorry, these guys have the right clearance. Why don't you wait in the lobby."

Ted's expression didn't change. He stood, nodded and said, "I understand," and left the room.

"Sorry about that," said Bell to the other two. "Rules. Foreign nationals and all." When the door closed, he said, "Now, to business. We've got a tentative but probably solid ID on that body at the French Trade Mission. Looks like a bomber to me. They got enough of a fingerprint to identify the ole corpus delicti. Seems his name is...or rather was...Pierre Blanchet. He's a former army enlisted man with suspect political leanings. He left the service six months ago. Apparently he's been here for a while."

"If so, I guess the next step would be to determine who his friends are," said Hank, adding, "unless he was a lone wolf."

"There's a lot to learn," said Bell. "I think we can give you a little more. Do you guys know Charlie Howell?"

Morrow shook his head while Hank flinched. "Howell? The Cultural Attaché?"

Bell paused for several seconds. "Yeah, that's right the Cultural Attaché." He then chuckled and gave them both an exaggerated wink.

Hank and Tom looked at each other. They said nothing but their raised eyebrows said, "Message received loud and clear." Five minutes later they were in Howell's office.

Hank didn't know if he'd ever met a CIA agent. By virtue of their jobs their occupation was generally not a matter of public knowledge. Hank was more certain than ever, after that wink from Bell, that in the unlikely event people in his line of work carried business cards, Howell's would read "CIA."

Hank had the Hollywood stereotype image in mind of what a Central Intelligence Agency officer might look like. He imagined the chiseled image of an Army Ranger, Navy SEAL or Marlboro Man. What he found in Howell was Orson Welles at the back end of his career, after he had pulled the rip cord. He spilled over his chair and never moved to get up when he bellowed, "sit down" to his visitors.

Howell grunted as they exchanged introductions and he reached across his desk to shake hands. In a voice that was deep and assertive he got right to the point. "Okay, you guys are cleared for secret, so we can talk. What we say here stays here. Got that?"

The two nodded.

"This is an off-the-record moment. You're in on it because as journalists you might stumble across some of this on your own. If you do, we want you to get it straight when you can use it, how to use it, and keep the lid on when it has to be kept on. Understood?" He studied each man closely. "If I read or hear anything that came out of this office, you're on the first boat back to the good old U.S. of A. And, your next job will be selling pencils on the sidewalk. In case you doubt it, rest assured, I'm not kidding."

Both visitors nodded though both were troubled by the 'keep the lid on' comment. Hank and Tom were impressed that this guy, who would give Fatty Arbuckle a run for his money, could pull off such a commanding, even threatening, presence. Howell sat back in his chair, shifting slightly to accommodate his bulk between the armrests.

"I'm sure Bell told you we have an identification on the Frenchie whose body parts were found at that French Trade Mission. We have every reason to believe he has OAS connections and that he was part of a small cell here in Munich or someplace in Germany. We've got some work to do on that.

"What I want to impress on you guys is that this is a touchy deal. The Germans and the French are not exactly best buddies. Our friend de Gaulle gets his nose out of joint pretty easily...especially when it comes to an organization that's tried to take him out more than once... and take out his government at the same time. He's not crazy about Americans right now either.

"The fact that there is a cell...or cells...operating in Germany is not sitting well in Paris. And this, after Argoud set up shop here, has just made a bad situation worse. The Krauts...I mean Germans," he said derisively..."are also antsy. Keep that in mind in anything you might be writing in the future.

"We need to get to the bottom of these French groups here and find out if the Russians are working with them. That's a big complication we don't need and won't know about until we identify the cells and have a friendly little chat with some of their members."

Hank and Tom were thinking the same thing. Howell was giving them a great story they could not use...yet.

"The FBI has a team in town working on the bombing, and working with us on all of this."

"Us?" asked Tom. "Who is us? What do you mean by us?"

"Us. Just us," said Howell slyly. "Us as in U.S. okay? Leave it at that."

"Does the FBI have any jurisdiction or authority here?" asked Hank.

"Let me just say that the Germans and the State Department are very happy to have them here. They were invited by Bonn. The French are also on board. The welcome mat is out. If the agents learn anything useful, they'll pass it along and the Germans will take it from there.

"Another little tidbit for you. You'll be hearing about it. Pierre Blanchet had a brother...in the army...French Army...stationed in Baden Baden."

"And," asked Hank, "is he helpful? Involved?"

"He's not helpful at all. He's dead. He was pulled out of the Oos River yesterday with a bullet in his head. Involved? That's the sixty-four dollar question. Maybe it's coincidence. If not, it's a big complication. The Germans and French are going to release it. They hope it will shake the tree and get someone talking. Keep your ears open boys. And, keep you mouths shut. As you can see it's a tough nut to crack with a couple of complications riding shotgun that have a lot more riding on them than a good news story is worth."

"You're asking us to put some ethical issues aside," said Tom who surprised Hank with his outspokenness. "You've put us in a box that's making difficult for us to cover this story at all."

"Screw ethics," said Howell. "Maybe that's where I want you...in a box. I want to be able to keep an eye on you before you come up with something on your own that could be...what shall we say...problematic."

"So what are we supposed to do?" asked Hank, "run stuff by you? That sounds a lot like censorship."

"We all have the same boss. Don't think of it as censorship. Think of me as an editor. The editor in chief is in Washington."

Tom didn't seem cowed. "As in John McCone? Let's face it, the Cultural Attaché in Munich seems to be overstepping his...portfolio."

"Next question," snapped Howell, his face suddenly as stony as a block of granite. "You're way ahead of your skis." It wasn't just a comment. It was a warning.

Hank and Tom realized this was a battle they weren't going to win. Hank thought they'd be better off trying to get along with Howell than by knocking heads with him. He could be a real obstacle as well as nuisance. But he also held all the cards, some of which might be useful down the road, wherever that road was taking them all. Nonetheless, Hank thought he'd take a chance.

"I guess you're briefing RFE too," he said. "I saw Ilse Stengel here earlier this morning."

Howell leaned toward Hank, looking at him suspiciously. "You know Ilse?"

Hank nodded.

"She does archives, not news. We swap notes from time to time."

"She wants to be a reporter," said Hank.

Howell looked closely and hard at him, a slow smile appeared. "You look like you're under Ilse's spell," he said. "You wouldn't be the first."

"Spell?" questioned Hank.

"Spell, as in infatuated. And, why not. She's lovely, smart and nice to be around. Lots of personality. Men like her. As I say, why not? But, charming as she is, if I need to talk to news...I'll talk to Talbot...not Ilse. I do want to talk to one of her friends though."

On a longshot impulse, Hank asked, "Lucky?"

"Interesting background. He's Alsatian. Lots of French friends. He's back in town. Got back last night."

"Ah," said Hank, surprised at the comment. Ilse had told him an hour earlier that Lucky was coming back tomorrow. Ilse *is* charming he thought. Is she also a liar? And, why would she lie?

Hank and Tom left the consulate without speaking, each was depressed after Howell's lecture and admonition. Hank had a double dose of cheerlessness because of what he'd learned about Ilse and Lucky.

They didn't speak until they were outside and Tom offered Hank a lift back to his office. They were in the car and in traffic when Tom asked Hank about his reaction to the earlier conversation.

"It's pretty clear he's a spook," said Hank. "Cultural Attaché my ass. I think he has our hands tied. He told us just enough to prevent us from reporting almost anything. If we do, he'll hammer us saying we were using information we got from him."

"On the other hand, without saying so, he is now a source," said Tom. "If we get something we need to check out, we can go to him."

"So he can put it off the record," said Hank glumly. "I wonder if there have been similar conversations with the correspondents in Bonn? I haven't even seen any mention of the bombing in the Times or Trib. My guess is they'll all be kept in the dark when they start asking questions. *If* they start asking questions. We probably know as much about it as anyone on the inside of the investigation. They choose to be silent. We've essentially been ordered to keep quiet."

"I believe it's called a muzzle."

"This business of Blanchet's brother being found dead is something. A hell of a coincidence, or some deep shit," said Hank.

"It's not like covering a local crime story," said Tom. "This is international. That, and the fact CIA spooks are on it, makes it big. Very big. It won't be long before the boys in Bonn start reading the Munich papers and get curious."

"Well, we read the Munich the newspapers too," said Hank. "We can report on what they local papers are reporting. Howell can't do anything about that, can he?"

"We'll see," said Tom. "Much as I hate to say it, I think we'll to have to keep in close touch with him whatever we do with this story." He jabbed Hank in the ribs. "Unless you want to become Baltimore's best-selling street corner pencil salesman."

CHAPTER 8

For the next two days, Hank and Tom independently checked the Munich papers looking for anything on the story they might use. Queries to the German police yielded nothing. The two Frenchmen who had answered questions about the bombing the morning after it had occurred, were unavailable for further questioning. The lid's on thought Hank.

A spokesman at the French Consulate indicated the two had returned to Paris to work out next steps and whether to reopen the Munich Trade Mission. That gave Hank a chance to advance the story, but beyond raising questions about the future of the office and a limited recounting of basic details, there was not much meat to be put on the bone. That depressed him because he knew he could write a much bigger and better story if Howell didn't cast such a big shadow.

Hank was surprised when Ted held the office phone in his extended hand and said softly that it was Ilse on the line. It surprised Hank. She had never called him before. They hadn't spoken since their impromptu lunch. He'd been busy and also gloomy, knowing Lucky was back in town. Ilse had taken a day off work the day before and he visualized them frolicking in any number of imagined ways. He knew he had no right to be angry, but he was: angry at Ilse. Angry at Lucky. And angry at himself for being angry, because deep down he felt he did have a right, knowing he had fallen for Ilse. And fallen hard.

His mood lifted at the sound of her voice. As usual it was breezy and cheerful. They exchanged the usual pleasantries when she said, "aren't you wondering why I'm calling?"

He told her he was and she explained that she had talked it over with Lucky and that he was happy to do the interview that Hank had suggested. They made arrangements to meet that evening at their favorite Gasthaus on Leopoldstrasse. Hank was both eager and anxious to meet Lucky with Ilse. He wanted to see how they connected. At the same time, he was anxious, fearing they might be connected too well. In reality, he couldn't care less about profiling him.

They were already seated at a sidewalk

table when Hank arrived. His heart fell as he approached. They were sitting next to each other, chatting and smiling warmly before they saw him. Ilse spotted him first and lightly touched Lucky's arm and waved Hank over with the other hand. Hank tried to smile in return and hoped it looked genuine. Lucky stood and extended his hand as Hank got to the table.

Hank was surprised at how short Lucky was. He can't be more than five foot five or six, he thought. Ilse stood too. She was taller. Hank was impressed by Lucky's firm grip as they shook hands. He may be on the small side thought Hank, but he's strong. And, in shape. He had not often thought of race car drivers as athletic, but Lucky Manon clearly was.

He was dressed in a T-shirt and jeans, revealing broad shoulders and a narrow waist. He was handsome, with an easy smile revealing strong white teeth framed by an even, tan complexion. He looked as if he were in his mid-thirties. A little old for Ilse thought Hank, while also grudgingly admitting to himself that Lucky and Ilse made a handsome couple. His greeting was friendly. This is a guy it would be hard to dislike thought Hank much as he had been prepared to feel otherwise.

Ilse introduced the two and sat down with a bounce. "We're having wine," she said cheerily. "Wine or beer for you? It's our treat."

"Beer." Said Hank signaling a waiter.

"She always spends my money easily," joked Lucky looking at her fondly. "She knows I have a little extra when I win a race." His English was good.

"Congratulations," said Hank. "Where did you race?"

"At Monteblanco in Spain. Not much money but I did get a good tan." Ilse looked at him proudly like a proud mother reveling in a child's accomplishment.

"Thanks in advance," said Hank laughing. "When you win in Indianapolis maybe you can buy us all dinner."

"Indianapolis?" asked Ilse.

"Big race there every year," explained Hank. "Big paycheck."

"I'm trying to get to Watkins Glen," said Lucky. "Then Indianapolis." Again an easy laugh. "Finding sponsors is more difficult than the races."

Hank pulled out his notebook as his beer arrived. "Let's find out a little more about the next winner of the Indy 500."

They chatted for an hour and Hank was impressed with Lucky's story. As an Alsatian, he had been caught between two worlds...literally. It was historically French but bordered Germany. The two countries wrestled for it over the centuries.

His parents were both French. In World

War Two, it was occupied by Germany. Thousands of young Alsatian men were drafted into the German army, including young Matthieu Manon's father, who never returned. His family never knew where he died or how he died. They had hoped through the years that he might one day return home. But that hope finally waned into despair.

His mother's heart, said Lucky, broke into smaller and smaller pieces until she finally died, old beyond her years at the age of forty one. Young Matthieu was raised by relatives.

Hank asked him how he had gotten into auto racing and Lucky laughed, explaining that he often watched American soldiers who had liberated Alsace race in their jeeps. It had fascinated him. When they left he found a job in a local garage and learned about cars. From there it was only a few steps to racing them with friends in nearby fields. He found he was good at it. In the fifties he hung around local race tracks helping mechanics and pit crews until he finally got a chance to drive himself. "They got tired of me in the pit so they put me on the track," he laughed.

In the years since he had won some big races on small tracks and done well in others until he spun out in Monaco and broke both legs. It was a long road back.

Hank was enjoying Lucky's story and knew it would make a nice feature for the "Stripes." He recognized that Lucky enjoyed talking about himself but he saw none of the arrogance or narcissism that Ted had suggested.

Ilse had sat silently as Lucky responded to Hank's questions. Finally, Hank put down his notepad and looked at her as he asked Lucky, "And how did you meet this lovely lady?"

Manon put his hand on hers. "They call me Lucky because I survived that crash in Monaco. I call myself Lucky because I met Ilse. She is very special."

Hank fought to maintain a smile. He had come to this meeting expecting to dislike Lucky Manon. Instead he found himself jealously admiring him.

"Spoken like a true Frenchman. I'm surprised she's not in a swoon after a line like that," he said.

Ilse was beaming.

"We met at the airport, both of us waiting for a plane to Berlin. This was before The Wall. We got to talking, sat together on the flight, had dinner on the Kurfürstendamm, went our separate ways then ran into each other again here in Munich a month or two later. Kismet," he said, "Fate."

He's in love thought Hank, looking over at Ilse. She was enjoying the conversation. Hank was not. Every comment stung.

"Have you had a chance to talk with our mutual friend, Charles Howell over at the consulate?" he asked, changing the subject. "I know he wanted to talk to you."

Ilse looked surprised. "I didn't know you knew Charlie," she said before Manon had a chance to respond. "I thought you hadn't met,"

"I hadn't last time I saw you, but Tom Morrow and I had a meeting with him the other day."

"We met," said Lucky suddenly subdued. "I can't talk much about it. They are investigating that bombing at the French office. Because I'm French, they hope I might know something or somebody who was involved. I don't. I don't know that many Frenchmen in Munich. I wish I did know something. I love my country. I would like to help."

"They think there are some OAS cells in Germany and here in Munich. It's touchy diplomatically, and obviously dangerous."

"Well," said Lucky, "I don't think we should have given up Algeria, and de Gaulle can be a horse's ass, but... c'est la vie."

"These anti-Gaullists are disgusting and evil," said Ilse in an unexpectedly bitter tone that Hank found totally out of character.

"Ilse, I'm surprised you have such passion for France," said Hank. "Where does that come from?"

"I love their history, I love their food, I love their wine, I love their fashion, and I love their women."

"Their women?" exclaimed Hank.

"Yes. They were so brave during the occupation. So many of them undermined the German occupiers. They were the backbone of the underground...the Resistance."

"And, many of them weren't." said Lucky coldly.

"And they paid a price," snapped Ilse.

"Pretty intense for a German," said Hank. "Whose side were you on during the war?" He meant to tease but she took him seriously.

"I was too young to be on anybody's side," she said sharply. "But when I was older and understood what Hitler's Germans were all about, I realized I could have never been one of them."

"Hitler's Germans?" asked Hank.

"There were two kinds of Germans. "His," she said contemptuously, "and the rest. The good Germans." The two men exchanged glances as she caught her breath. "Did you know he wanted to destroy Paris...burn it down?" Hank nodded. "It wasn't enough that he pounded Poland and Czechoslovakia into dust, then took the coward's way out when Berlin was a rubble pile. To think that he wanted to destroy Paris just so the Americans would have nothing to liberate. Such insanity." She wiped a tear from her eye. "Imagine," she said, "if he had taken London and issued such an order? Or Washington."

She was breathing as heavily as if she had

just ended a race. Lucky and Hank looked at each other but dared not roll their eyes. Ilse's emotional outburst signaled to each of them that she would not have excused it. They sat in silent response, hearing only the humming of cars in the street and the muffled footsteps of passersby.

After a moment or two, she whispered, "Sorry for the outburst. There are times when I'm embarrassed to be German. I consider myself only part German because I was born in Czecho-slovakia. I'm only German because Hitler said I was."

Hank took a deep swallow of beer. "I think we've got to lighten this up a little," said Hank, then raising his glass to Lucky and Ilse. It struck her as funny and she broke out in full-bodied laughter. There thought Hank, she's Ilse again at the same time wondering where her emotional outburst had come from.

"What do I have to do to get to Watkins Glen?" asked Lucky trying to keep the mood at the table lighter. "I know I just can't show up."

"I would think that your contacts in the racing world here would be able to help," said Hank, grateful that the subject matter had changed. "Have you tried any of them?"

"I have but they're most influential in Europe and weak in the states. And," he said with a hint of self-satisfaction, "most don't want someone with my skills leaving the European circuit."

"Well, all I can suggest then is to have another discussion with our favorite Cultural Attaché at the Consulate. He might have some ideas. Although," he chuckled, "he seems to have his mind on things more confrontational than cultural these days." For some reason that made Ilse laugh.

Hank stood and told Lucky that he would let him know when the profile would be published. He asked if Lucky had any pictures he could use for the story and they made arrangements for Hank to get them from Ilse on one of his runs to RFE to pick up the daily budget. He shook hands with Lucky and gave a quick hug to Ilse and they were all off.

Hank watched the two of them walk away in the opposite direction. They were hand in hand. I hope he finds a way to get to Watkins Glen thought Hank. And if he does, I hope he goes alone. As he stood there watching them he could still feel her body against his when they'd hugged while also regretting that he was not in Lucky's place walking away with her hand in hand.

"I met Lucky Manon yesterday," he said to Ted when they were sitting in their shared office. "I thought he was a pretty nice guy. Not into himself at all."

"If you get to know him better you'll see that side of him. He just seems a little off center. The conversation's fine as long as it's about him.

And, he's more than a little controlling with Ilse. I don't like that one bit. I'm surprised she takes it."

"Boy, I didn't see any sign of that at all. He talked about himself but that was because I was asking questions about him and his background. Ilse seemed to enjoy the company. They left hand in hand. Seemed like a happy couple."

"She made a joke about his size once," said Ted. "Something about her being taller. It was a joke. He almost bit her head off. He was furious...scary furious...but she didn't seem to mind. I did. I haven't had a very good feeling about him since."

Hank stared out the office window for a few minutes as Ted busied himself going through the daily newspapers as he did every morning. The sound of pages being turned was the only sound in the room until Hank spoke.

"I saw another Ilse when we met yesterday. I was surprised at how passionately she feels about the anti-Gaullists. She loves France and the French. I'd never heard her speak that way before. And, she hates what she calls 'Hitler's Germans.' She even went so far as to dismiss her own German identity. What's that all about?"

"She's always been emotional about these things. She despises the authoritarian world and blames it for her life's low points, directly or indirectly. Especially the deaths of her mother and sister. Normally, she keeps the feelings to herself. I think she's taken by Manon because of the French thing. But all during the Algerian troubles she was always agitated. She insisted France and de Gaulle were doing the right thing to bring OAS terrorism to an end. When OAS people melted away and brought their activities to Europe, she was especially upset...especially when we started hearing about cells in Germany." His paper rustled as he folded it and put it on the desk.

"She was fearful that the anti-Gaullist people would hook up with fascist elements here and in France and that the situation would lead to death and destruction on a much higher level. She worried that another Hitler might emerge. She was really worked up."

"And apparently still is," said Hank.

"There are plenty of people still around who would work very well with the OAS. The war's long over, but there are lots of people with Nazi and other fascist sympathies here and in France. And in other parts of Europe for that matter. The Russians would like nothing better than to see political unrest in the West...violent political unrest.

"At one point she was talking about going to Paris and signing on with French intelligence operations, internal and external, to do what she could to upend any plots brewing here."

"Did she?"

"I think I talked her out of it," said Ted. "But

with her, you never know." He shook his head, looking dismayed. "I try to keep an eye on her but that has its own challenges."

"Do you think Manon fans the flames?" asked Hank. "He seemed pretty moderate during our conversation yesterday...a *comme ci comme ça* kind of guy."

"Hard to say. Like I say, I don't necessarily trust him. But he does travel a lot and he seems more interested in his career than politics. That said, he's smart enough not to give himself away to a stranger.

"But he is French. I'm sure that's why Ilse likes to be with him. Remember," Ted cautioned, "she's young and passionate. That could be a bad combination in the wrong hands. She would be easy to manipulate in the orbit of someone like Manon." He picked up his paper again but looked closely at Hank. "If that's what Manon wanted," he added, leaving Hank to wonder if, in fact, Manon could be, or would be, that manipulative.

"One final question asked Ted, "What did you mean when you said a while back that if I wanted to know more about the CIA I should ask Ilse?"

"Hah," said Ted, with a subtle smile. "She spends a fair amount of time with your new friend...the Cultural Attaché. I'm sure you've figured him out by now."

"How long have you known about him?"

"Since he spent a couple of hours asking me lots of questions about who I knew, and who I was still in contact with in the East. It was intense. Everything but a rubber hose. Looks can be deceiving."

The following day the morning broadcasts and daily papers swooped in on the story of Marcel Blanchet whose body had been found almost a week earlier. It was obvious to Hank that the French, Germans, and probably the Americans had sat on the story trying to put the pieces together before opening the lid. Now, they wanted it out, undoubtedly hoping that someone might come forward with information they could use in their investigation. Did that mean, wondered Hank, that they didn't know much, or that they were using the story as bait of some sort?

Not surprisingly, the story made much of the connection between the French Trade Mission bomber and the dead French Army Sergeant. The question was obvious? Was Marcel also connected with the bombing? Coincidence? It was food for discussion in homes, cafés, and shops. It seemed that everyone had an opinion. It was also clear that no one knew, except for the ones who did.

Albert LeClerc knew. He read the papers carefully trying to determine how much the authorities had been able to put together. But he did not join in the gossip.

Hank considered it an opportunity. Ilse had gotten word to Hank through Ted that she had the Lucky Manon photos Hank wanted for his profile. The Marcel Blanchet story was a chance to broach the subject and learn more about the depth of the feelings she expressed the other day. It was also an opportunity to try and see what he could learn about the extent of Manon's political views and how he might, or might not, be in a position to influence her.

CHAPTER 9

"I want to apologize for the other day." They were the first words out of her mouth when he entered her tiny, shared office. He looked at her quizzically although he knew what the reference was.

"You were a little worked up," he said. "You've chosen sides and are passionate about it. Nothing wrong with that."

"Well, I shouldn't have been so dramatic. I just hate the thought of those people running around Europe blowing up things…"

"And, maybe killing people," he interrupted. "What do you make of them finding someone dead in Baden Baden who they think might be the French Trade Mission bomber's brother? It looks like murder."

"I don't think the OAS people are responsible. Why? The bomber was doing their work. I don't see a reason to kill the brother. Probably just a coincidence. He owed money? A woman?"

"We'll probably never know," said Hank as she handed him a large envelope.

"Here are the pictures of Lucky you wanted. Keep them as long as you want, but he does want them back."

Hank opened the envelope and examined the photos one by one. Most featured smiling Lucky posing in or next to colorful sports cars featuring big bold numbers. A few showed him holding trophies. There was a close-up head shot, and even Hank could see he was wearing makeup. "Did he borrow your Cover Girl or Max Factor for this one?"" he asked holding the picture for her to see.

"I think he has plenty of his own," she chortled. "He doesn't mind having his picture taken."

"Wow," said Hank as he shuffled through a series showing Lucky after his accident. In a smoking car. On a stretcher. In a hospital bed. In a wheelchair with an arm and both legs in casts. "He really got beaten up."

Ilse just nodded. "I can't even look at them," she said sadly.

Then she brightened. "Apparently things are in motion for Watkins Glen. Howell's organizing a packet of forms and other stuff he needs to make the trip, look for sponsors and enter the race there."

"That's good news. When does he leave?"

He asked perhaps more enthusiastically than he intended. That brought a smile from Ilse.

"A couple of weeks. He's got a race in Portugal. He left for Lisbon last night."

"Ah. You know, I was wondering something. In our conversation the other day, he didn't seem to have the kind of political concerns you do. That surprised me."

"Why?"

"Well, you know...birds of a feather. I'd have thought with you two being close you'd have such things in common. He was like he couldn't have cared less...a *c'est la vie* kind of guy."

"Well Mr. Hank..." she said, her face turning red,.."I don't have to have my feelings reinforced by my friends. I'm entitled to my own opinions and if somebody...anybody...doesn't like them, they can go to hell. Truth be told, as much as I care for Lucky Manon, I think he doesn't think about much more than the next race...and about himself."

"Sounds kind of harsh."

"I mean he thinks about himself...and how he's going to win the next race. That's what I mean."

"I thought you were true soul mates, that's all."

"Friends Hank. Just friends," she said sharply.

Live in friends thought Hank. That makes it

different. "Sorry. I didn't mean to get under your skin." They stood silently for a moment, each having nothing left to say, until Hank thanked her for the photos and excused himself, wishing that he had been more diplomatic with Ilse. He left thinking that he had learned nothing new about Manon, and had clearly pissed her off.

The next stop was the office of J. Harding Bell. Hank was hopeful that he could stitch together a story to follow up on the day's news about Marcel Blanchet. Bell was not of much use, although he did tell him that Hank Trewhitt of the Baltimore Sun had just left his office. He had been drawn to Munich from his office in Bonn by the Blanchet story. So, thought Hank, the big boys from Bonn and possibly Berlin, were on the story. That meant he would likely by playing catch up from now on. Their clout and celebrity gave them a much longer journalistic reach than his. Bell told him that Trewhitt had come to Munich to pick up the scent and was already off to Baden Baden to see what he could learn there. He told Hank that Daniel Schorr of CBS has been calling from Bonn too.

"Do we know anything new about the Marcel Blanchet case?" asked Hank, standing at the doorway to Charles Howell's office.

"Yeah, I can report definitively that he is still dead. Everybody's still trying to figure it out.

Investigators are convinced that he was murdered and that's where it all stops." He paused for a moment. "And that's where I stop. Nothing more for you."

"Was he the bomber's brother?"

"Could be. Don't know."

"What's Hank Trewhitt like?" asked Hank, on a bit of a fishing expedition.

"Good writer, good guy, good questions. And gone. He's off to Baden Baden."

"I wish I had had a chance to meet him," said Hank, somewhat disheartened that Hank Trewhitt had already found Howell. If he had, could the other correspondents be far behind? And could...would...Charles Howell...whom Ilse called Charlie...be kept in the dark by investigators? Not likely thought Hank.

Was it Murder?
By Hank Tollar

Munich---International officials investigating the death of a French Army Sergeant in Baden Baden are convinced that he was murdered according to sources familiar with the investigation. Marcel Blanchet's body was found one week ago. He had been shot in the head.

Munich newspapers are reporting that Blanchet may possibly be the brother of Pierre Blanchet, the man identified as the bomber at the French Trade Mission office in Munich earlier this month. That has not been officially confirmed.

Pierre Blanchet was killed in the explosion and was the only fatality although damage was extensive to the building which included several residences. The building has not yet been declared habitable by German authorities. Several residents were displaced.

The deaths of Pierre and Marcel Blanchet are being investigated by law enforcement officials of France, Germany and the United States. The FBI has teams in Munich and Baden Baden at the request of the Bonn government. There is nothing, according to press reports, to definitively link the deaths of the two men, although there is an apparent working assumption that they are related.

The Munich bombing is believed connected to the long-standing anti-Gaullist movement that emerged during the struggle for Algerian independence. Officials believe the Secret Army Organization, OAS, a right wing organization comprised of dissident French military personnel and various European fascist organizations, is behind the attack. OAS cells are believed operating in France, Germany and throughout Europe.

Earlier this year, former French Army Col. Antoine Argoud, an OAS leader, was kidnaped while in hiding in Munich and spirited to Paris where he was arrested.

Local newspapers are speculating that the Munich bombing may have been in retaliation for the Argoud kidnap incident.

The Munich and Baden Baden investigations are continuing with officials promising more information as it becomes available.

Hank was nursing a beer and reading Newsweek that evening at a café on Leopoldstrasse when Tom Morrow surprised him by sliding into a chair across from him. He asked to join him and Hank was happy for conversation with a fellow journalist. Tom lamented that he was being told by the "powers that be" at headquarters in Frankfurt that he was to keep his distance from what he called the "French bombing" story unless he had officially released information from the US Army, the State Department, the French or German governments, or the CIA.

"That shows you how much they know," he

said. "When was the last time you had a news release from the CIA? And, what's the Army got to do with any of it?"

They both laughed and Hank had to admit he was under no such directive from his editors, but that he felt similarly constrained because no one was talking, much less putting out news releases. At least I can report what the local papers are saying.

"Let's face it. They're all skittish as hell," said Hank. They're worried about international fallout and a little friendly fire from Bonn, Paris or Washington. They want to play ball and not rock the boat. If we do, we'll wind up selling pencils, remember?"

They commiserated and ordered more and more beer, hanging out until waiters began to turn out the lights. Each of them was more than a little wobbly when they stood. While they had not solved any professional problem, they had identified many. The beer was a kind of self medication that each found easy to take. They had, at one point, decided on one course of action that had a lot of appeal in the midst of the standoff on the "French bombing." They decided to take a long weekend trip to Berlin. Neither had been there since construction had begun on the Berlin Wall. They decided to take a look and enjoy some of the city's celebrated night life. They agreed to fly up two days later on Friday...if they could get the time off. Neither suspected that would be a problem inasmuch as their bosses were eager for them to rein in their enterprise reporting inclinations.

"Ever driven in?" asked Tom.

"No. Just flying."

"Driving in's a real trip...sorry no pun intended. It's interesting to see those surly East German police...the VoPos (People's Police)...give Americans the stink eye at check points. It's a couple of hundred miles of the Soviet Zone. I swear you don't see any color but gray or grayer, mixed with a spot of black or dark brown."

"I like flying," said Hank. "It's faster and the descent over the center of town below rooftop level is an amazing sensation. You can actually see into some of the apartments as you're flying by."

"I can't wait," said Morrow. "Sounds incredible."

"I think we'll be able to hitch a ride on a military plane without any trouble. I'll work it out through our friend Bell at the Consulate."

The two shook hands and, unsteadily, went their separate ways.

J. Harding Bell was in a very good mood when Hank arrived the next day with his request for assistance for the Berlin trip. He had transportation arranged and accommodations at a military transient hotel in downtown Berlin set up within a matter of minutes.

"Just a word of advice. Are you planning on taking a look at East Berlin...seeing what the other half looks like?" he asked laughing. "I'll tell you it's interesting but not much to do or look at."

"I was there before The Wall," said Hank. "I pretty much know what to expect."

Bell shook his head and explained that things were a lot different now with The Wall cutting off the sectors administered by the Americans, French and British from the one controlled by the Russians. He explained that now the only access was through Checkpoint Charlie which was manned by US military police. They'll record your crossing, give you a friendly tap you on your butt, wish you well, and point you toward a concrete path on the other side of The Wall that will "take you into paradise," he told Hank.

"But here's the thing," he said seriously. "We have this ying and yang thing going with the East Germans and the Russians. They think they've got a separate country going over there because Berlin's in East Germany. We don't consider the GDR (German Democratic Republic) a legitimate entity. And they're trying to act like one. It's a Russian puppet state. Berlin is still an occupied city. You'll have no trouble getting in. They hope you'll spend dollars or marks...a little hard currency while you're sightseeing."

"They won't get rich on us," said Hank.

"This is important," said Bell. "If anyone over there asks for your passport, forget it. Only bona fide countries get to do that. If you show a passport it's like admitting they're for real. They would like nothing better than to have photos of their border people checking western passports. It would give them a look of legitimacy. The State Department doesn't want to see any pictures like that. Got it?"

Hank nodded.

"The only thing you can show is your Defense Department ID. That's all you need. It just reinforces the fact that we, the French and the Brits have the right to move around Berlin and all of Germany...conquered Germany. We're all hoping that one day we'll all become part of one big happy family. One Germany." He folded his hands in mock exasperation. "It's a game, but once again, we've all got to play it."

"Got it," said Hank. "Fun and games."

"End of sermon," said Bell. "It's like required reading. Gotta do it."

Hank thanked Bell for his help.

The next stop for Hank was the daily trip to RFE. He would pick up the daily news budget and pay for the privilege with a large can of Prince Albert pipe tobacco for his friend Talbot. Hank was heady with the knowledge that he was getting away for a while and would have a chance to relax.

He joked with Talbot who wondered why, with all the wonderful places in Western Europe within a few hours of Munich he would choose Berlin. "You've got Paris, Zurich or Amsterdam right around the corner," he said. "Only spies go to Berlin." He thanked Hank for the tobacco and admonished him to be careful when "on the other side."

Next stop. A quick hello and goodbye to Ilse. He had finished with the Lucky Manon photos. Returning them was a good excuse to see her. She didn't hear him when he entered her tiny office. The door was always open in the hope more air would circulate. It was adjacent to a much larger room in which the temperature was controlled by noisy fans to protect shelves of documents housed in heavy cardboard storage boxes.

"Hello," he said startling her and drawing her attention away from a file she was studying. He waved the envelope with the photos.

"Oh, I didn't hear you. I was just taking a look at Enver Hosha's latest five year plan in Albania," she said affecting a bored expression.

"He's apparently going to keep them coming until he gets it right," said Hank. They both chuckled as she slapped the file down on her desk.

"I don't know how you can work in here," he said. "It's dark. No air. It's like a wine cellar without the wine."

"That's why you keep running into me someplace else. Any excuse is enough for me to find something else to do and someplace else to do it."

He handed her the photographs. "Thanks for these. You can tell Lucky the piece will run next Monday."

"He's still in Portugal and will be for a while. I'll get some copies for him for when he gets back."

"I just wanted to say hi and let you know that I'm going to be out of town for a couple of days. Tom and I are going to Berlin."

"Work or play?" she asked. "It's a good place to play."

"Just for the fun of it," he said. "We're both a little depressed. Our bosses are on us to stay away from the French bombing story and the death of that French Army Sergeant in Baden Baden. They call the shots."

Ilse leaned toward him, suddenly a little less playful and a lot more serious. "Why?" she asked. "A lot of people are wondering about it. Does anyone know if the sergeant in Baden Baden and the bomber here are related. That's what I've been reading."

"Apparently," said Hank, who went on to explain that everybody in his professional world was uptight about the story, There were fears there could be diplomatic consequences in the midst of Cold War tension, and given touchy relations between Germany and France. An anxious Washington was wringing its hands on the sidelines. The last thing Washington wants, he explained, is to be caught in the middle between its two friends while the Russian bear loomed. And Washington wanted least of all to be surprised. He speculated that "there are spooks all over the place trying to get ahead of the story."

"Well, you know where I am on all of that," she said. "The OAS types have got to be rounded up and taken out of circulation. Period!"

"Okay, let's not go down that road again. I prefer it when you smile."

"You can make me smile if you'll buy me a beer after work."

"Sold."

"The usual place? Around five?

He gave the okay sign as he turned to leave. Just what he needed, he thought. Three cheers for serendipity.

Once again, she arrived at the street side café, amidst a field of turned heads from men passing by, and at nearby tables, admiring her openly. The women looked at her as if they were conceding territory. They never had a chance thought Hank as she slid into a chair across from him.

"Nothing serious," he said, hoping to keep the conversation light. "I want to leave in a good mood and with a memory of you smiling rather than your declaring war on terrorism."

"Deal," she said unveiling her brightest smile.

They spent the next hour enjoying a nice evening and making small talk about the things that made Berlin a special place to visit, and not a special place to visit, and joking about noisy students a few tables away. They laughed a lot and Hank realized again how smitten he was with Ilse Stengel. She made him forget the things that, at the moment, needed forgetting. And, made him remember that he was a young man with a healthy supply of all the hormones that went along with all of the other.

One of the things about spending time with her was that there were also moments when they said nothing at all. It reminded Hank of times when his father and mother, who were unabashedly in love, could sit together silently. It had always seemed to Hank that that was a sign of a healthy and positive relationship, that neither felt he or she *had* to talk. They could be comfortable just being together. He wondered if he was getting ahead of himself thinking that way. She seemed equally comfortable.

But as the sun dipped in the west casting long shadows on the busy Leopoldstrasse she said, "I wish we could see the stars. It's such a clear evening. I'm sure the sky is alive with them tonight." She looked at him dreamily. "I wish we were sitting in the country, without the lights and traffic. If we were, I bet we could count them all."

"Let's make it a point to do that when I get back. Would you?"

"Of course," she answered, again putting her hand on his. It was a gesture she had made before. Hank wasn't sure if it signaled affection, friendship, or was just an automatic response to a moment. Whatever it was, it warmed him, and again kick-started a hormonal response.

"I have a favor to ask," she said after another long pause.

He lifted his eyebrows in response.

"What would you think about lending me your car when you are away?"

He was surprised. It was a question he would never have expected and for a moment he was speechless.

"That kind of came out of nowhere," he said. "Why would you want to use my car."

"Well," she answered, speaking quietly, "I have to go to Augsburg. It just occurred to me that if you're flying to Berlin, I could go with you and Tom to the airport, take the car, and pick you up when you get back." She waited for a response. When she got none, she went on, "I can drive...in case you're wondering...even your stick shift. I just thought that rather than your car just sitting there at the airport, I could put it to good use without having to worry about bus or train schedules. The idea just popped into my head."

He thought for a moment. "I guess I have no problem with it," he said, "but I'm not sure I can. I have military plates and it may not be legal for a German national, or non-military person to drive it. I think they have rules about that sort of thing."

She frowned. "I never thought of that. Oh well, it was just an idea."

"Let me ask," he said.

Her expression brightened. "I don't want to get you into any trouble."

He studied her for a moment. "What the hell. Why not. If I ask and am told 'no' then I can't do it. If I don't ask and it's a problem I can always say I didn't know I couldn't."

Her smile was all he needed to see that he was doing the right thing. It might have been the wrong thing, but at that moment, there was no doubt in his mind it was exactly the right thing to do. What wouldn't he do for her, he thought, this wasn't really a big deal at all.

"I'll have her gassed up," he said. "No sense taking a chance on questions asked at the military gas stations. And you can avoid the German gas stations. They're way more expensive.

"You're just such a nice guy," she said. "Please ask around to make sure it's not a...a...capital crime or something. It's not worth it."

"Let's finish our drinks and you can drive me around the block. I want to make sure you know how to drive."

She laughed loudly. "Do you think I could know someone like Lucky Manon and not know how to drive?"

It wasn't exactly what Hank wanted to hear. He shook his head. Why did she have to put a blemish on a nice evening by mentioning his name?

She passed his driving test and he decided just to keep her use of the car between the two of them. As a precaution he wrote and signed a brief note explaining that she had his full authorization to drive the car. That should take care of it, he thought, if there were any challenges to her using it along the way.

CHAPTER 10

He and Tom turned just before boarding the plane and waved to her as she stood responding with swooping goodbye gestures from behind a security fence. The door closed behind them and they could see her return to Hank's car. She was out of sight before the plane had taxied to the runway for takeoff.

The flight was uneventful as the plane made its way through a narrow air corridor of restricted airspace to the former German capital.

The descent into Berlin was breathtaking as the big transport flew the last miles at rooftop level before landing at the historic Templehof Airport. It was at Templehof a decade and a half earlier that the Allies had airlifted more than two million tons of food, fuel and other supplies to the city that had been isolated by a Soviet blockade. The Russians attempted, as one reporter put it, "to starve out the city" and turn Berliners against the Allies. Neither happened as thousands of Allied flights, with planes landing every thirty to forty-five seconds for the better part of a year, broke the back of the blockade, and established Berlin as a major thorn in Soviet Russia's side.

The two reporters mused over the scope and drama of the Airlift mission when their own plane touched down as thousands had done during the massive supply effort. It had been almost fifteen years since the blockade and West Berlin had thrived ever since. It had become even more of a city of contrasts when Hank and Tom arrived. The Western Sector had become a stable and vibrant sanctuary for democracy, while the Eastern Sector had continued as testimony to a failed system.

The two reporters had a chance to see it all first hand. Their first night included a dinner at one of West Berlin's many fine restaurants. They walked around well lighted and busy streets, visited one of the many cabarets that seemed to be everywhere. People were out and about and enjoying themselves at the uncountable number of cafés, theaters, and other places of entertainment and relaxation. It was difficult to grasp that they were on an island of prosperity one hundred miles inside Soviet controlled territory. They strolled to The Wall. It was still under construction but nonetheless still a formidable and ugly stone, concrete and barbed wire structure that snaked its way along the sector border.

Expressionless border policemen, cradling machine pistols in their arms, stared westward watching another world from their places on the eastern side of the structure. What must they think thought Hank and Tom, as they viewed life on the other side from their own desolate vantage point? Did they, wondered Hank, understand that The Wall was being built not to keep people out, but that it was constructed to keep people in? And, those men who glared from the darkness were among those who were, in fact, imprisoned.

That night Tom and Hank ventured to the roof of the building where they would spend the night. If the difference between the sectors was apparent on the ground, it was even more so from the roof. The difference was between darkness and light. West Berlin was ablaze with light. East Berlin was in virtual darkness. What light could be seen seemed dim. Even in the darkness, little spots of yellow were bullied by darkness. Nothing was fully illuminated. It was as if the street lamps were struggling to stay awake. It was hard to imagine the light that could be seen inside the few windows of apartments visible from the west, was even sufficient to create shadows. It was a study in darkness and light...day and night...black and white.

"How," asked Tom, "could the people living over there not want out...not be drawn to the light here like moths to a fire?"

"They are...or at least were," said Hank. "That's just one reason for the Wall. Too many people were leaving. Now they can't. The VoPo border guards we saw have orders to shoot to kill if anyone tries to breach the Wall. They've proved willing and able to do it time after time. People have tried to swim across where the sectors are divided by water. They've tried to tunnel. If there was ever evidence that Uncle Joe's society doesn't work, Berlin is it."

The following day...the two decided to "have a beer" in East Berlin to take a closer look. There was a sense of excitement knowing they were going to visit a different world where they would be welcomed with suspicion, curiosity, and scorn.

They checked in at Checkpoint Charlie, their only open door to East Berlin. It amounted to little more than a small shed set in the middle of Friedrichstrasse, which since 1961 had become one of the Cold War's most iconic sites. When construction began on The Wall, Soviet and American tanks had faced off against each other at that spot while the world held its breath.

An Army Sergeant, sitting in the small enclosure, examined their ID cards and suggested they mind their own business during the visit. "No international incidents," he warned, only half joking.

Nervously, the two headed for the breach in the Wall and toward the barriers familiar at border crossing points around the globe. Their hearts beat a little faster as they walked eastward through the sector border's no man's land. It was watched carefully by the VoPos who had them under surveillance from the moment they left the Checkpoint Charlie shed.

There was no attempt to interfere with their movement as they wandered into that part of the city. Human and motor traffic was at a minimum. An occasional military jeep squealed by. The people were colorless, like the buildings. Even the few people they did see did not make eye contact with the strangers. Their expressions were set and both men would later agree there seemed to be an overall universal joylessness. Even in the middle of the day the neighborhood seemed dark.

They found a small Gasthaus blocks from the border. A few of the patrons got up and left when the two men, easily recognizable as Americans, entered the room and sat at a table. A listless waiter approached and they ordered beers. A tattered menu was placed before them. The fare was limited, and featured items rich in fats and starches. They decided to wait for their return to eat.

Their beer came in thick glass mugs. Hank commented that it was like everything else they'd seen...a more colorless version of what they were used to. "I used to think beer was beer," said Hank, "but this tastes watered down. Maybe it's just my imagination."

Each was aware, as they sat talking, that the few folks who remained in the room, were watching them closely. Whenever one of the two Americans looked around the room, the Germans who had been watching them looked away. "I feel like an animal in a zoo," said Tom. "A freak."

After half an hour or so of this, the two decided to go back. They'd had more than enough of the "experience" and were eager to return to a more familiar, welcoming world. They said their *auf wiedersehens* to unenthusiastic, grunted responses, and were on their way.

The return to Checkpoint Charlie was more adventuresome. The East Germans had their own routine for departing visitors. As Hank and Tom approached the border for what they assumed would require nothing more than stepping past the barrier, two VoPo guards stood in their path and signaled for them to stop. Each carried weapons held like babies across their chests.

"Your passports," one of them said harshly in heavily accented English.

Hank and Tom looked at each other in surprise.

After a moment, Hank said, "No, we don't show passports." He pulled out his wallet and extracted his military ID card. He showed it to the one officer, who disregarded it.

"Passports," he again demanded more firmly than before.

"No," said Tom as he presented his own identification. "This is all we need."

"No...you need passport," said second border guard stridently. "Show passport."

The two reporters became aware that a third VoPo officer had joined his colleagues. He was carrying a camera. Hank remembered what J. Harding Bell had told him about passports, photographs and international incidents. He was feeling an extreme sense of nervousness as the three East Germans stood near them, at the ready to block any movement toward Checkpoint Charlie.

"What do you think?" asked Tom who was also familiar with State Department directives regarding Berlin border protocols. "They don't seem in the mood to negotiate."

"We want to talk to a Russian officer," said Hank. "He'll know that this identification is all we need," he said holding his ID card in front of the East German he assumed was in charge.

The German waved at it dismissively. "There are no Russians here," he said. "This is the German Democratic Republic. No Russians. No Russians," he said smiling, showing tobacco-stained teeth. "You think we have Russians here?"

His English was labored.

He turned to his colleagues and in rapid German said to them, "These Americans think there are Russians here. He" he said, gesturing toward Hank, "thinks we can provide a Russian officer, just for him." All three of the East Germans began to laugh heartily.

As suddenly as the laughter had started, it ended abruptly with the lead East German saying to Hank in a menacing tone, "You two...move over there." He pointed to an area behind them.

"You are *free* to wait here," he said as they stepped to the designated spot. "See, we have freedoms here." The two reporters were increasingly nervous knowing they were now farther from Checkpoint Charlie rather than closer. They were torn between showing their passports and being allowed to the free side of the Wall, or continuing a stalemate yards from it.

"You may stay here as long as you like. We welcome you to the GDR. But let me warn you," he paused and cocked his weapon with a menacing click. The other two followed suit. "Let me warn you," he repeated, "if you take one step toward your famous Checkpoint Charlie," he said gesturing toward the border, "we will shoot. As I say, stay as long as you like." He and his colleagues moved a few feet away, continuing to watch the two Americans closely.

Hank and Ted were beyond nervous. They

were frightened now that they had been threatened. "I still want to see a Russian," shouted Hank. The VoPos just smiled. Hank and Ted stood in bright sunlight wondering what they could or should do,

An hour later it was more than clear to them that their VoPo minders were not going to change their minds and that there would never be a Russian to negotiate with. Tom halfheartedly waved the East Germans over. Reluctantly, the two Americans pulled their passports from their jackets and handed them to the now smiling VoPo officer. He went through motions of examining them thoroughly, happy to give his colleague time to take many photographs.

He finally handed them back, tipped his cap, and said, "Thank you. I hope your enjoyed your visit to the GDR. Please come again."

Hank and Tom looked at each other dejectedly, nodded, and walked toward Checkpoint Charlie. They could hear the East Germans behind them laughing. Hank thought to himself that the incident with Jim Garner at the Munich student demonstrations in which Tom Morrow and Garner were threatened with expulsion from Germany, was nothing compared to what this could lead to. And, Garner's celebrity was not available this time to help.

The same sergeant who had ushered them through the checkpoint three hours earlier was still on duty. The two explained what had happened and that that they felt they had no choice but to show their passports in violation of official policy. The young sergeant grunted, "Don't worry about it," he said. "Everybody does it. It's all a big show."

"The question is, do we write about it when we get back?" asked Hank. "It's a story."

"But is it one we should tell?" wondered Tom. "I know it would never get past my editors."

"Mine too," said Hank. "I'm going to write it just for the heck of it and see what happens."

"Get those pencils ready," joked Tom, though he was only half joking.

"I'll write it third person and see," said Hank, still frustrated over the border incident.

> *What is our Border Policy in Berlin?*
> *By Hank Tollar*
> *West Berlin---What is our border policy in Berlin? Well, apparently it all depends on whom you ask.*
> *Ask the State Department and the answer is very firm. Because the allied governments do not recognize the so called GDR, German Democratic Republic, as a legitimate state, US passports are not required to be presented by military or government personnel when*

crossing from West to East Berlin. Not only are they not required, the State Department says, as a matter of official policy, it is not permissible for Americans to show passports. Other forms of identification are permissible.

Ask the GDR. It demands that passports be presented because it believes it is a legitimate entity.

The Allied policy is in place because the governments of Britain, France and the US believe presenting passports would suggest recognition of the GDR as a legitimate government.

Ask two American employees of the Defense Department who were recently caught in the middle of these conflicting arguments. They learned the system does not always work as intended by the Allies.

When returning from a brief visit to East Berlin, the two were stopped at the border by armed East German border guards who demanded to see their US passports. The two refused, and instead presented their Defense Department identification cards. The East Germans refused to accept them as acceptable alternatives to passports.

The two Americans asked to see a

173

Russian officer to resolve the dispute. They were mocked for suggesting that Russians had any authority for East Berlin, which is, of course, administered by the Soviet Union under Four Power agreements.

The American visitors were told they were free to remain in the Eastern Sector for as long as they liked, but warned they would be shot if they attempted to return to West Berlin without providing proper documentation.

The standoff continued for an hour before the Americans reluctantly relented and presented their passports. They were then allowed to return unimpeded through The Wall to Checkpoint Charlie.

Upon their return, they reported the incident to US military authorities. They were told that in spite of US passport policy at the border, most US visitors do, in fact, present their passports as demanded by the East Germans.

The bottom line seems to be that the Allied (US) policy neither works nor is enforced.

In this case, GDR 1---USA 0

"What do you think?" Hank asked Tom

when he'd finished his draft which he said he was going to file at the Berlin Stars and Stripes Bureau that afternoon.

"Good luck with it." said Tom. "Five bucks says they spike it."

Hank's visit to the Bureau an hour later proved Tom right. The editor studied the copy, smiled when he finished, and told Hank that he'd run it up the proverbial flagpole. That was the last Hank saw of it.

CHAPTER 11

Hank was still glum the following morning on the return flight to Munich. His mood brightened considerably when he spotted Ilse standing next to his car on the other side of the security fence. Two minutes after the props stopped spinning, he and Tom were giving her a quick hug and thanks for being there for them.

On the drive to town, they told her about their "adventure" on the other side of The Wall. She listened silently shaking her head. "I'm not surprised," she said. "It's easier for one government to stick to a policy than it is for three."

Hank and Tom looked at each other, surprised. "I thought you were on our side," said Hank.

"I am," she said with a chuckle. "I've just seen how the system works longer than you have."

They drove in silence for a while when Hank asked, "Any problems with the car? Any questions from anybody about your driving it?"

"Nope. No questions asked. Of course, I was in Augsburg. It's crawling with Americans. So nothing looked out of place."

"What was going on in Augsburg?" asked Tom. "You know somebody in the 24-th Infantry Division?"

"I do now," she laughed. "No, I just picked up some paperwork we needed in the archives. Just a little road trip," she said. Hank wondered what paperwork the US military would have in Augsburg that would be important for the Radio Free Europe files?

When Hank got back to the office he was welcomed by Ted who handed him an envelope from the office of J. Harding Bell at the Consulate. It was an invitation for Hank and a guest to attend a July 4th reception at Bell's home. "Something to look forward to," said Hank.

"I got one too, said Ted. "Sounds nice."

"I'll RSVP for both of us if you like when I'm over there tomorrow."

"I already have," said Ted. "I wanted to get back to him before he changed his mind. I went last year. It's a nice party."

Hank stuck his head through the door to

Bell's office, thanked him for the invitation and told him how much he looked forward to it. He turned to leave and Bell stopped him, saying that Charles Howell wanted him to stop by before he left the building. Hank left wondering what it might be all about.

He didn't have long to wait. From the moment he entered the Cultural Attaché's office it was clear he was not there for another party invitation. When Howell saw who it was he sat back in his chair scowling. He said nothing and just pointed to the chair on the other side of his desk.

"So, you're doing diplomatic analysis pieces now?" he said sarcastically. "What the hell were you thinking?"

Hank wasn't sure what Howell meant and gestured accordingly.

"That piece you tried to file in Berlin."

"Ah," said Hank, wondering how the Cultural Attaché in Munich would know about his spiked piece less than 24 hours after he'd tried to file in Berlin.

"You know, I think I'm going to have to work harder to get you to understand the difference between important policy and a flippant news article. There's a lot at stake up there, and in all of Germany. We all have to be careful, not only about what we say, but how we say it."

"I think it's valid to report a border incident, and that's what this was, a border incident."

"Valid? I'll tell you what's NOT valid. Any story that ends 'GDR one---USA nothing.'"

Hank's head dropped slightly. "So, kill that line," he said talking to his shoes.

"Nope. No story that looks like the GDR, or the goddam Russians have any authority at all on the border, or are intimidating on that border, is going to see the light of day. Because they don't."

"Well, when a guy with a machine pistol and no apparent sense of humor says he's going to shoot you, that's intimidating. It intimidated me."

"As far as I'm concerned, it's not an incident unless he does shoot you. Do you follow?"

"Whatever happened to freedom of the press?" Asked Hank.

"Same thing that happened in W-W Two. It gets spiked when it's against national interests."

"How the hell did you even know about the piece," asked Hank heatedly.

"A little birdie told me. Now, let me tell you one more time. Think before you file. Think about potential ramifications. Like I said before, we both have the same boss. We have to play by his rules, like it or not. And, if not, time to look for a different boss. Or for the boss to look for a different employee. That's just the way it is."

Hank got up from his chair slowly and angrily shoved it toward the desk. "Nice talking to you. Except for the threat," he said with as much cynicism as he could muster. "I guess I'll just go do a feature on the zoo."

"Do that," said Howell. "Just stay away from the gators. One might bite you."

Hank turned away, slamming the door as he left.

It was a bright and sunny day when Hank, with his date Ilse, arrived at Howell's home. It was more like an estate...a large stucco house on three or four acres set in a lightly forested area that Hank guessed even Howell could never have afforded back home, especially in DC. Fifteen rooms at least guessed Hank. Ilse was clearly impressed. American flags were set like sentries around the front of the property. A large crowd of Germans and Americans was milling around a brick patio in social formation. Most were drinking wine, though a few of the younger Americans were swigging from long necks.

"Wow," whispered Ilse. "I think I could get to like living here," she said as they made their way to the bar at the far end of the patio. "Thanks for inviting me." She asked the bartender for a white wine, as did Hank, although he would have preferred a beer.

"Ted's here someplace I guess," said Hank. "He said he was invited and that he'd be here."

"He'll arrive late and leave early. And, he'll be networking," she said. "He loves to work rooms like this. He'll come to the office with a pile of names and numbers."

"I'm all for that."

"What's going on over there?" she asked pointing to a gaggle of guests on the far side of the patio. Curious, they wandered over. "Oh my God," said Ilse. "I don't believe it."

Holding court with twenty or so guests hanging on his every word was Willy Brandt, the popular Socialist Party Mayor of West Berlin. The day's host, J. Harding Bell stood nearby like a proud father. Brandt had become an instantly recognizable figure all over the world because of his prominent position in one of, if not the world's foremost hot spots.

"Do you think I should file a complaint about my treatment in his city?" joked Hank.

Reacting as if she hadn't heard him, Ilse didn't respond. She was part of another audience...transfixed as Brandt chatted easily with his patio admirers. He was a formidable presence. He was above average in size. His head seemed slightly larger and out of proportion with the rest of his body. His smile was contagious. His audience leaned in as he spoke, trying to catch every word. Hank and Ilse joined the others and listened as he talked about German reunification, the European economy, and other subjects that don't make it to most lawn parties.

"Don't sell the East Germans short," he

said. "They have the strongest economy in the Soviet bloc. With reunification, Germany would be an economic colossus." He laughed, adding, "I should be careful saying such things. A lot of people don't like the idea of a 'German Colossus' at all."

His audience chuckled, some nervously, no doubt remembering how the colossus of the last generation had turned out. A few drifted away as others arrived. Brandt seemed to enjoy his role on center stage.

"You've got to give it to Howell," said Hank. "He's managed to put together a pretty good guest list. Including us, of course," he joked.

He caught the eye of Charles Howell standing by himself a few yards away. They wandered over in his direction. Ilse gave him a big smile and got one in return. Hank and Howell nodded perfunctorily. They made small talk for a few minutes with Ilse doing most of the talking, until she excused herself and broke away, leaving the two men.

"I didn't know that you knew the lovely Ilse," said Howell. "I like her. She's charming." He stared at her as she disappeared into the crowd. "I'm not so sure about some of her friends though."

"Thanks a lot," said Hank. "I suppose you mean me."

"Nope. Not you. You're actually okay. I'm

talking about some of her other friends."

"Like?"

"I won't burden you with that," he said, taking a large swallow of his drink. Hank wondered what he meant while noticing Howell wasn't drinking alcohol like everyone else. It looked like he held a glass of seltzer water with a wedge of lemon.

"Don't you drink?" Hank asked absently as he looked around for Ilse.

"Not when I'm on the job," answered Howell.

"Are you on the job now?" asked Hank.

"I'm always on the job," said Howell matter-of-factly. "Speaking of friends, it looks like Ilse has a new one." He gestured with his head in the direction Ilse had taken when she excused herself.

Hank turned, surprised to see Ilse standing with, and talking alone to, the Mayor of Berlin.

A moment later Brandt was at a microphone, again with a button- poppingly proud Bell standing next to him. The Mayor thanked everyone for being there, as if it were his party. Bell didn't seem to mind that his role as host had been preempted. The Mayor wished the guests...and America...a happy birthday, explaining that he had to leave to join the American Ambassador at his reception in Bonn. After a quick wave to Ilse he was on his way.

She wandered back to Hank and Howell

smiling brightly. She had forgone her usual fitted ski pants and sweater and was dressed for the occasion in a colorful sun dress that exposed a colony of freckles on her shoulders. "Isn't he nice," she said watching a convoy of Mercedes limos whisking the mayor down the long driveway.

You've got a new buddy," said Hank. "What in the world were you two chatting about."

"I'm not sure I'm at liberty to say," she giggled. "It might be classified."

Hank rolled his eyes. Howell didn't crack a smile.

"Charlie, you don't seem to be having fun," she said, turning to Hank.

"Actually, I wanted to know if the French in Berlin were having any incidents involving anti-Gaullists...the OAS?"

Now interested, Howell leaned in toward her. "And?" he asked.

"Charlie, I'm sure you know more about it than I do."

Hank looked at Howell waiting for a reaction. But the stone face was back and he just shook his head.

"Actually they have had a couple of incidents. Two bombings at offices in the French Sector. Two dead, one of them French military. It's a problem and Brandt says they're on full alert for terrorist activity. He thinks our friends on the other side of The Wall, and beyond, might have a hand in it." Serious now, she looked at Howell. "Sound right to you Charlie?" Hank couldn't tell if she were teasing or trespassing.

"No question these folks are a problem. And a problem we've got to solve before it gets more serious than it already is. Now, if you'll excuse me." He nodded dramatically as if were about to bow, then abruptly walked away.

"He knows plenty," said Ilse. "He may have his office in Munich, but he has his finger on things all over Germany."

"He is a spook then."

Ilse shot him a dark glance. "Don't use that word. Never around him. Just say he's a Cultural Attaché with a broad portfolio."

She said it in such a way that Hank felt like a teacher being lectured to by a student, realizing that he really didn't know whether she had a portfolio of some sort too. There was a momentary silence until Hank said, "How about something to eat? The buffet table looks incredible."

Many of the guests had the same idea at the same time, so there was a crowd forming a buffet line. Hank and Ilse chatted lazily awaiting their turn. Each nodded to people they knew as they watched them pass by with full plates and full wine glasses. Ilse was surprised that she recognized so many of the guests. There was a full contingent from RFE.

It was obvious to them both it would be

several minutes before they had their chance to attack the table. Noting that, Ilse asked if Hank would excuse her for a moment. He assumed she was looking for the "facilities," and was surprised when he saw her chatting with Charles Howell. It didn't look like a friendly interlude. His face was red and he was doing most of the talking. Once again the teacher-student metaphor crossed his mind. Except this time Howell was the teacher, she the student, and he appeared ready to send her to detention. He walked away and she stood in place and watched him amble down the path.

She returned to her place in line and stood silently next to Hank. "The food here had better be good," she finally said morosely, "because I suddenly have a bad taste in my mouth."

"Howell?"

"He thinks I should not have talked to Brandt and that I was out of line when I asked about what he might know about the attacks against the French." She looked up at Hank, her blue eyes glistening. "He said conversations like that should be left to the professionals. Humph."

"Why should he be concerned...or you for that matter? He's a consular officer. He has no power or responsibility over you."

"There's a little more to it than that," she muttered. "We work together from time to time. When we do, he's the boss."

She again turned to Hank. "Please don't ask

me any more." She looked up and tried to smile. "Hey, we're almost there. I'm starving."

Hank was too...but not for potato salad or ribs.

They loaded their plates and found a table that had just been vacated. Hank went to the bar and brought back fresh drinks. "I didn't wait," Ilse laughed, causing barbecue sauce to dribble from the side of her mouth. "Sorry."

They ate mostly in silence as each bowed to their appetites. Eventually they both sat back and took deep breaths.

"Don't even say the word if you're going to suggest dessert," she said.

"I wouldn't dare," he answered. "Not if it meant that I'd have to get up to get it."

They had fun watching other people at other tables overdoing it just as they had. The sun had started to go down, casting long shadows across the lawn and the patio. The sound of quiet conversation and laughter drifted across the area. A gentle breeze animated the numerous American flags overseeing the event. Music stirred softly from an unseen source. Show tunes. Mostly My Fair Lady. Cool jazz would come later.

"There's going to be dancing later," said Hank. "Want to stay around for that?"

"I do. I'd like to see what you've got on the dance floor," she said playfully.

"Not much, I'm afraid. Count me out if

they're doing The Twist. If it's Harlem Nocturne...Moon River... slow dancing...I'm your man. Forget the other stuff."

Ilse pretended to be disappointed. And they joked about it. "I'll make a man of you yet," she said. "But with this crowd, I'm thinking Moon River's going to get a workout."

"Phew. That's a relief," he teased.

An hour later they were practically standing in place, their hips the only movement as they swayed to a show tunes playbook. He had both hands cupped in the small of her back. Her arms were on his shoulders, her fingers locked at the back of his neck. Their cheeks touched. They both felt each other's heat. They were oblivious to the world around them. It was a dream world. His heart was beating at a rate out of sync with the music.

Her eyes were closed as if she were drifting on a cloud looking down at him, and at herself, together. At one point she leaned back, looked at him closely, then leaned forward to touch his lips with hers. Softly at first, then with more mutual pressure. Their tongues touched. At that moment, the movement of their hips stopped. They both leaned back. His eyes locked on hers. Again they brought their lips together.

She stepped back, smiled, took his hands from behind her neck and held them in hers.

"Let's get out of here." she said. "We can do better than this."

Neither saw Ted at a table well off the dance floor, talking with Charles Howell. The two of them watched as Ilse and Hank walked slowly from the dance floor hand in hand. Their eyes followed until the two were out of sight.

"That's what I was afraid of," said Howell. "He's too inquisitive and she knows too much."

PART THREE

CHAPTER 12

Albert LeClerc was experiencing a period that for him had always been elusive: one of extreme confidence. The one armed anti-Gaullist was proving himself a moderately successful leader of men and tactician. His plot to attack a French site in Munich was a double-barreled success. The French Trade Mission suffered considerable damage in a late-night bombing and was still closed for business. The bomber, Pierre Blanchet was killed, just as planned while placing the bomb. It had been armed for an instantaneous rather than delayed detonation to ensure Blanchet's death. It was regrettable to lose one of the members of his own small terrorist cell, but Blanchet had lost the trust of his commander.

Other successes had been registered in West Berlin where two terrorist explosions had been successfully carried out, including the death of a French Army captain. Every success emboldened him.

LeClerc was certain that such activities would prompt intense investigative response, but, he rationalized, this was war. At times, chances had to be taken. None would be more risky than his next objective, the elimination of Marcel Blanchet, the Munich bomber's brother. He was a non-commissioned officer stationed in Baden Baden with the French garrison.

His brother had made it clear that Marcel was a de Gaulle loyalist. Pierre's loyalty to the anti-government cause was unquestioned. However, he had likely spoken too much to his brother of anti-Gaullist activity in Germany and that, in turn, posed unacceptable risks. LeClerc's meeting with the two brothers had not convinced him that they might have, inadvertently or not, been the leak that had led to Argoud's capture. Nonetheless, he could not risk a security rupture that would lead authorities to him.

LeClerc's small unit had also grown. He now had a dozen French dissidents working for, and with, him. He had also added two Germans who had joined, not out of support for a French Algeria or opposition to de Gaulle, but rather for a lingering taste for violence that had been acquired a generation earlier. While an increase in number could pose security risks, the additional manpower also enabled a broader range of actions. The priority at the moment was the elimination of Marcel Blanchet. The Germans could prove useful in resolving that problem.

It wouldn't be easy. The young sergeant would certainly be on high alert following the death of his brother. It would not have taken too much imagination to infer that Pierre's death was more than an accident. And, Marcel would most likely be inclined toward vengeance, necessitating a rapid response. That alone put dealing with him at the highest priority.

LeClerc put a simple plan in place in which he would contact Marcel and ask for a meeting to explain exactly what had happened to his brother. An accident, he would say, during a midnight bombing that was designed to send a message: not an attack to harm anyone. They would meet at a place of Marcel's choice in Baden Baden. They would have their conversation. LeClerc would leave and one or two of his henchmen would follow Marcel when he left the café. They would do what LeClerc insisted had to be done.

Driven more by curiosity than by a desire to have personal contact with LeClerc again, Marcel Blanchet agreed to the meeting.

He was furious on several levels when he'd learned of his brother's death. He recognized from the details he knew, that it was the result of his brother's terrorist affiliation. It had obviously been a risky and symbolic attack against an insignificant target. It sickened him to think that his younger brother would have been involved in such an absurd action. He thought of it as a waste on all levels. There was no legitimate expectation that such attacks would have an impact on the French government beyond their nuisance value: a flea on an elephant.

It wasn't difficult to recognize the rag tag nature of whatever organization was behind the bombing. He could see it in his brother's dismal apartment and lifestyle, along with the unimpressive demeanor of the one-armed "leader" of the group. He was a commander with apparent delusions of grandeur. It all suggested a group that was ill-equipped, ill-prepared and badly led.

On the one hand therefore, it was easy to understand how an operation run by a gang of misfits could go so wrong. On the other hand, given recent discussions between his brother, himself, and LeClerc, coupled with LeClerc's obvious suspicions that the Blanchets were not to be trusted, it wasn't difficult to build a case against the LeClerc cell choosing murder to seal loose lips. If that were the case, thought Marcel, then he was also in danger. He had to approach a meeting with LeClerc, even in a public place on his own turf apprehensively and alertly.

Curiosity prevailed. Marcel trusted his own military instincts and training to anticipate and overcome any attempted move against him. He considered bringing a fellow officer to the meeting as protection. He discounted that rather quickly. Although he assumed LeClerc's cell was beyond borderline incompetent, he could not dismiss the possibility that LeClerc's reach might include the French officer corps in Baden Baden. There were still plenty of Frenchmen in and out of the military with grievances against the French government in general, and Charles de Gaulle specifically.

Blanchet was confident he'd be able to read LeClerc quickly and react accordingly. He had to know whether his brother was the victim of the LeClerc group's incompetence, or whether he was a victim of its paranoia, and killed intentionally to guarantee his silence. If he determined that that was the case, he'd be prepared.

There was no cordial greeting when the two men met at Wiener Stuben, a brightly lighted restaurant in the center of town. Business was brisk. LeClerc had arrived first and had arranged a table in a far corner of the public room. A noisy clientele ensured they would not be overheard.

Marcel nodded as he sat down, noisily dragging his chair. "Your meeting," said Blanchet brusquely. "Why?"

"I wanted to personally offer my condolences over the death of your brother. We too were brothers...brothers in arms. We served together in Algeria and were of like mind when it came to politics." He looked around as if to convince himself that there were no eavesdroppers.

"I am asking for your discretion in what I am about to say." It was a meaningless comment, given what he had planned for Marcel.

Marcel offered an unenthusiastic nod. "Go ahead."

"I suspect you know we are an anti-government organization. Your brother was enthusiastic and believed in our mission..."

"And that mission is what?" interrupted Marcel.

"We want a new government in Paris, and a reevaluation of our country's policies in Northern Africa."

"And you think that amateur bombings in Munich carried out by small groups, will bring you closer to those objectives? Ridiculous."

LeClerc momentarily stiffened at the rebuke. He finally said, "Your brother didn't think so," he said harshly, more so than intended.

"My brother was a child who became caught up in something I'm sure he did not fully understand."

"I think he understood fully well."

"I don't think he understood that he was carrying a bomb that would blow up in his face."

'It was an accident."

"He had no experience with bombs."

"Actually, he did. In Algeria."

"Fuck Algeria. That's yesterday's news. Algerians got what they deserved, Independence."

LeClerc bristled.

"I am here," said Marcel, "for one reason only. You were clearly concerned that Pierre, through me, had tipped off Paris that Argoud, and other people...people like you...were running around Munich plotting against de Gaulle. I can write a scenario in which you wanted to silence him because of that. Murder him."

"No, no, no," protested LeClerc. "Never. We don't murder our own." He slammed his palm on the table so loudly adjacent diners turned to stare.

"I think there's a pretty clear record that you've done more than your share of that." He stared intensely at LeClerc.

"Are you prepared to tell me right now that my brother's death was accidental?"

LeClerc licked his lips and waited several seconds before responding. It was the kind of pause Marcel had seen before during interrogations in Oran. Without words from LeClerc, it was the answer to the question he had come to Baden Baden for.

Slowly, he pushed back his chair. "I think I have my answer," said Marcel. "Your little group is pitiful. First you turn on your country, then on your colleagues. You are pathetic." He stood over LeClerc, his face broadcasting his anger and disrespect for the man seated before him.

"I'm leaving," he barked, "but you have not heard the last from me."

LeClerc was churning inside. The threat was out in the open. There was no more questioning the other man's intentions. He could form no words. With a quick nod of his head, Marcel Blanchet turned and left the room quickly, unaware that his fate had just been officially sealed.

Marcel Blanchet grew more and more angry as he walked to his car, no longer needing to be convinced that his brother was the victim of his misguided colleagues. LeClerc, as leader of the tiny anti-Gaullist cell, bore the responsibility, reasoned Marcel. It was he who had the most to lose.

While he may have spoken out of turn to military colleagues in careless conversations he could not remember about anti-government cells in Munich, he could not imagine words uttered in discussions could have made their way to high authorities and led to action against Argoud.

However, Marcel now realized that innocent talk over too much wine, may have led indirectly to the death of his brother. He was overcome with sudden dizzying guilt. What would his next step be? What should it be?

He could go to the ranking officers in his unit and report the LeClerc operation in Munich. He could even take investigators to LeClerc's apartment. However, he realized that the French military was rife with anti-Gaullist sentiment. He was uncertain whether even his superiors could be trusted?

There was also another risk. Questions would be raised as to his earlier silence. If he were aware through Pierre of the anti-Gaullist sentiment and terrorist cells in Munich, why would he not have reported it earlier? That would be an obvious question. Wasn't it, therefore, possible he could be accused of being an accessory?

The questions defied easy answers as he made his way to his car. He was oblivious to his immediate surroundings and unaware of two burly men approaching him from behind. As they seemed ready to pass him on either side, they reached out simultaneously with each grabbing an arm. Marcel was startled, and tried to pull away. But in that instant he knew what was happening just as clearly as he knew escape was impossible.

There were no other pedestrians on the sidewalks. Motor traffic was light. It was the perfect time and place for an ambush-abduction. He started to shout for help, but his throat had gone dry, and he could not. He looked from side to side at each of his assailants, each of whom was a head taller than himself.

They were strong and were lifting him by his arms as if escorting a drunk as they guided him brusquely to his car. The rusting Peugeot sat in darkness around the corner. Once there, they opened the back door and shoved him inside. One of the two followed him in and grabbed his shirt by the collar pulling him to a sitting position. All three were breathing loudly.

"Keys," said the man holding him. It was the first word that had been spoken since they had intercepted him on the street, while he'd been preoccupied with his thoughts about LeClerc. This is LeClerc's response he thought as he dug for the car keys in his pocket. He did not resist. What would be the point? I am done for he thought to himself as the man next to him took the keys, handed them to his partner, then proceeded to forcefully pull a crude canvas sack over Marcel's head, shutting out all of the limited light coming from a distant lamppost.

All he could hear was the heavy breathing of himself and the two others in the car, then came the hum of the engine turning as the Peugeot hummed to life. He could feel it pull away from the curb and move into the traffic lane. With his head under the hood he could smell his own breath. It was vile, like the acidic taste in his mouth.

Moments later, the car coasted to a stop. Marcel could tell they had parked in a quiet place. There was a strange calm in sharp contrast to his wildly beating heart. He could hear the sound of insects, but there were no city noises. There was another sound it took him a moment to identify. Water. The river. The Oos. They were in the park adjacent to the Oos river.

It was his last thought as a single bullet was fired into his brain exploding his head inside the canvas sack.

LeClerc was ecstatic when he received word of Marcel Blanchet's death. It was several days before word of it was reported in Munich's newspapers. The Press and authorities eventually determined that Marcel may have been related to the man killed in the French Trade Mission bombing, but they could take it no further than that. That uncertainty served to fuel the Frenchman's belief that he had managed to successfully ensure operational security for himself and his organization. It was also a boost to his self-confidence which had always been hungry for reinforcement.

But all the self-confidence he could muster would not fund the enterprises he envisioned for his organization. He needed weapons and explosives. And that meant he needed money. He also recognized the need to provide some form of compensation to members of his growing cell. The men who had joined him had poor German language skills and limited proficiency for joining a civilian workforce. They were all ex-military, enlisted men of low rank.

The Germans were more capable of finding employment, but seemed less inclined to do so. They were content to be quasi-military mercenaries. But LeClerc realized their contentment would be short lived if they were not paid, especially after committing murder for sport rather than for a cause. He had to find a revenue source.

LeClerc knew that his choices were limited and that the only options were illegal. Any criminal expansion of his already illicit enterprise would put the entire operation at greater risk. Given the limited intelligence of his compatriots, the solution would have to be simple. Maybe simple is best he thought. Fewer things could go wrong, except that every criminal event would result in an investigation, each of which would bring with it a security threat.

LeClerc reasoned that simple street crime would be his best option. Street robberies and holdups could be controlled, carried out at times and places of choice offering minimum risk of failure.

Within a week his men had struck successfully eleven times. The take? A paltry thousand marks ($250) and a little over one hundred US dollars. The dollars had been taken from two tipsy GIs leaving a Gasthaus. The two Germans had held them up at gunpoint in direct violation of LeClerc's orders that the street bandits stay away from Americans. Exacerbating the situation was the fact one of the Germans had pistol-whipped one of the American victims. The last thing LeClerc wanted was Ami investigators looking for his men. Crimes against Americans would routinely be investigated more vigorously than crimes against Germans or immigrants. At the same time, he realized that it was the Americans who could always be counted on to be carrying larger amounts of cash than the average German.

As to the German members of his group, LeClerc felt increasingly boxed in. He could not discipline them effectively. They had murdered a French soldier on his instruction. They could turn on him if so motivated. Arrest might be just such a motivation. And blackmail might be another option.

GI INJURED IN STREET HOLDUP
By Hank Tollar
An American soldier suffered severe head injuries in a street holdup near downtown Munich late Thursday.

SP4 Armond Crawford is being treated at the US Army Hospital in Munich. His injuries are described as serious but non-life-threatening. He is expected to remain hospitalized for 24-48 hours.

Crawford and his companion, PVT Jackson Pittage were approached by two *gunmen outside the Alpenstück Gasthaus on Hohenzollernstrasse. The two holdup men demanded money. When Crawford refused, one of the two gunmen hit him on the head with his weapon. Crawford remained conscious and gave the men more than $50 in cash.*

Pittage also turned over an estimated at $40 in cash. He was unharmed.

The two assailants are described as German, about six feet tall, burly, unshaven, dressed in typical worker's garb: blue flannel shirts and gray trousers.

US Military Police and the Munich Police Department are investigating.

The Munich papers reported much shorter versions of the story.

LeClerc was dismayed to read them. The last thing he needed or wanted was media sunlight on members of his organization. His operation needed to remain in the shadows to succeed. He had no choice but to stand down...for the time being. He called his men to a meeting to explain the need for new caution following the publicity over the street assault-robbery of the Americans. They will investigate, he told them, and will turn on the heat if there are more street attacks against GIs.

He was speaking to all of his men, but was

directing his message primarily to the Germans. They stood aside from the rest of the men who had been shifting nervously and listened impassively as he spoke. LeClerc had little confidence that his message was getting through to them. He ended the meeting telling his men that there were to be no more robberies until he gave the word. They mumbled assent.

The men became impatient after several days. The small amount of cash they had managed to steal in the first days was quickly gone. The men needed cash. They had to eat, pay rent, and pay for their transportation.

Less than a week after calling off the street robberies, LeClerc okayed a resumption of the activity. He outlined a formula whereby the men would keep most of their loot, but would be required to turn over a percentage of their take to him to run the cell. "But," he admonished them again, "stay away from the Americans." The two Germans looked at each other without saying a word, but each could read in the other's eyes that they were not taking orders from a one-armed "Dummkopf."

It took some weeks before an increase in street crimes came to the attention of German and American authorities. It was not that the amount stolen was so high. What brought incidents to the attention was that victims were saying increasingly that the holdup men had French accents. This information made its way up the law enforcement food chain where investigators of French terrorist activity had run into a series of dead ends. Was this street crime activity, they wondered, the work of underground anti-Gaullists in Munich? Was it coincidence? Was the information even accurate? If so, they wondered, could they could pull the threads that might lead them to the terrorist cells?

Charles Howell was especially interested in the crime statistics. Munich was not a high crime city. But there had been an obvious increase in holdups and the French connection was intriguing to him.

When it was brought to his attention, he called a meeting of interested parties who had established an informal working group focusing on French anti-Gaullist activity.

They gathered in his office on a rainy morning. There had been an explosion outside a French restaurant the night before. It was not a powerful blast and the device had been badly placed. No one was hurt, but the target seemed to reinforce concerns that they were witnessing a spike in anti-Gaullist activity.

Those invited to the meeting had been specially chosen. All were intelligence officers in their respective organizations. Their briefs went far beyond common street crimes. Sitting at the table with Howell were Lt. Hans Erbach of the Munich Police Department and Captain Dieter Krausweg of the Bavarian State Police. Major Todd Zwilling represented the Munich Army Command Criminal Investigation Division (CID). Guy Dupuis was a representative from the French Consulate. Representing the FBI team that had been brought in after the Trade Mission bombing was Special Agent Graham Bell, who had long since tired of people making fun of his name. Each of the men looked the part: fit, erect posture, steely-eyed. Sitting in, in sharp contrast, was J. Harding Bell who was no relation to the FBI man.

They had all worked together individually and as a group on various matters of mutual concern. They had met several times on the issue of the suspected OAS presence in Munich and beyond. Meetings had started with the abduction of Col. Argoud. All participants agreed that Argoud's presence in Munich was an obvious signal that anti-Gaullists were operating underground in the city. The bombing at the French Trade Mission seemed to confirm it. The questions hung like ripe fruit just out of reach. How many? Who were the leaders? What were the objectives? How were they funded? And what did the spike in street robberies apparently, involving French thugs, mean?

The gatherings took on a new urgency with a major assassination attempt against de Gaulle.

A paramilitary team fired some two hundred rounds at his car as he sped by with his entourage outside Paris. Miraculously, he was not hit. There was concern it represented the beginning of a new offensive by the OAS and its allies. Participants wondered whether a modern Reign of Terror was emerging?

"So, what cultural matters do we have to discuss today?" joked Major Zwilling with a straight face as the men got comfortable at a big conference table.

"French theater and bad comedy," responded Howell without missing a beat. "Shall we get on with it?"

The rain splashed noisily against a big window.

"Okay, we've all seen the news stories and know what's on the agenda," said Howell. "Let me ask each one of you how you read it? Lt. Erbach?"

"We know they're here. Argoud and the bombings leave no doubt. They are like rats coming out at night. They're hungry. With Argoud gone, it looks like they have no leadership. They're stuck in Germany."

"Captain Krausweg?"

"Sounds right to me. We have to pick one of them up and find out for certain. Difficult. They are active all over Germany. Especially here. We have our eyes open outside of the city. And, our ears are open listening for strangers with French accents. They may be headquartered outside of town. So far, nothing."

"Our intelligence sources have nothing," said Dupuis forlornly. "We have looked closely at the French citizens we know are here...those who have registered with us. We suspect the ones we want to find are unregistered. We are looking for them."

"Agent Bell?"

"I can't offer much about the holdups. The bomb last night looks like a cheapo. Amateur. Not as sophisticated as the earlier one. Good thing. Broke some windows but that's about it. I can't say the signature's the same on both bombs. We're still looking at that."

"Major?"

"We've had half a dozen attacks against GIs. One guy hurt pretty badly. In every case, the bad guys were German. Not French. I don't know what that means."

"Maybe nothing. Maybe that they have some local help," said Howell. He cracked his knuckles as he scanned the faces of the men at the table. "We've got to round up someone and get to the bottom of this. We don't want any more attacks, or anyone getting hurt."

"Any ideas?" asked Krausweg.

"Yeah," said Howell. "We've got to pick up one or two. Squeeze and squeeze hard."

The men talked for more than an hour.

They agreed that the randomness of the criminal events made it difficult to establish a coherent plan. Lt. Erbach promised to put more officers on the street hoping for a lucky break. He would also make use of various street informants. He shrugged his shoulders admitting that odds of success were slim.

Captain Krausweg promised to get the word out throughout Bavaria to keep track of strangers...especially those with French accents. "That's about all I can think to do," he said solemnly. "That, and keep our eyes open."

Major Zwilling said he'd put as many of his men that he could in bars and taverns acting drunk, hoping one or more of them might be considered easy targets on the street. "I've got some tough guys with martial arts skills. But the odds?..." his voice trailed off.

The FBI man scratched his head saying he hoped bomb forensics would provide something of use.

As the meeting wound down, Howell reminded the group that there was an issue of delicacy, diplomatic and otherwise, involved in their mission. Relations between Washington and Paris were strained at the moment. De Gaulle was suspicious of US intelligence reports alleging Russian moles in the French military and even within the highest levels of government.

"Arrest or harass an innocent Frenchman

or German and it will hit the fan. Make sure your men know that," Howell said somberly. "All we need is one to interrogate. All we need is one" he repeated, standing as he spoke. It was his signal the meeting was over. The others followed suit, and pushed their chairs back noisily. They looked at each other as they headed for the door, their expressions anything but hopeful or optimistic.

Howell and his colleague Bell watched them leave. "Well, what do you think?" asked Howell. "They hardly look like a hungry football team coming out for the second half."

"They know," said Bell, "that they are looking for a needle that's not only in a haystack. It's a needle in a moving haystack."

Frustration for the allied working group continued for days, then weeks. Isolated incidents of street robberies following the same pattern continued with no leads. There was no violence in any of the holdups though it was always threatened. A few GIs were robbed but most of those incidents involved Germans, not French thugs. There were no bomb attacks.

There was one deviation from the pattern when a US military gas station was robbed by two Germans. The haul was significant. Two thousand dollars. Witnesses gave descriptions that more or less matched those of GIs who'd been robbed. But then again they also matched those

of an entire population of German working men.
Working group members wondered, if they were
the same men who had held up servicemen?

That robbery and the ongoing street holdups produced little or nothing in the way of information that might lead to the arrest of any of the
criminals. It was a dry hole.

But, there was frustration on the other
side too. LeClerc was not only frustrated. He
was becoming increasingly impatient. His band
of holdup men had been bringing in limited
amounts of cash. The Germans had made the
biggest haul with their successful gas station robbery. While the cash was welcome, they took
most of it. And, it infuriated LeClerc that they
had acted against Americans, violating his specific orders. Street holdups were one thing. A
major robbery was another. It would certainly
receive a much higher investigative priority than
would a two-bit street robbery of a drunk GI.

But LeClerc's frustration was not only
about the limited amounts of cash coming in. It
was also in his need, and yet inability, to perform a significant act of defiance against France.
He needed something big. He needed to send a
message, something to prove to the other OAS
anti-Gaullists, as well as the French, Germans and
Americans that he was a force to be reckoned
with, that he should be taken seriously.

The frustration was fueled by the size of

his group. Some earlier recruits had drifted away. His cell now included only ten men, including the two Germans. The lack of resources, including cash and weapons, was also problematical.

There was also a dearth of meaningful targets. He needed a big success. There were rumors de Gaulle himself would be visiting Germany one day soon. He wanted to be at the table if and when what he assumed would be an inevitable attack against the French President was being planned. He yearned for a gaudy success that would help make that possible.

He recognized the opportunity immediately when he saw it. Lucky Manon had qualified for a big race in America, and was to race in another major event at someplace called Daytona. In between, he would be returning to Europe to solicit sponsorships. He was being hailed as Europe's next big star in auto racing.

Wonderful thought LeClerc. Lucky Manon is young, he is handsome, he lives in Munich, and...he is French.

"Lucky is coming home," said Ilse as she and Hank drank coffee on her rumpled bed. They had spent much of their free time in that bed in the weeks since he had brought her home from the Fourth of July party. Their relationship had been electric since that night.

They had said very little to each other on

the ride to her place from the party. Emotions exploded the instant she opened the door to her second floor apartment. Wildly impromptu, they embraced passionately, and frantically removed their clothes, leaving a trail behind them as they stumbled into her bedroom.

Their lovemaking was noisy and without restraint. Exhausted, they fell asleep near dawn. When they awoke at mid-morning, hungry for each other, they made love again. They showered together, laughing like two small children who had discovered a hidden box of treats.

In the subsequent weeks, they were together every night. They went to work reluctantly, and were impatient the rest of each day until they found each other's arms again at night.

At the end of their first month together, they sat drinking wine at their favorite café on Leopoldstrasse, when Hank suddenly said, "I love you Ilse." It was a simple statement. The drama was in the words, not in the way he said them. He looked at her dreamily.

"I know you do," she giggled. "I knew it from the first moment. A girl knows such things."

"That obvious, huh?"

"Yes. I thought it was sweet. Flattering and sweet," she added quickly. "I was more certain of your feelings than of my own."

"And, they are what?" he asked warily, worried her answer could be anything but what he wanted to hear.

She looked at him closely for several seconds. He's handsome, she thought. His nose is a bit too small, but his eyes, gray and alert, are alive and intelligent. He's smart. He sometimes acts like a little boy...a loveable little boy. And he loves me. But, she wondered, how do I feel?

"I'm trying to figure that out," she said coyly. "I've never been in love before. I don't know whether what I feel is love. What does love feel like? That's what I'm asking myself."

"I'll tell you what it feels like. It feels like I feel. It feels like I want to be with you every moment I'm not. It feels like I want to have you in my arms all the time. I want to listen to your laugh. It feels like I'm floating. It feels like I'm high."

"Okay, so far so good," she replied giggling again. "I think I'm passing that test."

"If you think of it as a test," he said, "don't think of the questions. Think of the answers. The way I feel about you is not a question...it's all of the answers I just mentioned describing the way I feel."

She raised her eyebrows as if she were about to respond, but Hank went on. "While we're at it, what about Lucky? I feel he's in the middle of this conversation without being mentioned. Is Lucky a silent partner to the discussion...to our relationship?"

"Hah," she exclaimed. "Here's something I know how to answer and I know about my feelings." She was serious now. "I know you've wondered about my relationship with Lucky. We do have a relationship. We've known each other forever. I love him. But I love him like a sister loves a brother. He's a good guy. He lives...loves...his profession. That's his first and only love. Second. He's quite fond of himself. I don't know if he has any love left over for others." She was speaking rapidly.

"He's proud of what he's accomplished, but he wants more. He's a little boy playing at life. He was almost killed racing. It's like he wants to prove that he's tougher than death itself, accomplish all he can, and live life to the fullest before the next accident."

"So, is he living life at the fullest when he stays with you when he's in town?" asked Hank. "Is he one of the complications you once mentioned?"

She shook her head. "He's a friend. He sleeps on the couch. And, when he brings home one of his 'admirers,' I sleep on the couch and he gets the bed. That's a friend," she said, "not a lover." She took a deep swallow of wine. "I think," she said, "that I can tell you a lot more about friendship than I can tell you about love."

"So, friendship is giving up the bed for the couch?" he said wryly.

"Finish your wine," she said. "We'll start on the couch, and wind up in bed. Does that answer your question?"

"Forget the wine," he said. "Let's go."

"When's he coming?" he asked cautiously taking a sip of his coffee.

"In the next couple of days," she said. "I'm not certain. He called me and didn't have much time. The French Federation of Automobile Sport is giving him an award in Paris which he hopes will help him with sponsorships. Then he'll come here to beg for money from his German contacts. He's excited. He only has a few days before he goes back to the states to get ready for the race. He needs to build his own team first and doesn't have much time."

"He know about us?"

"Yes."

"And?"

"Nothing. He just said he hoped I was happy, then went on and on about his plans."

"Shall I stay with you when he's here?" Hank asked almost timidly.

"Like I said, when he's here, he gets the couch."

"And if he brings home a girlfriend?"

"Then," she laughed, "he'll have to learn how to use it the way we did the other night."

Lucky Manon's return to Munich was something of a personal triumph, though even with some press attention, not much noticed beyond Ilse, Hank, some other friends, and Albert LeClerc. Hank wrote a few lines as a follow up to his recent feature on the race car driver. The Munich morning paper carried a short local-resident-makes-good story with a photo of Manon receiving his award in Paris.

While Lucky's return to Paris and Munich was of limited interest to the average reader, Manon's publicity was noted with pleasure by LeClerc. The Munich paper's headline, *French Race Car Driver Returns with Honor,* was enough to make LeClerc chuckle.

For the first few days after his return to Munich, Manon was busy trying to fulfill his sport's constant demand for sponsorship money. It is an expensive sport on many levels, especially in putting together a first- rate team to attend to a first-rate car.

Manon could be charming when on the financial crusade. The movers and shakers at Porsche received him with open arms and wallets in Stuttgart, promising significant financial and technical support. And a vehicle. It was a bigger win in many ways than any on the track so far.

It was reported with some fanfare in local papers, all of which was a cause for celebration for Manon who reveled in the success of his effort. And, for LeClerc who felt he finally had a local target that would garner the kind of attention he'd been looking for.

CHAPTER 13

Hank was both envious and jealous when he saw how enthusiastically Ilse greeted Lucky, but he tried not to show it. Lucky was all smiles with arms held wide as he beckoned her to him. In one hand he held the trophy he'd been awarded in Paris. She complied willingly, shrieking happily as she wrapped her arms around his waist and snuggled against his chest before kissing him on each cheek. "I'm so happy for you," she gushed. "You are a star." Hank watched the reunion with a forced smile and wondered, as an only child, if this was the way brothers and sisters typically greeted one another.

"And you," said a clearly relaxed Lucky finally pointing at Hank and smiling..."you did not waste any time moving into Ilse's life when I was away."

"You got your prize and I got mine," said

Hank. "That makes us even."

Manon laughed heartily. "Ah, but mine does not talk back," he said holding up his trophy, "or tell me to drink less wine." He laughed again.

"I learned a long time ago," said Ilse, "that asking you to drink less wine was what the Americans call a fools errand."

She grabbed Hank's hand. "Now, I'm working on Hank."

"You are finished, Hank" said Lucky, putting his trophy on the nearby table.

"I am happy for you both," he said with a sincerity that surprised Hank. It was even more surprising when Lucky stepped forward, put his arms around Hank and kissed him gently on both cheeks.

Hank congratulated Lucky for "living up to his name" in his racing success and his success with Porsche. There were grins all around, and Hank was feeling a lot better about Lucky's relationship with Ilse, and his own relationship with the Frenchman.

"We want to celebrate," shouted Ilse. "We are going to make reservations at La Bouche and celebrate in style."

"Wonderful," answered Lucky. "Do you mind if I bring a friend?"

Ilse raised her eyebrow.

"Yes, I have found a little songbird," he said.

"There is room on the couch for two," said

Ilse playfully, "I'm sure you can figure it out."

"Hah. She has her own place," he said, slapping Hank on the back. "She's an American journalist and wants to do a profile. She's staying at the Bayerischer Hof."

"*Oh là là*," exclaimed Ilse. "You are coming up in the world. And speaking of celebrating, I have some champagne to open," she said turning toward the kitchen.

"And who is your journalist friend?" asked Hank as she left the room. "I don't know of too many women in the business."

"Her name is Kay Montgomery. Her father is the Associated Press Bureau Chief in Frankfurt..."

"I know him and her," interrupted Hank. "She was just starting high school when I first met her."

"She's not little any more. Her father's giving her a chance to do a story. She's going off to college to become a journalist."

"I'm guessing she's going to learn a lot more than daddy bargained for in doing this one," Hank teased as Ilse returned holding the champagne bottle the same way Lucky had held his trophy.

"We have a reservation tomorrow at seven at La Bouche," said Ilse as she poured champagne for all. "It's not far from your hotel. Why don't we meet you there?"

They agreed on arrangements for meeting

the following evening. Lucky left more satisfied with life than ever with two glasses of champagne under his belt and a pretty girl waiting for him at her hotel.

"I have another bottle of champagne," said Ilse as they listened to Lucky clomp down the wooden stairs. "He must like the new girl. I was sure he'd stay for more. Would you like another glass?" she looked at Hank suggestively. He nodded approvingly. "Good" she said, "let's drink it in bed."

La Bouche is not an imposing restaurant from the outside. It's the food inside that had given it its outstanding reputation. And there were few complaints when the eyebrow-raising bill came. It was located in a simple stone building located on the corner of a small street. Blue awnings hovered over large glass windows giving passersby full view of how *the other half* lived. Bottles of expensive wine were positioned in racks along the walls, reflecting the intimate lighting. A colorful bar dominated the far end of the dining room, behind which shelves containing a mountain of bottles that proudly presented the labels of the world's finest spirits that beckoned discriminating drinkers. Lighting was soft and conversations were muted as diners savored the many award-winning house specialties.

In the first minutes after their arrival, the

Manon party, as the maître d' had christened the group, had settled in with great satisfaction and watched with delight as a gypsy violinist angled among the tables playing soft music designed for both aspiring and seasoned lovers.

"This is incredible," gushed Kay. "It sure beats the wurst and kraut places I get taken to in Frankfurt."

"I don't think you'll find either on the menu here," laughed Ilse who was quite taken by the young woman. Kay was pretty in a way that promised more when she flowered into full adulthood. At eighteen she had smooth skin, brown hair, a little too much lipstick, but an engaging smile and bright eyes. She's already pretty now at eighteen thought Ilse, assuming she'd be a turning everyone's head by the time she graduated from college.

Lucky was clearly smitten and nuzzled her ear at every opportunity. Hank hardly noticed as fixed as he was on Ilse, who, he thought, was gorgeous in a tight black sweater and slacks that fit her perfectly, and also matched the informality and good taste of a fine restaurant that worked very hard to give the impression it did not take itself too seriously.

It was an evening of small talk dominated by Lucky's recitations of how he intended to take the American racing world by storm.

Kay promised to be at the vanguard of a

wave of women making their way in television journalism. "Nancy Dickerson and Pauline Frederick are just the beginning," she said. "They opened the door and I intend to walk through it."

Everyone agreed that she should and that she could. Ilse spoke of her own reportorial ambition and suggested coyly that Hank might be able to help. "Television sounds good," she said, "but it will be a long time before German television will have any women around except for the Putzfrau."

Hank remained largely silent. He had wondered a lot recently about what *his* future might hold. Stars and Stripes was a good start, he thought, but recent interference with some of the stories he wanted to write had soured him. Was there room, he wondered, for truth, independence, and fairness when the government pulled the strings in its own interests?

Lucky ordered another bottle and announced that he was picking up the tab for the evening which was more than welcome to Hank who'd calculated that the price tag for the evening would be the equivalent of a week's pay for him. Kay was droopy-eyed and giggly when they emptied the bottle. Ilse was yawning and Hank was feeling slightly tipsy.

They'd just agreed it was time to go when a young American in a crew cut and glassy eyes came to the table. He was in civilian clothes but Hank thought he had all the earmarks a brand new 2nd lieutenant who's had one drink too many.

"Hey," he said talking to Lucky just as all were standing to leave. "Aren't you that race car driver that I read about in the Stripes?"

Lucky beamed and nodded.

The young man looked him up and down. "Congratulations," he said, adding, "You're a lot shorter that I thought you would be." He was smiling, but Lucky was not. He had a short fuse when he drank. Ilse could see immediately that there could be trouble ahead.

"Well," she said, "he was tall enough to hit the accelerator and brakes at Watkins Glen and he will be at Daytona too."

Everyone laughed, including the young American who slapped Lucky on the back and wished Lucky good luck.

It took everyone a moment to realize that a potentially embarrassing incident had been averted. They shrugged and walked out onto the street where they hugged and said their goodbyes.

Ilse and Hank watched Lucky and Kay get inside his car hoping that he hadn't had too much wine to be driving. Just as they turned toward Hank's car parked just a half block away, they heard the noisy sound of an old, gray automobile coming down the street. It slowed slightly and they saw that something dark was thrown from the vehicle toward Lucky's car. The old car then sped away noisily.

The late evening calm was shattered by an explosion that lifted Lucky's car off the ground. Hank and Ilse were buffeted by the blast and slammed against a building. Fire from what had probably been a hand grenade or small bomb broke out immediately at the rear of Lucky's car and seconds later, before anyone could react, the gas tank exploded covering the entire vehicle in a wave of flame. Screams could be heard from inside the car.

The blast had shattered the large windows of the restaurant. Stunned and confused diners, some of them screaming, gasped in disbelief as they looked through the broken windows at the ghastly, fiery scene at the curb. Everyone watched in horror as Lucky, on fire, tumbled from the car, seemingly in slow motion, before he collapsed in the street. Kay's shrieking stopped at the same time. It had all happened in a matter of seconds.

Hank and Ilse were shaken, unable to fully absorb what had just happened a few feet away. In a moment, the only sound was the eerie whooshing of what sounded like wind, as the fire relentlessly attacked the vehicle. Someone from the restaurant ran outside with a tablecloth and attempted to smother the flames that had enveloped Lucky's body. The heat from his burning clothes and the nearby car was too intense to get close and the would-be Samaritan was forced to back away. The fire was winning on all fronts.

There was nothing anyone could do but watch. Many of the stunned onlookers, stood slack-jawed in helpless disbelief at what was playing out before them.

Hank was speechless as he watched what had unfolded in just a few seconds. He put his arm around Ilse and pulled her away from the building and farther from the flames. He could hear her mumble again and again between sobs, "My god...my god...my god...this can't be happening...it just can't be happening." They had moved only a few feet when they began to hear sirens heralding help that would arrive much too late.

When fire engines arrived, onlookers remained transfixed on the scene as firefighters went about the business of dousing what flames remained. Police and medical personnel attended to the bodies.

As the remains of the young woman were pulled from the car, more gasps before dignity could be restored to the victim by firefighters covering the body. Police had begun the process of gathering information from people who had nothing substantive to give them.

Hank approached one of the uniformed officers and whispered that he and Ilse had been with the victims until just before the bomb had been detonated. Eventually, the officer called over his sergeant and explained who they were. There was another short wait until the sergeant eventually summoned a detective who escorted Hank and Ilse to a nearby police van. He and Hank sat in the back and Ilse settled in the front passenger seat positioned so she wouldn't have to look at the work going on around the wreckage of Lucky's car.

They explained their relationship to the victims. As the officer took notes, they detailed the evening's events prior to the explosion, then explained what had happened as they had seen it once they left the restaurant.

Ilse remained largely silent, her ongoing shock clearly evident. Hank tried to bring her into the conversation on a few occasions but gave up when her monosyllabic responses seemed more and more painful to her.

When the detective asked if either of them had any idea why anyone would launch such an attack, Hank and Ilse shook their heads whispering "no" in unison.

When the detective had finished and snapped his notebook shut, Ilse and Hank turned in response to a knock on the window. Both were surprised when they recognized Charles Howell. The Cultural Attaché gestured with his head, beckoning...or was it ordering... them out of the van.

"What the heck are you doing here?" asked Hank when they had stepped out of the vehicle. "This doesn't seem much like a cultural event," he sniped. At the same time he saw there were two uniformed American Army officers talking with the German Police.

Howell ignored him and turned to Ilse. "You okay Ilse?" he asked softly. Hank was surprised at the tenderness in Howell's voice. The older man was rubbing her arm gently much as a father might console a child.

Ilse nodded in response. Howell put his arm around her and walked her toward his car, gesturing with his head for Hank to follow.

"Get in the back," he said to Hank, the tenderness was gone. Howell and Ilse got in the front seat. A moment later Howell pulled the car into the street.

"Where are we going?" asked Hank. My car is back there."

"Pick it up tomorrow."

"What the heck is going on?" Hank asked again. "Where are we going?" he repeated.

"The consulate...after I drop you off. Where do you live?"

"I'm with her," said Hank sharply. "I'll take care of her. And, why are you taking her to the consulate?"

"Because I want to talk to her."

"And not to me?"

"There's time for that later."

He argued for a moment, but when it was clear it was a fruitless effort, Hank punched the palm of his left hand as he gave Howell his address. A tragic and deadly evening had turned even more inexplicably strange. They drove in silence until they reached Hank's apartment.

"You go write your story," said Howell as Hank was getting out of his car. "I'm sure that's a first order of business. Do not use Ilse's name...or mine" he commanded. "Just say German Police and the American Consulate are investigating. Call Bell for a statement. We'll be in touch."

"I'll call you," said Ilse weakly, just as Howell put the car in gear and squealed off.

Hank climbed the stairs to his apartment grappling with basic questions. Why had Ilse been spirited away to the consulate by an officer everyone surmised was CIA or State Department Intelligence? If it was for interrogation, why hadn't Hank been invited to the party? What was Ilse's relationship with Howell? How had Americans showed up at the crime scene so quickly? Why? They were questions that needed answers, but neither questions nor answers could be a part of the story he was about to write

American, Frenchman, Killed in Downtown
Munich Street Bombing
By Hank Tollar

A violent explosion has killed two
people in their car outside a fashionable

restaurant in downtown Munich. One of the victims is a young American identified by friends at the scene as 18 year old Kay Montgomery of Albany, New York.

The other victim is identified as Matthieu "Lucky" Manon, 35, a prominent Alsatian-born French race car driver who resided in Munich. The badly damaged auto was registered in his name.

Witnesses say the two had just left the La Bouche restaurant where they had dined with friends. Seconds after they'd entered Manon's car, an unknown person or persons in a passing automobile threw an explosive device under Manon's vehicle. It detonated immediately, badly damaging the car and igniting a fierce fire which caused the gas tank to explode almost immediately.

The young woman died trapped in the car. Manon, whose body was on fire, managed to get out of the vehicle, but died moments later in the street.

Witnesses say the car from which the bomb was thrown was an older gray sedan, possibly a Peugeot or an Opel.

There is no known motive for the attack. It is not known if the couple was targeted or whether they were random victims.

There was considerable damage to the restaurant's windows as a result of the blast. No one was injured inside.

American and German officials are investigating and say they have no further details at this time.

Ms. Montgomery is the daughter of Hollis Montgomery, the Associated Press Bureau Chief in Frankfurt. She was preparing to study journalism at Syracuse University next fall, and was working on a freelance assignment profiling Mr. Manon for the AP.

Manon has no known surviving family members.

Manon's stature in the racing world had been on the rise in recent months. He had only recently signed a sponsorship contract with the German automaker Porsche after he had won in the United States at Watkins Glen.

Earlier this month he had been signed to race at Daytona in Florida.

His win at Nürburgring in Rhineland-Palatinate two years ago was his best European showing after racing with limited success on minor circuits elsewhere in Europe.

A spokesman for the US Consulate in Munich says Miss Montgomery's father is arranging to accompany his daughter's remains to Albany for burial.

Authorities are asking anyone who might have information on the attack to contact the Munich Police Department or the US Consulate in Munich.

The German papers played the story slightly differently. The same basic information, but the focus was on Manon. The headlines were more along the line of...*French Celebrity Killed in Bombing...French Racing Star Manon Victim of Bombing...Was Manon Targeted For Being French?* They all made the point that there was no known motive for the bombing. If it was not a random killing speculated some writers, the bombing was all the more mysterious because "Manon was not known to be political."

"First, I have nothing to tell you, and second, I have nothing to tell you. You got that?" Howell was obviously in a bad mood when Hank entered his office the next day. He looked tired and was, as was Hank. Hank's temper, usually held in check by a fragile thread around Howell was released with Howell's remarks.

"You know Howell...*Mr. Howell*," he said sarcastically, "I'm getting a little tired of your attitude. You act like some kind of Grand Poobah...holier than fucking thou around me."

Howell sat back in his chair.

"You said yourself the other day," continued Hank, "that we both have the same boss. Well, you know who my boss is...and I have a pretty good idea who yours is...your real boss. So take off your goddam spook's coat and give me some sense of what's going on." He stopped momentarily to catch his breath as Howell sat unmoved, even looking slightly amused.

"What's going on with you and Ilse? How the fuck did you and the CID get to the scene last night almost before I did?"

"Settle down sonny," said Howell, red-faced and speaking in a brusque tone so low he was almost growling. "Don't think you can come barging in here and start making demands. And..." he almost shouted..."you can drop throwing the word 'spook' around. Otherwise you might find yourself on a slow boat to Baltimore." He angrily pushed around some papers on his desk before looking up at Hank.

"First, Ilse and I have had a kind of relationship..."

"Relationship?" interrupted Hank hotly.

"Not *that* kind of relationship," said Howell scowling. "You and she have *that* kind of relationship. Ours is different. Let it go at that.

"Second, we have an arrangement with local authorities. If there's any incident of violence involving an American, we are informed immediately. When the Germans realized the girl in the car was an American, we got the call right away."

"How did they know she was an American? She was apparently burned to a crisp."

"Her purse was blown out of the car. Her passport was in it."

"I want to know more about what's going on with Ilse," said Hank. "You're right. It is personal now."

"I'll bet you do. All I can say is she's a great gal, and, don't waste your time asking her about any of it. Now, I've answered your questions. Get the fuck out of here and go give her a hug. She's really shaken up over all of this." His expression had softened and Hank noticed.

"Who isn't," Hank said, followed by a momentary pause in which both men visibly relaxed. "I can't figure you out," he said shaking his head. "Seems like you're playing both the good cop and the bad cop at the same time in all of this. Which one is the real Charles Howell?"

"You're not supposed to figure me out," he said smugly. "It's in my contract. And Yes...good and bad cop. Time to go Hank."

"I am going, but keep the good cop hat on, because before I leave...one more thing. What do you make of the German paper questioning whether Manon was targeted for 'being French?'" he asked using air quotes. "They all mentioned the Trade Mission bombing. I didn't. Is it possible there's a connection?"

"Off the record...could be a stretch. But it is intriguing. And, by the way anything you and I discuss in this office is off the record. Always. I hope you understand that."

"Sure," responded Hank. "but you need to understand that anything you said before going 'off the record' is on the record. That's the way the game is played. And, anything the German papers report is fair game."

"This is no game Hank." said Howell somberly, adding, "and I make the rules."

CHAPTER 14

I t was with conflicting emotions that Albert LeClerc was responding to the newspaper headlines the day after the bombing. He was thrilled that the German press was playing the story as it was; that a French celebrity had been the victim, with one even suggesting that the incident might be connected to the anti-Gaullist movement and the OAS. It was little more than a suggestion, but it was one that was a source of pride in LeClerc. The message he intended to send was that no things French were safe, and would not be, until de Gaulle was gone and Algeria was back in the French fold. He was confident careful readers would be able to read between the lines.

But, there were unintended consequences that cast a shadow over his "success." The young American victim. In the days following what the German press was calling the "La Bouche Bombing" the public reaction was reaching crescendo proportions. Stories about the young woman who seemed so pretty and so promising and so presumably innocent, and unworthy of such a brutal attack, came to dominate the story. It was the American, Kay Montgomery, whose name was on everyone's lips, not that of Lucky Manon. She, not Manon, became the face of the attack.

Now LeClerc found himself hoping for a quick end to the publicity he had so craved. But it continued with photos of the young victim, and of her father coming to Munich to escort his daughter's body back home. He gave interviews and the German media was attentive to everything he said. He was emotional in calling on law enforcement to solve the crime and punish those responsible. It fueled demands for justice from a public outraged by the heinous attack that had taken the life of the pretty young woman, Kay Montgomery, and her companion.

None of this was lost on the other cells in the German anti-Gaullist network once they became aware of the LeClerc group's involvement. Their concern was less that an anti-Gaullist message had been diluted, but rather that American investigators were actively involved. They were looked upon as tenacious and committed to finding those responsible for the bombing. Because they were very good and thorough at that sort of thing, that could not bode well for the Frenchmen in Germany who were already struggling to establish traction in a mission that had been facing formidable odds since Algerian independence.

Messages were sent to LeClerc demanding he "clean up his mess" and curtail all operations until the dust had cleared. This had a demoralizing effect on his small band, some of whom had objected to targeting the emerging French hero, Lucky Manon. One by one the men broke away. The truly committed found homes in other likeminded groups. The two Germans disappeared entirely. LeClerc was relieved over their departure on the one hand. But on the other, realized their departure meant chances for successfully reconstituting his operation were less and less likely.

He became increasingly despondent when he learned that anti-Gaullists in Germany had been forced to make a move in the wake of the La Bouche Bombing. The other groups moved quickly to establish a central command to consolidate and collaborate more closely, and to coordinate future action inhibiting unilateral action on the part of individual cells or individual members of them. LeClerc was not invited to participate in the new command structure planning strategies and tactics, further bruising his increasingly fragile ego.

Within two weeks of the bombing, alone and fearing reprisal against him, he went deeper underground.

Hank read the German newspapers and duly reported what they were saying, especially because their reporting placed so much focus on Kay Montgomery. He could find no one in the American military or diplomatic communities willing to engage in the kind of undocumented speculation about a French terrorist bombing connection which was published daily in the German press. Howell was refusing to talk to him altogether. Bell offered little in the way of substantive news related to the bombing.

Hank was frustrated feeling he was surrounded by a good story that had the potential of becoming a very big story. Yet he felt powerless to pursue it.

His frustration was magnified with what he felt was his deteriorating relationship with Ilse. He had seen little of her since the bombing. When he had, her depression was painfully obvious.

"I feel responsible," she said during one of their infrequent discussions after the bombing. "I should not have suggested we celebrate...I should not have chosen that restaurant. If we had been someplace else, anyplace, any other time, Lucky and Kay would be alive right now." She began to sob. "That girl. That poor, beautiful girl, her life snuffed out, all because I chose that place and that night. It's like I killed her...and him."

Hank tried in vain to disabuse her of that notion. She frowned deeply and made it clear that she wanted to be alone. He was no longer welcomed to her apartment or her bed.

He saw her from time to time at RFE where it was obvious she was just going through the motions. Her energy and animation were gone. She was losing weight and dark circles had over-shadowed the usual liveliness of her eyes.

Had he looked closely would have seen the same things in himself. His heart was being broken piece by piece...bit by bit. He was being shut out of her life, and the helplessness he felt was increasingly painful, and, it seemed to him, just as increasingly insurmountable.

"I'm worried about Ilse," he said to Ted during their morning office routine. "I saw her yesterday at RFE. She hardly spoke to me. She looked awful and I'm worried. She's taking the deaths of Lucky and Kay very, very hard."

"I know she is," said Ted. "I've had some conversations with her."

Hank looked at Ted curiously. For a moment he was surprised, then wondered why he was surprised that he was surprised. Ted had known Ilse far longer than he and had a strong, apparently loving, relationship with her. Of course they would talk. Nonetheless, Hank felt a twinge of pain for yet again feeling excluded from her life at a time he wanted her to need and rely on him more than anyone.

"I think I can understand what's going on," Ted continued. "She's devastated that Lucky was killed. They were friends. But, it seems to me, her real pain is over the death of the young woman. There is a guilt. I believe she feels it should have been she in that car. And, at this moment, I truly feel that she would prefer that she had been."

"How can I get back into her life, Ted? I really believe I'm in love with her. I thought she was at least beginning to feel she might feel the same way." His eyes glistened. "But it seems all of that has evaporated as far as she is concerned."

"Ilse's a very complicated young lady. I've known her a long time. When she has feelings for a person or a cause, the feelings run deep and strong, and aren't easily shifted. If she had those feelings for you, they're still there. They've just gone underground...set aside...for the moment. I say 'if' because I don't know the extent of her feelings for you. We haven't talked about it. I do know where her greatest passion is at the moment."

"And?" said Hank warily. "Where is that?"

"She wants to find whoever did that bombing, find out exactly why, and take her revenge."

"Revenge?"

"She's capable of it," said Ted. His eyes narrowed as his jaw muscles tightened.

"How capable?"

"I think if she found whoever is responsible for that bombing, she is capable of killing them."

The man who *was* responsible was trying to reestablish a connection with former military colleagues scattered throughout Germany who were associated to a greater or lesser degree with anti-French activism. Those with whom his politics aligned supported his banishment, convinced that he was a rogue warrior with a knack for making bad decisions. He was considered a leader without leadership skills, and more importantly, without men to lead. Those who shared only nationality wanted little to do with him and considered him eccentric.

LeClerc's situation was not improved with word that the American Consulate was offering a ten-thousand-dollar reward for information leading to the apprehension of those responsible for the bombing. Leave it to the Americans to offer money, he thought, as the means to solving a problem. He was also aware, having seen enough American movies, that it was a strategy that often worked.

It worked on his paranoia as well. It was disquieting for him to consider how many of his former colleagues might now be tempted to deliver him to the Americans. Never the two Germans, he thought, for they had carried out the bombing mission. They might be strongly attracted to the money, but not likely to risk drawing authorities closer to themselves and closer to LeClerc pointing the finger at them. The Munich Frenchmen? That was a different story altogether.

Ted Domjan had few loyalties, but where those loyalties existed, they were unassailable. One was to himself. He was a survivor and had been since the war. His defection to Czechoslovakia after the Nazis had killed his loved ones, was only the beginning. He had defied the odds in his escape and promised himself to do what he could to help end the war and bring Nazis to justice.

He was loyal to Americans who had given him the chance to do that. They had given him satisfying work with the Stars and Stripes in return for his post-war intelligence work in which he was instrumental in the capture of several former Nazis. His distaste for Germans had dissipated over the years. He had moved from barely tolerating them to respecting their ability to rebound from self-inflicted military and political outrage and chaos. But he never lost his own outrage for those with any hint of Nazi background or the party's *Weltanschauung*.

He remained close to the intelligence community, and was a frequent visitor to the American Consulate where he conferred confidentially from time to time with Charles Howell just as he had with Howell's predecessors. Sometimes it was to provide information he felt they might find useful. And, at times it was at their request to gather specific information they were interested in at the time. His loyalty to America and Americans was strong.

He had become increasingly fond of the young man for whom he worked. Especially so when he realized the depth of Hank Tollar's genuine feelings of affection for Ilse Stengel. For if Ted Domjan's loyalties could be prioritized, number one on the list would be Ilse. He had known her for most of her life and almost half of his own. Her mother had helped him survive.

He had watched her grow from a curious and intelligent child, to a beautiful, principled young woman. She reminded him so much of his long- lost wife that it captivated him. He felt a responsibility for her and was ever vigilant as to her welfare. He sensed she knew that, but had never, ever sought to take advantage of it. She was his unshakable first loyalty. Before himself. Before the Americans. Before Hank. And before the Germans among whom he lived.

Ted was concerned about Ilse's well-being far beyond that which he would reveal to anyone, including Ilse herself. He knew there was only one way to help lift her from the fog of grief she was experiencing. She would only be assuaged, he knew, by bringing those responsible for her deep sorrow to justice.

Ted chose his German friends carefully. He needed them for his work gathering information for the newspaper and for the occasional detours into the sub rosa world of intelligence gathering. It was because of his familiarity with Germany and Germans that he was called into Charles Howell's office two days after the La Bouche bombing.

"We need to find the bomber," said Howell, "and I'm hoping you can help. We need to wrap this thing up quickly. I know you are just as interested in that as we are, if for no other reason than Ilse," he said, fully aware of Ted's closeness to her.

"You've talked to her?"

"As best I can. She's almost catatonic about it," said a shaken Howell.

"I know."

"She's been a lot of help to us in the past, and we're working on an important project now, but she can't seem to get it together on this. She's always been so strong. Unflappable."

"I know," said Ted. "She feels guilty...responsible."

"Getting her back on track is important, but one of the victims in that bombing was the goddam daughter of the AP Bureau Chief in Frankfurt. We don't want the AP or any press climbing up our ass on this. The longer it goes on the more flak. Plus, the Germans are making a lot of noise about a French involvement. Seems a stretch, but you never know. The FBI says there are some similarities between the device used the other night and the bomb at the French Trade Mission. Not conclusive but interesting. And not for publication," he added quickly. He hadn't intended to reveal that.

"Whoa. That puts a new wrinkle on it, doesn't it?"

"As I say, not conclusive, but as I've told you, we've got a lot of people working on it. The Germans have people out there, but they've come up dry so far. Many of those they might be talking to remember the bad old days and have problems interacting with other Germans in uniform." He pointed his finger at Ted. "But you've got street connections too. I'd appreciate anything you might be able to come up with."

"I'll try to help," said Ted. "But this is a tough one. I'll have to be lucky, but we'll try."

Howell nodded. "I know you will. Keep Hank out of it if you can. Old man Montgomery is all of the press I can handle now. Fortunately, the correspondents in Bonn have been happy to stay there and just call in for anything new. I don't want them coming in because of anything that catches their eye in the Stars and Stripes. If he's ever on to something, let me know, and I'll handle it."

"You know, he and Ilse have a thing going. He's just as interested in getting to the bottom of all this as we are. He's just as worried about her as I am."

"I know. It bothers me. We can't stop young love, but he can't know any more about her than he does now. Don't you agree?" Howell asked hopefully.

"I guess so Howell, but what is it they say? 'Love conquers all.' That can also mean no secrets. You may have to contend with that."

Howell looked at him sternly and took a deep breath. "If it comes to that, I'll deal with it. First things first. Let's do what we can to find that fucking bomber."

"Were probably looking for two," said Ted. "One driving the car, the other to deliver the bomb. It's hard to drive, arm and throw accurately at a target...especially from a car on the move. There had to be a second person in the car. Did any of the witnesses say the car slowed down when the bomb was thrown?"

"I don't think so," said Howell. "I'll check it out."

"If there were two, that might help us a little bit. It's a bigger footprint to look for."

"We need all the help we can get. And we need it fast."

CHAPTER 15

East German guards along the zonal border with the Federal Republic were better known for the frequency of shooting people trying to escape to the West than they were for stopping anyone attempting to enter the GDR. Traffic was all but universally one way. One exception occurred near the town of Mödlareuth where the border separated the West German State of Bavaria, and Thuringia in East Germany.

The eight hundred miles of inner German border was a heavily fortified, heavily patrolled boundary. Fortifications included stone walls in some places, barbed wire in others, as well as combinations of the two. Guard towers stood along the entire border and the men who manned them spent endless hours peering through binoculars toward the western part of the divided country. Frequently plowed ground on the eastern side was scanned constantly by patrols looking for telltale signs of activity by anyone trying to breach the border. Nighttime searchlights swept the frontier looking for anything that moved. The precautions made crossing the border close to impossible from either direction.

One East German who had crossed to the West before the inner German border was sealed, attempted to scale a barrier and make his way back into the GDR at the heavily fortified border separating the German states of Bavaria and Thuringia several days after the La Bouche bombing. He attracted the attention of border dogs in his effort. Searchlights relentlessly sweeping the barrier found him. He waved frantically in a gesture of surrender. Misreading his intention, alert border guards opened fire. He never had a chance. He fell dead on the western side of the barrier. He was identified as Klaus Richter.

Residents of the tiny village at the border told investigators that Richter had been seen with another man earlier in the day as they sat in an old automobile near the frontier. Sightseers at the border were not uncommon, so the two men did not attract much attention.

It was only after Richter's death that residents began to talk. Their gossip and speculation made its way to local authorities, and ultimately to American military officials in Bavaria. They sent investigators to the village where they corroborated details of Richter's attempt to cross the border. They mentioned a second man and an old car. The color was gray.

After extensive interviews with villagers conducted by Army CID officers and German police, they secured a partial license plate number from the car. A farmer's adult son remembered part of the number...8-1-6-7. As it happened, it caught his attention because his birthday was August 16, 1947.

"We have a partial on the plate," Howell told the working group of Americans and Germans, as well as the French consular official during a hastily called meeting.

"It's a longshot but the pieces fit, even if they are very small pieces. These could be the two who bombed the girl and the Frenchman at the restaurant. It's not much, but all we have to go on at the moment. That and the fact he was going the opposite way from just about everyone else trying to cross the inner-German border. Who would do that?"

"Someone running away from something. Someone who was scared," said the American Major, Zwilling, as the others nodded.

"Exactly," said Howell. "We've got to get everyone on it," he said, looking one by one at each of the men at the table. "That gray car fits what we know too. So, as I say...the pieces are small but..." his voice trailed off.

"What about Richter? What do we know

about him?" asked the Frenchman, Dupuis. "Anything?"

"Obviously, his name. We got that from the papers he was carrying. Something else interesting. The Waffen SS blood type tattoo on his left arm, meaning he was a good little Nazi. Most of them didn't have a problem with violence. We're seeing if we can find something in Nazi military records. And, we have his picture. Photos taken of dead men usually don't work too well but we're showing it to the GI who was beaten up in that street robbery a while back by two...count 'em...two German thugs." He held his hands up. "Another long shot."

The meeting broke up with the participants expressing a glimmer of guarded optimism that the sum of all the little parts they had might add up to something significant.

Two weeks after the La Bouche bombing the story had vanished from the American and the German press. The funeral ceremonies for Kay Montgomery and Lucky Manon were dutifully reported, but the lack of information on the bombing investigation had stopped the story cold. Hank's editors downplayed the story of the shooting of the German at the border. No one picked up on the fact that Richter was attempting to cross into the GDR rather than cross out of it. That might have given it a little more heft in the eyes of editors who were increasingly inured to border shootings, unless they were in Berlin. Hank was back to covering his beat's most mundane and routine stories. Ted was out and about beating the bushes but there was little to chew on for an enterprising reporter.

Talbot's news operation at RFE was also on auto pilot after the excitement of the Cuban Missile crisis and the Communist Bloc concerns that the confrontation could have been a prelude to World War III. The Germans had also been alarmed over the toe-to-toe standoff and the fact US forces in Europe were on high alert. There wasn't much for the two men to talk about after Hank had presented his usual can of Prince Albert Pipe tobacco.

He debated whether he should visit the archives and say hello to Ilse. He longed to see her, but dreaded the possibility that she would continue to shun him as she had mostly done since the bombing. He decided longing trumped apprehension.

He was pleasantly surprised when she greeted him with a smile and a kiss to the cheek when he surprised her in her work space. He was even more surprised that she looked so much better. Her color was back. The darkness around her eyes had faded. Time was apparently healing the wound of Lucky's and Kay's deaths. He told her she looked great and that he was glad to see that she was in a better place.

"I went to his funeral you know," she said. "I thought that was the least I could do."

"I didn't know that," he said. "I wish I had. I would have loved to go with you," he said wistfully.

She put her hands on his cheeks and brought her eyes close to his. "I'm sorry Hank. I only decided at the last minute. I know you have been busy."

He laughed to himself. There had been no point in the time that he had been in Munich when he had been less busy, but he said nothing admitting that to Ilse.

"I didn't even mention it to Ted," she said defensively.

"And, how was it?"

"Quite impressive, actually. There were a lot of people including many officials from Paris, a small parade including some of his fellow drivers. It was all quite touching and, of course, very depressing. I just spent the day."

She returned to her desk and held up a sheet of paper. "I wrote a story about it, but the desk wasn't interested. Old news...or something. I think they didn't think it was very good." She hesitated. "Would you like to read it? Maybe you could give me some pointers."

"Sure I'll take it with me," he said. It would, he hoped, give him an excuse to see her again.

"Would you like to have dinner?" he asked. "We could go over it then."

She looked slightly flustered. "Sure," she said. "Maybe in a day or two. I'm painting my apartment." She laughed. "A new look. Too many memories," she said, not realizing how those words stung Hank.

"What happened to us?" asked Hank after they'd settled into their seats at an outdoor table at their favorite Schwabing restaurant. Ilse looked nervous and more than a little uncomfortable when he asked the question. Her usual smile was gone. She scraped at a spot of paint on her hand with her fingernail.

"This is not the conversation I want to have," she said. "I can't tell you what happened to us before the bombing or after. I guess, thinking about it, that what happened to us is that bomb. I lost a dear friend. The world lost a beautiful and charming young woman who, who knows, might have helped change the world." She shook her head. "I'm not sure I'll ever get over it."

"We all feel the pain, but life goes on...painful or not...we have to move on."

"Hank, my life is complicated. As it happens, you are just one of the complications."

"That's it? I'm a complication?" A waiter who had come to take their order took a few steps backward. "That's good to hear," he said sarcastically. "I tell you I'm in love with you and you tell me I'm a complication."

Her eyes moistened. "I can't tell you every-thing that's going on in my life right now. But our relationship has to take a back seat...for the moment."

"For the moment? What does that mean? That we have a relationship? Or that you'll get back to it when you have time." His face was red. "And what are all these complications. For Christ sake don't I have any right to know? Maybe, what-ever they are, I can help."

"Hank, I know you care for me, and I care for you. Believe me. But this whole thing has to be put on hold for now. I need time. More time be-fore I can move on."

"Time? More time. That sounds like a line from every bad movie I've ever seen. Time for what?"

"Just time. I think I should go," she said standing.

"Please don't." Hank was desperate not to let her leave, much less leave angry. "We'll drop the conversation. Let's eat something and go over your story on the funeral." She tried to smile, then sat down. The waiter glided in like a plane that had been cleared for landing.

They ate in uncomfortable silence, each wondering how to steer the conversation away from continuing an uncomfortable discussion about their relationship. What little small talk took place referenced the food, the weather, the crazy outfits of many of the student passersby.

As they finished, Ilse asked Hank if he still wanted to go over her story about the Manon funeral. He nodded, pulling the manuscript from his jacket.

"How did you like it?" she asked managing a partial smile.

"First thing I need to say is that I respect and admire you for taking this on. Writing in a foreign language is hard. I can't imagine writing something like this in German. You did a lot better in my language than I would do writing a story in yours. I can't see myself even trying. So, good for you."

"Sounds like you're leading up to saying 'nice try.' That it?"

"No. It's better than a nice try. It's a well-written news story. But not so much as a feature."

She looked puzzled.

"They're different animals. A news piece is facts...just the facts. A feature is different. A feature relies on painting a different kind of picture. When you use paint you use color and texture to bring the picture to life." He held up the pages. "Your story is in black and white.

"Let me give you an example. You wrote that hundreds of people lined the streets along the procession route. Here's what's missing. Who was in the crowd? Young? Old? Men? Women? Were they weeping. How were they dressed? Stuff like that was missing. What was the weather like?

"When I read a feature like this, I want to see a picture in my mind of what it was like. I don't get a picture from this," he said again waving the pages. "I just get facts. Nothing wrong with facts, but features need more. Color."

"I understand," she said softly, looking hurt.

"But the biggest omission is the fact that you knew him and knew him well. You could have added a lot of color writing about the him you knew."

She looked surprised. "But I've always been told that reporters should never make themselves part of the story..."

"Part of a news story," he interrupted. "Features are different. For instance, when you were writing about the crowd you might have added something like, 'The men were grim. Most of the women were crying openly. Perhaps they were remembering the Lucky Manon I knew so well; the carefree, young man who never missed a chance to smile or to talk about racing, how excited he was when talking about racing in the U.S. Or food.

"Or...the casket was draped in the French flag, symbolic of the love for his country he often spoke about. Stuff like that. That's adding a dimension you won't find in a news story."

She laughed out loud. "Hank there was no flag on the casket. He would never have gone for that."

"I'm glad to see you smiling," he said. Just as quickly as he said it, it was gone.

"Should I try it again?" she asked. "I think I understand what you're saying. I can do better."

"I'm sure you can. But, the more time that passes between the funeral and when you turn in the story, the less chance the newsroom would want it. Old news."

"I thought you said it was a feature, not a news story."

"When it's old news, it's just that...old...no matter what the format is. But, if you want to tackle it again, it would be a good exercise for you. I'd be happy to go over it with you."

She looked into his eyes. "I will. I appreciate your help Hank. You're nicer to me than I deserve."

"You know why," he whispered tenderly.

"I do."

CHAPTER 16

The working group overseeing the bombing investigation was once again meeting in Charles Howell's office. A heavy rain was rapping on the widows and members of the group were shaking out their raincoats as they entered the room before sitting down.

"I have some good news," said Howell as all of the men settled into their chairs. "We've come up with something...I say we...the French Military has come up with something in Baden Baden. We think we have a name to go with that partial license plate number the kid gave us after the shooting at the border." The men at the table leaned in toward Howell. This was good news.

"It took some doing because no one was sure if it was a French military plate, a French civilian plate, a German plate or from someplace else. Seems like it was probably a French plate." Howell seemed to be enjoying taking his time with details even in the face of growing impatience on the part of his audience. The American, Major Zwilling, cleared his throat loudly as if cuing Howell to get to the point.

"Here's the bottom line," said Howell suddenly laconic. The car was registered to one Marcel Blanchet."

One of his visitors exhaled loudly.

"Marcel Blanchet," Howell added quickly. "Apparently and probably the brother of the man killed in the French Trade Mission bombing. Marcel was himself found murdered in Baden Baden a few days after the bombing."

"Are we making assumptions?" asked Lt. Erbach of the Munich Police Department.

"The one that comes most immediately to mind is that the person or persons who killed Marcel took his car after they killed him. It was a 1951 gray Peugeot which matches the description of the car at the border...at least the age and color of the car."

"So," said Zwilling, It's a good bet two men killed Blanchet. They were from the East or friendly with the folks over there, and were trying to get to the GDR after the La Bouche bombing."

"So, you assuming the same two were involved in that?" asked Erbach.

"All the pieces seem to fit," said Howell. "The only way we can be sure is by picking up the second guy...assuming he hasn't made it over the border yet. But, we don't have much to go on there. In fact we have nothing to go on."

"And," said Dupuis, the French Consulate representative, "because we're working with only a partial license plate number...and one that some kid gave us because it was his birthdate, there's always a chance it's not the right ID."

Two of the other men laughed. "Do you believe that it's just a coincidence?" one of them asked. "This information connects a lot of dots. Too many for a coincidence."

"Stranger things have been known to occur," said Dupuis, not disguising his irritation at being challenged. "It might turn out that the car belonged to a hat maker in Paris..."

"...Who had driven to Bavaria to watch an ex-Nazi try to climb over the wall?" scoffed the Bavarian State Police officer, Krausweg.

"Okay, okay," said Howell. "Let's relax. I think we're safe working on the assumption that it was not a Parisian hat maker..." he said looking at the Frenchman condescendingly..."that it was Blanchet's car...the guys who killed him stole it and were on the run." He looked around at the other men. "It really doesn't matter until we find that second guy...unless we don't find him." He laced his fingers and pushed his arms forward cracking his knuckles. "And, let me remind you the car at the La Bouche bombing was described as old and gray."

His audience exchanged glances around the table. "These coincidences are getting cheaper by the dozen," said the American, Zwilling. "Our best chance is that he fucks up somehow," he added. "How he might do that...if he does that...is anybody's guess...if he's still in the West."

"The next piece of information I have," said Howell, "is that we've shown the picture of the dead Nazi to the GI beaten up in that street robbery."

"*Und,*" asked Erbach.

"He wasn't sure. He said it could have been, but he just wasn't sure."

"And on that note," said Zwilling, "we wind up with a whole lot of nothing."

"Not exactly," said Howell. "We've got a whole lot of one thing." He again looked around the room at the expectant faces of his audience. "We've got a whole lot of shit coming down from on high. They want the murders of the Montgomery girl and the Frenchman solved. Period!"

They ended the meeting agreeing to "get the word out to their people" although none of those present was optimistic that it would lead to anything.

Ted Domjan had always operated as an independent agent. Dating back to his days in Hungary, Czechoslovakia, California and Germany. He had always operated as a loner who was more comfortable in the shadows where he could observe rather than be observed. It served several purposes. It kept most people at arms length, and allowed him to come and go as he chose, emerging from the shadows when it suited him. This tendency served him well in his job as Hank Tollar's assistant. He could operate with anonymity when it was the best way to gather information. Or flash press credentials and backslap when that suited the situation. He did not have a long list of friends, but did have a large number of acquaintances, many of whom, for a variety of reasons, also lived in the shadows.

Since his talk with Howell, Ted had kept his eyes and ears open for any hint of information on the La Bouche bombing. He asked pointed questions of some of those on the street he knew, and was especially primed after a private meeting with Howell. The American had briefed Ted on the new information about the missing German, and the very strong possibility that he was connected with the murder of Marcel Blanchet and, possibly, with the bombing that had killed the young American woman and the French auto racer. Ted carefully spread the word, not as an investigator seeking to track down a suspect, but rather as a street gossip which tended to encourage conversations.

Twenty four hours after Howell's meeting

with the bomb investigation working group, Ted was approached by one of his casual acquaintances, a fellow Hungarian named Istvan. He was a taxi driver who had fled Hungary in 1956 during the revolution. He and Ted had bonded because of their common cultural background. Ted had been fascinated to learn that this working class man had a multi-lingual son who had made good use of his German education and currently worked at Radio Free Europe.

Istvan and Ted chatted briefly over a beer when they ran into each other at a small out-of-the-way restaurant favored by Hungarian exiles. Ted frequented it often because it gave him a chance to speak his native language.

"The gossip at RFE," said Istvan, "is that the Americans and Germans are pulling out all stops to find the bombers at La Bouche."

"Well, the Americans don't take too kindly to one of their own being blown to bits. Especially a young girl."

"I'm hearing that it was the Frenchman who was the target, not the girl," said Istvan. "But who can tell when one hears such things. So many people who know nothing, but want to sound like they know everything, talk just to talk.

Ted was now extremely interested in this small talk. "Who is saying such things?" he asked. "Who would know?"

"I understand there were some Germans

working for French interests here, OAS types."
Ted was eager for more, but let Istvan talk at his
own pace.

"The Germans, from what I hear," said Istvan, unaware of Ted's piqued interest, "special-
ized in doing some of the dirty work because
they enjoyed it, and the French could sit back and
watch without getting dirty themselves."

"How many Germans?" asked Ted.

"I don't know. I hear two in particular.
Former Nazis. But that's all I know. And I don't
know. It's just what I hear."

"Your son's hearing this kind of thing at
RFE?"

"Oh yeah, Everyone gossips there."

"Does your son believe any of it?"

"He just says that there are a couple of guys
who seem to think they have it all figured out."

"Any chance you can get me their names?
There might be a story for me."

"I'll ask. You know how they are over there.
Security, security, security."

"What desk are they on?"

"Czech, I think. I think he said one of the
guys who does a lot of the talking is a Sudeten
Czech."

"Well," said Ted trying to act casual, "if you
get a name give me a call." As he spoke, Ted was
writing his phone number wondering if he'd ever
hear from Istvan. If not, he thought, as he handed

Istvan his number, I have another way to go.

Later that day Ted was once again in Charles Howell's office. Howell had made time for Ted when he was informed over the phone that he "might be on to something."

The two huddled for some thirty minutes going over their respective notes on the bombing case and on how to proceed with the new information that Ted had brought about the RFE gossip. Neither was totally convinced that the information was valid. Nor could they discount it. It had to be followed up.

"When do you expect to hear from him with names?" asked Howell, rubbing his hands together as if he were trying to keep them warm.

"I have no idea," said Ted. "I may never hear from him. We're not close. Just acquaintances. And, I don't think he has any idea that what he has might be of real importance to me. Our discussion was very casual."

"Let's give him until this time tomorrow. If we don't hear from him by then, we'll go to Plan B."

"Ilse?" asked Ted.

"Ilse," nodded Howell. "I'd like to avoid that. She's got a lot on her plate just now. But the people at RFE know her, she speaks the language, and..."

"...And she's pretty," said Ted. "The kind of pretty that men like...keeps them talking more than they should just to be around her. But you're right, she does have a lot going on. Upstairs, I mean. Upstairs," he repeated, pointing to his head.

"The people I'd send in to ask questions wouldn't get nearly as much. So, this time tomorrow I'll give her a call...unless you have some names for me."

Istvan did call with names. "Anton Vesely and Hynek Svoboda," he whispered to Ted almost conspiratorially as if he were afraid of being overheard. "Just don't mention my son's name if you talk to them," he added. "It might make them uneasy. Exiles are a suspicious lot. Anxious most of the time."

Ted assured him that he would not, and that there was no certainty that he would contact them at all, repeating that he might want to do a story with them. He thanked Istvan for getting the names to him so promptly. A moment later he was on the phone to Howell telling him he had the names, but wanted to talk to him before revealing them to the American.

"Much as I hate to say it, I think we should have Ilse approach these two," said Ted later as he sat across from Howell. "Istvan made a point of how anxious and suspicious some of these refugees are. I think professionals might cause them to back off if they think they're being investigated or under suspicion...singled out for any reason.

Ilse won't make it sound like she's asking questions. More like chatting...or flirting."

Ted took a deep breath. "Also, she's been depressed ever since the bombing and Manon's death. I think it would do her a lot of good to think she might be doing something helpful to find the bombers."

"I had been thinking the same thing," said Howell. "A feather's always better than a hammer." He looked toward the ceiling and closed his eyes as he spoke. "She's spent a lot of time making friends with the people on the Czech desk recently. It would be the most natural thing in the world to have her chatting them up."

"Why's she spending time with those folks?"

"Oh, just verifying vital statistics for the archives, and so on," said Howell rubbing his desk with both hands as if he were polishing it. Or as if he were erasing something.

"I'll talk to her. I'd like you to be with me when I do. Do you mind?"

Ted nodded knowing that if Howell had not asked, he would have.

Ilse was surprised an hour later when she arrived in Howell's office and found Ted sitting there. He stood as she entered and she kissed him on the cheek. She looked from one man to the other then back again. "Strange bedfellows," she joked. "I didn't know you two were sharing an office."

"Neither did I," said Howell, "but we get together from time to time to talk about you."

"Me?" she said, pressing her fingers against her chest, feigning surprise.

"Have a seat," said Howell. "We have a favor to ask of you,"

"We?" she looked at Ted who lifted his hand and gestured toward Howell.

"Go ahead Charlie."

"It wouldn't be fair to you to ask what we'd like you to do without filling you in on all the details. But, you must promise to keep them to yourself. There are only a few people in the loop. Can you do that?"

She nodded.

"Nothing. Not a word to anyone...including Hank Tollar in particular... this is not ready for the press yet."

She looked at Ted and nodded once again.

Howell outlined the whole story, detailing the incident at the border and the information they had about the license plate identification linking Marcel Blanchet's murder to the two Germans, who may, or may not have been involved in the La Bouche restaurant bombing. He underscored the importance of locating the missing German. He made a point of emphasizing that the surviving German was likely a former member of the SS, relying on his knowledge of how much she detested Nazis and hoping that would be helpful in convincing her to assist in the investigation. He told her of Ted's conversation with Istvan and Istvan's comments based on speculation from a couple of people on the Czech desk at RFE about the surviving German and a possible French connection. He explained why they thought she might have a more persuasive touch in gathering the information they needed.

"We need to know if they know more. Or, if it's just gossip and speculation. You know the people on the Czech desk. Do you know Anton Vesely and Hynek Svoboda?'

"Vaguely," she responded softly. "Do you really think this German was the bomber?"

"Very possibly. If so, he can tell us who gave the orders to kill Manon and the girl."

"Count me in," she said. "I'll find out what they know if I have to fuck them both."

Howell held up his hands. "That's not part of the scenario," he said. "If you think they know more than they're saying, let me know and I'll send in a team with rubber hoses. We just need you to unlock the door."

"We'll see," she said. "We'll see."

Ilse waited for Ted by the front desk. It was not a long wait. Perhaps ten minutes before he ambled out of the elevator. He was surprised to see her standing and waiting.

"So, are we collaborators now?" she asked as he approached. He signaled for her to keep quiet until they were outside. They stepped into a brisk breeze and both held their coats closed near the collar to avoid the chill.

"I didn't know you were so cozy with American intelligence," said Ilse looking slightly perturbed. "Who signs your paycheck, the CIA or the Stars and Stripes?" she asked as they started to walk toward the Englischer Garten.

"Sometimes we work pro bono," said Ted shrugging his shoulders. "I work for Howell the same way you do. He asks a favor, you say yes. Simple."

"This is a favor I'm happy to do," she said. "I'm more than happy to play a role in finding out who was behind the bombing. Both bombings for that matter." She looked at him closely. "It doesn't seem like they have a lot to go on at the moment."

"Don't get your hopes up. I think Vesely and Svoboda were probably just repeating street gossip or maybe even making it up."

"The thing about gossip," said Ilse, "is that it has to start somewhere and sometimes it starts with the truth."

"We'll see," answered Ted. "I hope that's the case." She was walking quickly and he, even being much taller, had to struggle to keep up.

"How well do you know Vesely and Svoboda?" he asked.

"Just well enough for friendly chit chat about the old country. They're both middle-aged analysts. Serious types. Interestingly, not the type to gossip. I'll have to find out where they first heard about the Germans and the French involvement."

"How are you going to go about it?"

"I don't know. I have to think about it."

They stopped at the corner were they'd go their separate ways. She gave him a hug. "Now that we're conspirators," she winked, "I'll keep you up to date."

He kissed her on the cheek, nodded, turned and walked away hoping she had not been put in a dangerous spot.

CHAPTER 17

"Thanks for taking a few minutes," Ilse said to Anton Vesely. They were sitting in her tiny, cramped office, surrounded by shelves of files. He nodded and looked at her suspiciously.

"What's this all about?" He tried to smile and appear friendly, but he sounded nervous and fidgeted. Finally, he folded his arms across his chest. It was body language that reminded Ilse that it was the universal plight of refugees from the East to always fear they were under suspicion for something, even when there was nothing to be suspicious of.

"Nothing more than making sure our paperwork is up to date," she said cheerily. "What would we do without paperwork?" She gave him her brightest smile. "Would you mind if we talked Czech?" she asked, hoping it would help put him at ease. "I have so little opportunity to do so. It keeps me from getting too homesick."

His expression brightened as he responded in their native language. Ilse was gratified that it seemed to relax him. She took the moment to inquire about his home town and family. They reminisced about life in the "old country," although Ilse had left at a very young age and her memories were vague at best. That seemed to endear her to him. She let him talk. He asked if he could have a cigarette. She told him it was forbidden in her work area because of all the important files and paperwork.

"Let's go to the lunchroom," she suggested. "I'll bring my forms and we can finish up in there. Plenty of ashtrays."

Halfway through his second cigarette, Anton seemed much more relaxed than he had been earlier. He was taking the initiative in their conversation. Ilse was used to that. Men liked to be with her and talk to her, something she could use, even manipulate, in a situation like this.

"Do you ever get used to living in a foreign country?" he asked. "I still find it strange after ten years."

"I've lived here a long time," she said. "But I've found it difficult recently."

He raised his eyebrows. "Oh...how so?"

"A good friend of mine was killed in that bombing outside La Bouche a few days ago. Such violence," she sighed. "Then there was that other bombing at the French office a while back. I just don't understand it."

"Germany has always been a place of violence," said Anton with more than a little contempt. "I wish I could do my work someplace else."

Ilse nodded in agreement. "I hope they'll find out who did it," she said. "I don't want to be afraid to go to a restaurant or walk the streets."

"My friend Hynek Svoboda thinks he knows something about it, but I don't know how he could. He says it was a Nazi who did it."

"A Nazi," said Ilse pretending disbelief. "I thought we were through with Nazis."

"Hah," snorted Anton. "They are all over the place. The war may be long over, but the infection is not."

"Ah, this is all so unpleasant," said Ilse. "But it's interesting you should mention Hynek Svoboda. I have to update some forms for him too. Is he in today?" she asked casually.

"His desk is right next to mine. I will be happy to let him know you want to see him." Then he said cheerfully, "I will tell him how nice you are. He already knows how pretty," he added blushing.

"Fine. How nice. Thank you. Now, let me get the rest of your information and you can go back and send me Svoboda." She tried not to show her excitement over the opportunity to find out how much Hynek Svoboda really new.

Hynek Svoboda was Anton Vesely's opposite. He was confident and loud. She didn't find it difficult to imagine him whispering secrets. If he was as nervous as his colleague had been, it showed only in his habit of licking his lips. Viper-like thought Ilse. He also brought into her office a cloud of body odor that she found difficult to endure. The armpits of his shirt were moist and stained. In short order, she invited him to the lunchroom where she had just recently been with Vesely, hoping the aroma of food and stale smoke would cover the hygienic flaw that almost made her nauseous.

How, she thought to herself could any woman make love to such a man? Yet the forms she held indicated he had six children. "That needs updating," he said proudly when she asked about his family.

"We are expecting our seventh child in a month."

Ilse congratulated him, and continued to ask questions verifying the information on file about his family, background, place of birth and other information.

"Do you miss Czechoslovakia?" she asked, hoping it would lead to where she wanted to go, and also hoping she would get there quickly. The ambient odors in the lunchroom were insufficient to mask his body odor.

"I do, but I am able to communicate with relatives who live outside of Kladno. We exchange letters and occasional phone calls. There are not many left, but I have some cousins and a few aunts and uncles who are still there. Much of my family was killed by the Nazis in the war. Now, the Communists," he said, obviously dispirited. "But I am making a life here. My kids have known nothing else. Do you miss it?"

"Not so much. I came out as a young child. I don't remember much. Germany has been fine. Until recently, at least."

"Oh?" he said as a question.

"I lost a very good friend recently." She went on to tell him in detail about her witnessing the bombing outside the restaurant and the loss of her friend and his companion. "I hope the police find who did it," she said. "As I told your colleague Anton, I am now afraid of going to restaurants and walking the streets. It was so sudden. So horrible. So random."

"Not random I think. My cousin tells me that it was the Frenchman who was the target of that bombing, not the girl."

"How would your cousin know?" she asked.

"He lives in a village outside of Kladno. He owns a small Gasthaus and hears all kinds of stories. He wrote me that a German has been coming in lately and getting quite drunk. My cousin hates

Germans. They brutalized Kladno during the war. They butchered our family.

"My cousin said the German bragged that he'd been living in Germany until recently but that he had had enough of it. He talked about French anti-Gaullists there not having the stomach to do their own dirty work. My cousin wrote about the two bombings because I live in Munich."

"Is he saying the OAS was behind the bombings?" asked Ilse.

"That's what he implied. Without saying so, he apparently even made it sound like he was involved. When my cousin asked the German point blank, the German just laughed. Nobody was paying much attention to the drunken German. Like I say, the people around there don't like Germans much. But my cousin had heard about the French race car driver getting killed on Radio Free Europe. He only mentioned it in a paragraph or two because the bombings happened here."

"Why would anyone want to kill him? He was my friend. He was not political."

"I don't know. Maybe it was personal. A grudge. Maybe symbolic. I don't know."

Ilse was excited. She believed what she was hearing. "The authorities here would love to talk to that German...or even your cousin. They badly want to solve the case."

"That's not going to happen. They're on the wrong side of the border for that."

"How about you?"

"No, I can't vouch for any of it and I don't want to get involved. The Frenchman plays rough. I've got kids...a wife...a job."

"The Frenchman?" asked Ilse trying to contain her excitement.

"My cousin says a Frenchman gives the orders here in Munich. The German says he lost his courage when he lost his arm. That's why he uses Germans."

"Lost his arm?"

Hynek nodded. "He referred to a one armed Frenchman but never mentioned any names. Like I say, it was just a few lines in a long letter. It's well known the mail is read by the authorities...the StB...the
Secret Police. You don't want them sniffing around."

A one armed Frenchman giving the orders is not much to go on, thought Ilse, but it's more than we had before. A Frenchman with one arm should be easier to find than a Frenchman with two.

She finished with Sovboda's forms and thanked him for taking the time to help her update his file. Her gratitude went far beyond that. Ten minutes later she was on the phone with Charles Howell.

"Okay, how do we find a one-armed Frenchman?" asked Howell in an office meeting at the consulate. Ted and Ilse, shook their heads.

"That was great work Ilse," said Howell. "It's something to go on, but not much. The frogs are spread out all over Bavaria. We don't know how many are here who don't want anybody to know they're here. They can go underground as quickly as sewer water."

"We can get the German cops to track down some of the French people we do know are here and see if they know anything about one-armed Frenchmen," said Ted. "I'll ask around myself."

"Good," said Howell. "I'll call my group together and see what we can come up with." He stood and looked first at Ted, then at Ilse. "Good work guys. Now, let's get on it."

There was a palpable excitement in the room when Howell told his working group about what Ilse had learned. They all felt that while it would not be easy, the chances had just increased exponentially. They agreed that they could spread out in their own bailiwicks and twist the arms of any Frenchmen they could find. Dupuis had names of French citizens who had registered at the consulate. He cautioned, however, that those involved in anti-government activity, some of whom were wanted men, would certainly not have registered. He promised to make those on file available with the caveat that the names of citizens who could be vouched for by consular officials would not be provided.

How French, thought Howell. "Get someone to ask those on file if they know of a one-armed Frenchman," he barked slapping his desk.

Major Zwilling added that the one they were looking for, because he had only on arm, was likely a veteran, especially if he was connected to the Secret Army Organization. He suggested contacting the French military and see if they could identify how many veterans were collecting pensions for losing limbs...especially arms...while in the service. That would undoubtedly take a lot of time, they all agreed, but was worth trying. Dupuis volunteered to follow up on that request.

They all left the office with a newfound spring to their step optimistic that their chances of finding a one-armed man were fairly good. The last one out was a participant who had said nothing, but had listened intently. It was Ted Domjan, whom Howell had invited as a courtesy given the assistance he had, and could, provide to the effort. He was all for this international dragnet, but desperately wanted to close the net on the suspect. He was not thinking so much of himself as he was for Ilse.

"Hey stranger," Hank said to Ted as the older man entered their office. "I haven't seen much of you lately. What's going on."

Ted lied that he had been asked by Charles Howell to sit in on the interrogation of a Hungarian defector who had shown up at the consulate. "They have no one with Hungarian language skills," he said. He didn't like lying to Hank, but security had to remain tight. He reasoned that one day he would be able to help Hank with information for one heck of a story.

"You don't look too good Hank," he said, changing the subject. "Your eyes are cloudy and you look tired."

"Not feeling so hot," said Hank. "Maybe coming down with the flu. I may go home and try and sleep it off, or sweat it out, whatever you do with the flu."

"Fluids. Always fluids...but no alcohol," quipped Ted, "proving the cure is often worse than the illness."

Hank stood and stretched. He yawned and complained about being so tired he was having trouble staying awake. He grabbed his jacket to leave, then turned to Ted.

"Have you seen Ilse lately? Is she okay?"

"I have. I wasn't going to mention it unless you asked. She's having a hard time of it right now."

"How so?" asked Hank.

"She's been hearing from her father. He's in Prague. You may know that when he got back from the war, as Ilse, her mother and sister, were getting ready to leave for Germany, he refused to go with them. He didn't want to leave his own country. He had no use for the Communists, but he thought he could keep out of their way." He stopped. "Do you know this?" he asked.

Hank shook his head. "I just know he refused to come to Germany."

"They were never close. All of a sudden he's making contact and it doesn't feel right to her. She thinks the StB...Secret Police...might be behind it. She's very upset. So that's what Ilse's dealing with now. She's working with Howell on what to do about it and how to do it. That's one of the things I've been talking with him about too."

"You're working with Ilse and Howell?"

"Howell knows I'm close to Ilse and wants me to keep an eye on her. He's concerned about the possible StB involvement."

"Jesus Christ," said Hank. "How long has this been going on?"

"Several weeks," said Ted solemnly.

"A lot of things make more sense to me now," said Hank.

"You've got to keep it to yourself until it's been worked out and Howell gives the green light. If he gives the green light."

"This is one hell of a deal. All I've been getting since I arrived in Germany is people...the Army, State Department...the CIA telling me what I can't do. I'm a reporter and everybody tells me to keep quiet...unless the general's wife is elected president of the garden club. It's ridiculous. It's like a game when everyone has cards but me."

"No one's playing games, Hank."

"I'd love to write about it."

"Your worst idea Hank. This may involve people who don't scare. They do the scaring. Remember, it's just conjecture at this point."

"Conjecture that's got her pretty uptight. I can't believe this is happening."

"That's because you're used to your world, not this world. Howell's got some people watching her. Just to be on the safe side, it's not a good idea for you to be around her with all that's going on. If the StB is involved somehow, they've got eyes here. They might get nervous if she hangs around with a reporter. Best for you and Ilse to play stay away. She knows that."

Hank sat down and cupped his face in his hands. He was silent for several seconds. "Holy shit," he bellowed, pulling out his handkerchief and blowing his nose loudly. "I feel so fucking helpless," he whispered.

He took a deep breath. "Thanks for leveling with me Ted. I'll go with the program. Not because I want to, but obviously I have no choice for a lot of reasons." He put on his coat. "I've got to go. I feel like shit."

He left shutting the door noisily behind him. Ted sat in his chair listening to the sound of

Hank's footsteps fade, wondering if he had told Hank too much, and knowing there was so much more to the story that he couldn't tell.

PART FOUR

CHAPTER 18

"I've got a name," said Ilse, greeting Ted at her apartment. "I've come up with the name LeClec...Albert LeClerc. One arm. Army veteran. He's been outspoken in opposition to Algerian independence and de Gaulle since the very beginning. He was here in Munich as recently as a few weeks ago, but he dropped out of sight. Probably gone underground after the bombing and the departure of the Germans. I don't think Howell and his group have got it yet."

"How did you get it Ilse? Everybody's looking for the name."

"A priest," she said. "German-born just across the Rhine from Strasbourg, but brought up in Alsace. He considers himself more French than German. Lucky introduced me to him. Father Gabriel."

"So he's not registered at the French Consulate?"

"No, he's German. He was great friends with Lucky. They grew up together." She looked reflective for a moment, as if replaying an old scene.

"Lucky used to make fun of him for going into the priesthood. He always told Lucky that 'when it comes to the race for heaven, I'll beat you even if you're driving one of your fancy race cars.' That's the way they joked. Lucky loved to tell the story.

"He's not at all political, but was just devastated when he read about the bombing. He told me, 'I guess he'll get to heaven first after all.' He's sad, but more than that, he's angry. When I asked him about a one-armed Frenchman he knew immediately who I was talking about. He lived in a tiny apartment in Giesing. Father Gabriel knew some of his colleagues."

"But we don't know where he is now?"

"He's probably gone underground since the bombing. Gabriel...Father Gabriel...says his colleagues have more or less deserted him. He's an outcast. Considered incompetent. The Father says he'll see if he can find out where he is."

"If he does, what then?"

Ilse flushed, her eyes narrowed, her jaw muscles tightened. "Then we will have a party...a coming out party at his expense. I want him punished for what he did. I want the ultimate punishment."

Ted looked at her closely, surprised at her sudden display of vitriol and at the level of her contempt. Strangely, it made him feel proud of her, and at the same time more than a little frightened. He had never seen Ilse like this before. He wondered where this was going to lead her...and him.

It was a nervous twelve hours for Ilse and Ted. They had hoped to hear from the priest, but there was no contact. She went to work the morning after her conversation with Ted, hoping the day would be interrupted with news from Father Gabriel.

Ted was in the office early when he received a call from a military doctor at the army hospital. Hank, he reported, was in the hospital. He'd gotten feverish and headachy overnight, called the hospital and was gurneyed into an ambulance less than ten minutes later.

He felt a little better said the doctor, who told Ted that Hank's temperature, as he put it, "was well above the boiling point" when he was admitted. It had gone down a bit, but Hank had been told that he would be hospitalized for "a few" days. "No visitors until tomorrow," said the doctor. "He's a sick one, a nice dose of pneumonia, but antibiotics should do the trick. And rest."

Ted called the editors in Frankfurt, told them the news that Hank was out of action, and that he was going to "take some time" as long as Hank was out of the office...but be "on call" if something broke. He sat down, impatiently waiting for the phone to ring, not with word about a good news story to cover, but rather with good news from Ilse. He assumed he and Ilse were still ahead of Howell and company in tracking down the Frenchman. How far ahead was the question? Then what?

Her call came around noon. The ringing of the office phone startled him when it broke the silence of the quiet office. "We've got an address," she said without even saying hello. He could hear excitement in her voice. They arranged for a place to meet. Ted's heartbeat quickened as he realized they had reached a tipping point. The decision had to be made. Would he and Ilse move in on Le-Clerc independently, or would they turn their information over to the Americans? One approach was safe. The other was fraught with dangerous uncertainty.

They met in an out of the way café where they were unlikely to be seen by her colleagues at RFE, or by anyone from the American Consulate who might have questions. It was not lost on Ted that they were taking precautions before they had made any decisions or taken any action. It was another signal that both understood the implications of their situation. If precautions were already being put into place, then what lay ahead?

They met with a quick hug and furtive glances at the few occupied tables. They sat next to each other and leaned in closely so they could converse in shallow whispers.

"He's alone in a small apartment in Moosinning. It's a quiet area. He doesn't go out much. He has no money, no friends, and apparently has become quite paranoid," reported Ilse. "Father Gabriel says his old friends have abandoned him. They feel he's toxic."

"The CIA could use Father Gabriel," said Ted. "He moves fast."

"Like I said, he's angry."

"Now what? I could have him picked up for questioning through Howell's working group. The Germans would love to get their hands on him."

"So would the French. I'm guessing they would try a lot harder to find out what he knows about the anti-government activity in Germany. He must know...even being on the outs...what the whole network is like...how it's structured...leadership...in Germany. He could name names. And, because everyone has turned on him, he might be more willing to talk. Turning him over to the Germans means months of legal crap."

"Well, we can't mail him to Paris."

"Maybe Baden Baden and the French military would take him."

"Can the military be trusted? He has friends. Many in the military lean in his direction on de Gaulle and Algeria. He might just disappear?"

The two sat silently weighing their options, occasionally taking a sip of coffee, deep in thought. Neither was enthusiastic about the choices.

Finally, Ted said, "I think the best thing is to turn him over to Howell's group. Let them handle it and we can get on with other things." He watched her closely for a reaction. When he said "other things," she winced as if in pain.

"The 'other things' are problematic," she said. "Prague is putting on the pressure. But Howell's confident he can find a way. He's thinking about ways to take the heat off. He wants me to play games. The idea is to provide misinformation to the StB and hope to gain some advantage, like maybe some idea as to how they'd use it. Very complicated. Very risky."

Ted agreed and thought to himself that in a way, Ilse was no better off than LeClerc. Both of them had one foot in a snare than could snap shut at any moment with lethal consequences.

"By the way, I have told Hank about your situation," he said slowly and softly. She was taken aback and put her hand over her mouth in surprise. "I thought it was only fair that he know. No details. Just that you are under pressure from your father."

She looked angry. "Fair to whom? Fair to me? It's none of his business. You just put him in the mix...in danger...if there is to be danger and there likely will be. God knows what he might try and do to help. He will try to help, I know it. Damn Ted. Why couldn't you keep your mouth shut? He's a reporter for Christ's sake."

"Because he loves you, or thinks he does. He's known something's out of whack and he's been wondering about it. Now he knows that you're dealing with a problem, but that's all he knows. I think he has a right to know."

"But it is not your right to tell him. Only I have that right." She stood as if she were getting ready to leave. "Damn. All I need now is another complication." She said it loudly enough that people at other tables turned toward her. "How could you?" She sat down heavily and put her head in her hands.

It was what Ted had feared; a reaction just like the one he had just experienced. "I'm sorry," he said. "Naturally, he wants to help somehow, but he knows to be quiet about it. He's upset, of course. At the moment he's not going to be doing anything. He's sick. Quite sick. In the hospital."

She lifted her eyes to his. "Sick? What's wrong?"

"He's was taken to the hospital last night. He has pneumonia. He'll be there for a few days, probably until the end of the week. He'll be okay, but he is sick."

Her eyes glistened. The anger in them had left, replaced by a helpless sadness that promised tears that never came. She remained silent, but only momentarily. The sadness in her eyes faded. "Are you sure?" she said.

"The doctor said he'd be fine."

"No, not about that," she answered with a cagey look. "Are you sure he'll be in the hospital for several days?"

Ted wondered what she was getting at. "That's what the doctor said."

"Can I visit him?"

"Tomorrow. He can have visitors tomorrow."

"Well, maybe he can help...at least with Le-Clerc." She leaned toward Ted conspiratorially and began to whisper. As she continued, his eyes got wider and he stifled a smile, wondering where this new version of Ilse had come from?

Hank was still feeling lousy, but his spirits brightened when he saw Ilse at his door. He fleetingly wished he had known she was coming, although in his present state there was not much he could do to prepare for a visitor. Shave perhaps. Brush his teeth. It would have been a struggle to do either.

She was proceeded by her brightest smile,

and clutching a single red rose. She held it out to him like a trophy. He took it, smelled it, and croaked a thank you. His voice was hoarse.

"I wish I could say you looked great," she said, still smiling brightly, "but you look like you've been hit by a honey wagon. Sorry."

"I'd rather be hit by a honey wagon," he replied. "This has not been fun. Until now," he quickly added. "You're about the best medicine I can think of." She reached for his hand.

"Warm," she said. "Still have a fever."

"I guess so," he said. "Doc says it will take a couple of days to shake it."

"Well, when you do, let's get together," she said, keeping her hand on his. "I'd like to have a long talk." She explained that she knew that Ted had told him about the complications in her life at the moment. She explained that she was not happy that Ted had done so, that any issues she had did not need to be shared with those that "she cared for." Hank brightened at those words.

A nurse came in, saw the rose, and put it in a tall water glass on his bedside table. Hank and Ilse continued to chat, making small talk about hospital food, mutual friends, and RFE gossip, all the while she held his hand and stroked it tenderly.

The subject of the bombings and the search for those responsible came up. Ilse did not offer what she knew. Hank could add little because he knew so little. When their conversation began to stall, Hank brought up what was, with her visit, foremost on his mind.

"Do you think Ilse, when I get out of here, we might go back to where we were...where we were before the bombing? I want that. I want it very much. I have the feeling you need someone now, and I want to be that someone."

"Let's talk about that when you get out of here," she said happily. "We can cover all the bases," she added playfully. She put a finger to her lips, kissed it, then placed the finger on his lips. And with that gesture, Hank was happier than he had been in weeks.

"I have to go," she said. "They said I shouldn't wear you out."

"Wear me out. That's a laugh. I want you to wear me out," he said laughing.

"Something else to talk about when you get better." she teased, squeezing his hand.

"Oh. Before I go, I have a favor to ask," she said turning serious.

"Sure."

"Remember when you let me borrow your car last time...to go to Augsburg?

He nodded.

"I'd like to borrow it again if I can. As long as you're going to be in here or a few days, you won't be needing it," she said playfully. "Would you mind?"

"Sure. Going back to Augsburg?"

"No. Hamburg."

Confounded, he said, "Hamburg? That's a thousand miles away. What are you going to Hamburg for?"

"It's only a few hundred miles, actually. I feel I need to get away for a while with everything that's going on. There's a British rock band that is all the rage up there. The Beatles. Everybody says they're great. Ted and I want to drive up and see them."

"Beatles. Never heard of them. Ted wants to go?" he asked, surprised. "I didn't know he was into rock bands."

"He's not, but he's very protective of me and thinks getting away is a good idea. We'll drive up, see a concert, and drive back the next day. We'll be back before you're released. Then I'll tell you all about it when we get together," she said as she leaned in closely to give him a kiss on his cheek. "Okay?" she asked. "I'll take good care of the car."

"If that's what you want," he answered. "Of course. Just be careful."

"Thanks," she said standing to go. "What would I do without you."

I hope you never have to find out he thought.

"The keys to the car are in my jacket in the closet," he said, waving weakly in that direction.

She left him in the bed buoyed with pleasure and the restoration of hope her visit had brought. So much to look forward to, he thought. He stared at the lone red rose next to his bed. He had the feeling that the gulf that had separated him and Ilse these past weeks had been bridged. If not fully, then it certainly would be upon her return, and his release from the hospital.

The Beatles, he thought, what a strange name for a rock band.

CHAPTER 19

Ilse was more concerned about threats from Czechoslovakia than she was willing to reveal. She had little in the way of loving feelings for her father. She could scarcely remember what he looked like. She had never forgiven him for his choice in forsaking her, her mother and sister in favor of remaining in Czechoslovakia. Now, she thought, he may be paying the price for that decision, as a pawn in a dangerous international game. If so, so was she.

She had become increasingly paranoid and was limiting her exposure in public, attentive to who was around her at all times. She was as uncomfortable at work as she was coming and going around Munich. Who could know, she thought, how many people were already trapped in an StB web and available to do its bidding...including hurting her. She sought to put herself into the shadows but knew it was impossible to remain invisible full- time. She had to come out and into full view from time to time, possibly exposing herself to an enemy that was even more invisible than she could hope to be.

She and Ted met at her apartment. Ted was shocked at how much in disarray she had let her small place go. Dishes in the sink, clothes tossed about, the unmade bed. He took it all in sweeping his eyes around her place as she offered him the couch. Once again, a surprise from the usually fastidious Ilse.

She told him with some satisfaction how she had talked Hank into giving her the use of his car. She told him how she planned to use it to abduct LeClerc. Ted listened to her plan with growing misgivings as each detail emerged.

"It's simple," she said, reading his doubts as she repeated how it would work. They would confront LeClerc, subdue him, put him in the trunk of Hank's car, and drive him to Paris à la Argoud. There, they would dump him where he would be sure to be found. She said she'd pin a nice note on his shirt explaining all that he'd been up to. Then it would be up to French justice to take it from there, saying, "I'll make it easy for them." She waited for approval from Ted who looked skeptical.

"We could do it all within twenty-four hours," she said. She went on to explain that it would be the best kind of revenge. LeClerc would be out of the game. He would likely reveal the identities and locations of those in Germany plotting against de Gaulle. He would, she thought, probably be executed for murdering Lucky and for crimes against the state. Or, she calculated, he'd at least spend the rest of his life in prison.

Ted was unconvinced. "I see you have it all worked out...or do you?" he asked. "When Antoine Argoud was abducted in Munich, it was by French Security agents. No problem for them," he said sarcastically, "popping across the border unchallenged."

"We can do it," she said. "I borrowed Hank's car once before and drove it to Salzburg. One look at the military plates...and a big smile...and they waved me through. No problem."

"Austria is not France," growled Ted. "Austria's not at war with terrorists."

"Ah, but I think I have what the Americans call 'an ace in the hole.' Someone who can be a big help at the border."

Ted looked at her, his expression a mixture of curiosity and doubt.

"Father Gabriel," she continued. "He's agreed to go with me. We'll cross the border at Strasbourg. He's back and forth all the time and practically knows the first names of border guards. With that, his collar, and Hank's car with US military plates, I think we'll get through."

"Unless an ambitious customs guard wants

to look in the trunk."

"Ted, I think it will work. This is bigger than you or me. It has to be done. If it doesn't work, and the French arrest me, it may not be the worst thing in the world for me to spend some time in a French prison right now. But," she hastily added, "I don't think that's going to happen. And, even if they do find LeClerc in the car, he'll be in France, and they'll still have him. He'll be right where we want him to be.

"Want to go along for the ride?" she asked. "It should be fun."

"I'm not so sure I want to spend any time with you in a French prison. I think it's a long shot." She looked at him, obviously disappointed.

"And, what about the car?" he asked. "It's Hank's car. If they stop you, they'll take the car at least for a little while. It will probably cost him his job. And maybe some time in jail himself."

She waved with a dismissive gesture and didn't respond to the question. "Will you at least help me with LeClerc when we confront him?" she asked. "Father Gabriel said he'd help, but I feel funny about that."

Ted took a long time before answering. He was not relishing his own potential involvement in Ilse's plan. "You feel funny about the priest, but aren't concerned about Hank," he said as a statement, not a question. She remained stubbornly silent.

Ted was wresting with myriad thoughts. He did not want to be involved, but at the same time he had promised Howell that he would keep an eye on Ilse. He felt protective of her for that reason, and for the reasons for which he had always felt a responsibility her. As unappealing as the prospect was, he agreed to give it some thought.

"There's no time for that," she said. "We've got to confront LeClerc almost immediately. I only have the car for a couple of days and it will take us a full day to drive to Paris and back." She stood impatiently with her arms folded, adding, "We won't even have to pack."

"I'm going to say it one more time," he said. "I think the best thing we can do is tell Howell where LeClerc is and let him and his group deal with it. He's got all the contacts and all the diplomatic tools to see that LeClerc is returned to France. And, he added firmly and deliberately, "He can do it with none of the risk."

"I want to do it myself," she said. "I want to see him squirm. I want my own form of justice."

He did not recognize this young woman he had known for so many years. She had always been so pretty, so bright, so level-headed. A woman who had always put others first. She had become a selfish bitch, he thought. She is like a woman possessed who was putting herself on a potentially destructive course. She was more in need than ever of his protection he thought. But now it might be protection from herself.

He remembered old vows to her mother. Yet, he asked himself, would he be able to provide it on a mission that seemed to him so filled with flaws that it would be impossible to fulfill successfully. Nonetheless, he nodded slowly and said to her reluctantly, "Okay. I'll go."

Ilse leaped from her chair and gave him a big hug. "Thank you, thank you, thank you. We'll make it work. I know we will."

He gave her an unconvincing smile and somberly thought to himself God help us if it doesn't.

Their next step was to contact Father Gabriel and tell him that they were moving ahead. He agreed to find out if LeClerc was at home. If so, he told them that he was ready to begin the "adventure," as he called it, as soon as possible.

Within an hour there was no longer any time for Ted's doubts. Father Gabriel's contacts told him that LeClerc had not been out of his apartment for two days. He was there now. They could begin their operation at once. It was decided that they would go for him at dawn, then leave immediately for Paris. They wanted to time it so they arrived in the French capital after dark. It would be a drive of ten hours or so, depending on how long it would take them to cross the border. They were counting on entering France quickly. Any delay crossing into Strasbourg could disrupt everything.

They knocked on LeClerc's door before the sun was up like friendly neighbors. He answered cautiously, rubbing the sleep from his eyes with his only hand. Even Ilse was struck by the Frenchman's appearance. She, like the others, felt a modicum of sympathy for him.

He was gaunt, dirty and unshaven. His deep-set, red-rimmed eyes revealed a momentary flicker of fear as he considered the three strangers before him. His eyes stayed on Ilse for a split second longer than the others as he wondered what this pretty woman would want with him. There was no such question as his gaze went from Ted and his stern countenance, to the priest who was making the sign of the cross. It was that reflexive act by Father Gabriel that frightened LeClerc the most.

The three of them moved toward LeClerc, backing him up slowly. His mouth moved as if he were trying to form words of protest, but there was no sound. The three intruders remained silent. Father Gabriel, who now seemed to be taking charge, pointed toward a wooden chair. LeClerc stumbled backwards to sit in it almost knocking the chair over. His eyes betrayed his fear. Beads of sweat appeared on his forehead.

"We are not going to be patient with you," said a menacing Father Gabriel. Ted was again surprised at his tone. It was the voice of command, not a voice from the pulpit. Ted thought in that instant that there must be far more to this man of God than he had reckoned. LeClerc was, he thought, no doubt thinking along the same lines. He was terrified, but at the same time, it was likely he was asking the same questions that were occurring to Ted.

"I'll ask you once," said the priest. "Did you order the bombing at La Bouche?"

LeClerc remained silent. So that's what this was about he thought. When the priest had spoken to him in perfect French, he had assumed it was most likely a French security agent who had taken him because of LeClerc's anti-government activity. The question he asked would not have been his first if that were the case. No, this was something else. And, he wondered, why a priest...if he is a priest...was asking the questions?

When he did not respond immediately, Ilse leaned close and asked, "Did you order the death of Manon...the race car driver? Were the bombers...the Germans...your men?" Her tone was intimidating.

They know about the Germans thought LeClerc. How much do they know? He remained silent. Let them talk he was thinking to himself.

Ted watched and wondered how the scene

would play out. It occurred to him that they might never have to make that trip to France. The priest was obviously impatient. Ilse was rosy with rage. If she had a weapon, she would kill him right now thought Ted, who found himself strangely sympathetic toward the pathetic Frenchman, a helpless captive.

"I am not answering any questions," said LeClerc finally. "I don't know who you are, but I have friends…"

"No you don't," said the priest. "You have no one. No one except us. And we are hardly your friends. We have your fate in our hands. Answer my question." His demand was emphatically impatient.

LeClerc's mind was spinning as he weighed the possible consequences for not responding. Or for answering honestly. Or for lying.

"I was aware of the Germans' plan," he said, his voice shaking. "But that's all I know. I don't know why they targeted Manon."

"Once again, did you order it?" asked the priest.

LeClerc did not respond.

"The fact you don't answer answers for me," said the priest, reaching into the deep pocket of his cassock. "It tells me all I need to know. Silence is the same as a confession. I think it's time to quit the game and get you to some people who will know how to get you to talk and talk truthfully."

LeClerc remained mute, his eyes fixed on what Father Gabriel was withdrawing from the cassock. He never quite saw what the priest was doing as Father Gabriel turned his back to Le-Clerc. Ted was uncertain also, until the priest turned suddenly and placed a white cloth against the nose and mouth of the Frenchman. He tried to push the priest away, but LeClerc went limp within a few seconds. Ted grabbed him to keep him from falling off the chair.

"Chloroform?" he asked. The scent of the anesthetic reached him, answering the question before the priest could respond.

"Chloroform-plus" said the priest nodding. "A special concoction. Enough to keep him out for a couple of hours. Let's get him to the car."

Ilse took the wheel and drove the car smoothly toward the highway that would take them to Strasbourg. They were silent for several minutes as she navigated the quiet, pre-dawn streets.

"That was quite a performance," Ted said to the priest from the back seat of the car. "They teach you all of that in the seminary?"

Father Gabriel laughed. "No."

The sun was now high enough that Ted could closely examine Father Gabriel for the first time. He had appeared youthful when they had picked him up in the dark outside the church where the priest lived. Looking at him in the early light of day, he could see he was older than he had appeared earlier. He was handsome with a sharp nose, deep-set dark eyes, curly hair and a slight scar on his left cheek.

"The Resistance?" Ted was guessing. "You acted more like a field commander than a man of the cloth back there," said Ted gesturing with his head in the direction from which they had just come.

Father Gabriel looked straight ahead at the road. "Is there any reason one could not be both?" He said. It wasn't really a question.

"Well, that holy water you carry around in your robe seems to serve both well."

The priest laughed heartily as did Ilse. Ted chuckled to himself. Questions or other small talk on this subject is over he thought. He has a story, but he's not going to tell it.

They were on the road for an hour when Father Gabriel announced that LeClerc would be coming out of his "sleep" somewhere between Stuttgart and Karlsruhe. "We'll stop at a quiet spot and let him get a little air. I'll give him another dose of my...holy water," he said with amusement. "That should keep him quiet until we're well into France."

As if on cue, a few minutes later, they heard

loud banging from the trunk. It continued for a few minutes until they found a quiet stretch of road.

The priest and Ted helped LeClerc, who now seemed more angry than frightened, out of the trunk. Ilse watched as Ted held his arm and walked him around the area. LeClerc, wondering where they were and what they were going to do with him, futilely protested his captivity.

"Did you order the killing of Manon? Or the Trade Mission bombing?" asked the priest. It was the first time he had mentioned the Trade Mission incident.

LeClerc shook his head.

"You should know," said Ted, "that one of the Germans who worked for you was killed at the border with the GDR. The other made it across and is telling people that they acted under your orders."

"Then why are you asking me?" LeClerc scoffed. "Is he coming back to testify? Hah. I don't think so."

"Testify?" said Ted. "You think there's going to be a trial? No. You're just going to disappear."

"And you're going to believe the word of a German?" asked LeClerc desperately.

Father Gabriel sneered. "Being German, I would," he said, stunning the confused LeClerc.

The priest grabbed LeClerc's arm from Ted and spun the Frenchman around to face him. "Because we're taking you to France, if you tell us that you gave the order for the bombings, it will go easier for you than if they have to beat it out of you."

Hapless and hopeless, LeClerc's head dropped. He was sore from the long cramped ride in the trunk of the car. His head ached from the chemical cocktail that had knocked him out. He was increasingly terrified knowing he was returning to France, where he knew the priest was right. He would not be treated well by the de Gaulle government. Some of his former military colleagues in Algeria had been executed for their anti-government activities that had included bombings and even assassination attempts against de Gaulle himself. The terrorism had intensified since the signing of peace accords with Algeria at Evian. The French would be more hostile than ever.

"I was a soldier," he said. "In the field you have to do what you have to do to fight the enemy. The enemy is France and the government of Charles de Gaulle. There are Frenchman all over Europe in this fight."

"But," said Ted, "Manon was not with the government. He had no politics. His allegiance was only to cars and the track."

"He was French," said LeClerc. "And he was a hero. A symbol that made him important to them."

Ted looked at the priest who turned to Ilse. The priest said to her, "Have you heard enough?"

She nodded and looked at LeClerc with disdain. "Whatever happens to you is too good for you." She turned to Ted and the priest. "Let's go and get this pig home where he belongs."

They approached the border crossing point less than an hour later. Their captive was drugged, bound and gagged in the trunk. The tacit confession from LaClerc and the routine activity along the Rhine River at the crossing point was like a tonic for the three of them.

When they were stopped the priest got out of the car and waved toward the familiar face of a young man in uniform. They chatted for a moment, laughed a little, and with the slight gesture of his hand, the young man casually waved the car into France.

CHAPTER 20

The drive to Paris through the French countryside was uneventful aside from the immense feeling of relief at having gotten across the border unchallenged. Once across, Ilse and the priest were chatty the way people sometimes are when they experience a rush of relief after having bypassed danger on one hand, while preparing to confront the unknown on the other. It was not clear to either Ilse or the priest how they could most effectively turn LeClerc over to the authorities. Ted sat quietly in the back seat, listening, occasionally dozing, and wondering throughout the drive what lay ahead.

As they neared Paris there was more activity as rural farms gave way to suburban villages and small towns. It became increasingly commercial as more shops and cafés lined the streets the closer they got to the city. Workers and shoppers were scurrying home for the evening meal.

The three travelers stopped for something to eat at a village café on the Paris outskirts where they would wait for the sun to go down.

For reasons they could not explain, the three of them seemed more nervous as they were about to complete their mission than they had been at the border where the chances of failure were high. The ebullience over their border-crossing success had eroded with time, replaced by uncertainty. They didn't know who would receive them and their captive, much less how they would be received.

They shunned wine for mineral water to keep their heads clear. They enjoyed a cold meal primarily in silence. They decided that their best plan was to find a police station and simply walk into it with their captive.

They paid their bill and saved a crust of bread for LeClerc who was still lying senseless in the car trunk. They knew he would be regaining consciousness at any moment. Indeed, when they got back to the car, they could hear him thumping with his feet against the inside of the trunk.

Foot traffic was light and no one seemed to notice the noise he was making. Nonetheless, although pedestrian traffic was limited, it made them even more jittery. They drove to a wooded area on the Paris route where they fed LeClerc and re-secured his bonds. Once satisfied he was secure, they let him walk a bit to work stiffness out of his joints. Then they put him in the back seat of the car with Ted.

LeClerc was stoic throughout. The three of them supposed that he was undoubtedly and desperately attempting to devise a plan that would enable him to avoid whatever lay ahead. He scanned the faces of people who passed on the sidewalks, his eyes darting from one to another as if somehow they might see him and know that he needed help. Alas, they were more interested in themselves and each other than they were with the occupants of a passing car with American license plates. Americans were no longer a curiosity in France. Certainly not in metropolitan Paris. One or two youngsters did wave. But as the fleeting car passed in the growing darkness, no one noticed the man in the back seat whose eyes spoke to his fear and his desperation. Nor could they hear his pounding heart.

The outskirts of the city were not busy with early evening activity. Auto traffic was light and only a few pedestrians were on the sidewalks. "Perfect for us," said the priest. "We don't need a crowd." They drove around for several minutes once they'd entered the city proper hoping to find a district police station. "I don't know this part of the city," said Father Gabriel. "I'm going to have to ask, otherwise this will take all night."

When they saw a pretty young woman walking arm-in-arm with a smiling young man, the priest called to them asking for the location of the nearest police station. He was cheerfully told that there was a district station just a few blocks away.

They found it without difficulty and waited outside for several minutes, hoping an officer would emerge and they could turn LeClerc over to him. None came.

"I'll go inside and get someone," said Ilse finally, opening the car door as she spoke. "I don't think this will take long." She walked up the steps of the ancient stone building rapidly and was quickly out of sight through a door showing a dimly lit hallway as she opened it.

Moments later she emerged with two burly officers laughing loudly like old friends. As they reached the steps, the priest and Ted pulled a shaking LeClerc from the back seat. He stood unsteadily between them as the police officers approached, their smiles fading.

"We bring you a gift from Germany," said Father Gabriel soberly. "This man is a killer and a terrorist and has been active with others in the OAS." He turned to Ilse.

"Ilse do you have your notes?" She gave him an awkward look and pulled several sheets of paper from her coat.

"Here, this will tell you everything you need to know about him," she said handing the policemen the papers, "including newspaper articles about his activity. He is a wanted man. If you check, you will be able to confirm it. The Sûreté certainly has a dossier on him."

As she spoke her two companions pushed LeClerc toward the bewildered officers. He protested loudly. "I've been abducted," he shouted. "They are criminals." The policemen ignored him.

The second officer exchanged glances with his partner, took LeClerc by the arm while the other glanced at the papers Ilse had given him. He studied them for a moment, turned to LeClerc then to Ilse, then to his partner. "Get him inside," he said firmly to his colleague, tipping his cap to the other three. "Thank you Father."

They all nodded politely and turned toward the car. The officer added, "I must ask you to come inside. This requires a report. I will need you with me when I write it."

It was exactly what they feared and needed to avoid. They had no desire to accompany LeClerc inside the station and be subjected to questions from the police. "I'll have to come back," said Father Gabriel. "We have some urgent church business to attend to. I will return a little later. I'm sure that will be okay. Right?" he said backing away. "Bless you both. Go with God," he added before they could respond. They all kept moving, with the priest gesturing and blessing the officers with the sign of the cross.

The two baffled policemen watched them

get into their car and drive away. They were out
of sight before the two officers had gotten LeClerc
inside the district station.

They drove out of the city much faster than
they had come in, eager to put as much distance
between themselves and French authorities as
quickly as they could. They were on the road for
five minutes before anyone spoke.

"Do you think they will try and stop us
from leaving the country?" asked a concerned
Ilse. Her voice was shaking. Her earlier confidence was gone.

"Let's get to the border quickly and get back
on German soil," said the priest. "Crossing this
time may be a little more difficult than it was
coming into France. I hope LeClerc is screaming
like a stuck pig. That will keep them occupied for
a while."

In fact, LeClerc was doing just that. He was
protesting loudly and almost incoherently saying
that he had been kidnapped unjustly, that he was
not the man they said he was, and that he was a
veteran who had served honorably. It took more
than an hour to settle him down. By then, the
three who had brought him to Paris were almost
halfway to the border.

"I guess that went about as well as we could
hope," said Ted finally. "One more bridge to cross.
Literally."

Ilse was somber until she finally said to the

priest, "I wish you had not mentioned my name Father Gabriel."

He looked surprised. "I don't think I did, did I"

"Yes, you did." She looked at him seriously. "I wish you hadn't."

"Why? He asked.

"Because now they know it," she blurted turning angrily back to the road. "And, I wish they didn't." She tightened her grip on the wheel. Instead of elation over the transfer of LeClerc, she found herself feeling uneasy and frightened.

Ted sat quietly in the back seat. He was not surprised that Ilse was upset. He had been too when the priest had carelessly called her by name.

Everything seemed to have fallen into place. LeClerc's outbursts had preoccupied the police who had not given the three who had delivered him to them any thought, especially since they had been assured by Father Gabriel that all would return. Ilse, the priest and Ted were at the border before anyone in the district police station began to wonder about them.

The unofficially casual, hands-off treatment of vehicles bearing American plates, and German familiarity in dealing with Americans, made for smooth sailing across the Rhine and into the Federal Republic. Ilse, Ted and the priest collectively exclaimed relief when they were waved through.

They drove into Munich just as the sun was rising, twenty four hours after their departure the previous morning. Ted was at the wheel, his turn, as they had been sharing driving chores. The rising sun woke Ilse and the priest and they watched it wash familiar buildings with a red and golden glow as the medieval city began to come alive. They drove first to Father Gabriel's residence. It was a stone cottage set behind a modest 16th century church in an even more modest neighborhood. With words of sincere appreciation, Ilse and Ted thanked the priest for his assistance, realizing the outcome might have been quite different had he not been a part of their plot.

Ted drove to his apartment. He turned over the car keys to Ilse. They were both yawning and exhausted and separated with few words. A few minutes later he was sound asleep, sleeping better than he had in days.

An exhausted Ilse was in her own bed a few minutes later and fell asleep with conflicting emotions. She had accomplished a major objective in avenging the death of Lucky and the girl by turning LeClerc over to the French. She was confident it would result in prison, or worse, for Leclerc as well as the disruption of whatever opposition to the French government was embedded in Germany. She drifted off to sleep, hoping to learn soon whether Charles Howell could find a solution to her Czechoslovakian problem, realizing it could prove considerably more dangerous than the most recent adventure with LeClerc. Then there was Hank. Then there was sleep.

When she woke, she tried to contact Howell but he was in Berlin and not available until the next day or the day after that. She called the hospital to enquire about Hank and learned that he would likely be released the next day. She could, she was told, visit any time.

She knocked on the door to his room in late afternoon well aware that she was going to have to put on an act. He called her in and she found him sitting in a big chair with a magazine in his lap. His face lighted up when he saw Ilse. She went to him and kissed him on both cheeks.

"Welcome back," he said as she pulled up a chair. "How were the Beatles?"

She gave him a fabricated account of the "Hamburg concert," that included a rave review of the young band. She told him about the long, uneventful drive north, the dank weather near the coast, and how she and Ted had had a chance to bond once again while recalling old memories. "It was great fun," she said.

"But what about you. You look and sound

much better, and they told me at the nurse's station that you will likely be released tomorrow."

"That's the plan," he said, assuring her that he felt great and that if he had his way he would walk out with her then and there.

"I'm looking forward to being with you when I get out," he said, watching her closely for her reaction.

"Me too," she replied touching his cheek. "Me too. We have a lot to talk about."

He could not read all that she meant by that. It could cover a lot of ground including the future of their relationship and the disquieting situation with her father. He was about to say something to that effect when a nurse came into the room carrying a tray with his evening meal. She smiled pleasantly as she placed the tray on a bedside table.

Ilse stood and offered her goodbye. "I'm not going to interrupt your dinner," she said. "I'll come back tomorrow to get you home. Please get a good rest." She touched his cheek again. She nodded to the nurse, and asked, "What time are you letting him go tomorrow?"

"Early afternoon," said the nurse. "After the doctor finishes his rounds."

"I'll be here then," said Ilse, blowing a kiss to Hank before turning and leaving.

"She's beautiful," said the nurse as she left. "Is she your wife?"

"Hah," exclaimed Hank. "You're right about her being beautiful. She's not my wife. I'm not even sure she's my girlfriend," although he felt he had more reason to believe that she was than he'd had before he was admitted to the hospital.

At the very moment he spoke the words, unbeknownst to Hank, Ilse, Ted and the priest, nor to any members of Charles Howell's working group investigating the bombings, two French newspapers were about to come to the attention of all of them. Le Monde, the afternoon paper, was on the street carrying a short story recounting the apprehension of Albert LeClerc. Le Parisien was preparing an even more detailed version for its edition the following morning. While the news was of only moderate interest to most Frenchmen, the reports were about to have a major impact in Munich.

CHAPTER 21

Charles Howell was back from Berlin and in his office early the next morning. He found his colleague, J. Harding Bell, the press officer, waiting for him. He held two newspapers in his hand. "You haven't seen this yet, I'm sure. French dailies. I'm sure once the local papers here get wind of this and the local connection, they'll be jumping on them...probably tomorrow."

"I don't read French," said Howell frowning. "What is it?"

Bell held out a typed sheet of paper. "I had Marcella translate and transcribe the Le Parisien version. It's longer and more complete than Le Monde...which I'm guessing will have more this afternoon.

Howell took the transcript and read it with a scowl.

SUSPECTED OAS TERRORIST

ARRESTED
By Gideon Jean-Pierre

Paris--- Paris Police have detained a former captain in the French military who is believed to have part of an anti-government campaign in Algeria prior to independence. He's suspected of having continued that effort in Munich where he is believed to have carried out several acts of terrorism.

Albert LeClerc was taken into custody in Paris Tuesday evening when he was presented to two officers in the 19th Arrondissement by three Germans who had driven him to Paris from Munich.

LeClerc is believed to have led a small group of OAS sympathizers in Munich. The Germans brought with them information linking the former officer with two bombings in the Bavarian capital. He's accused of masterminding the bombing of the French Trade Mission in March, and of engineering the bombing that took the lives of celebrated French auto racer Matthieu "Lucky" Manon and a young American woman, Kay Montgomery earlier this month.

LeClerc is said to have been a staff

associate of General Charles de Gaulle before deGaulle founded the Fifth Republic. LeClerc resigned after the two had a falling- out over the now president's policies on Algeria.

LeClerc is himself a veteran of the war in Algeria. He lost an arm in combat there. He had been accused while in service of torturing members of the National Liberation Front, the FLN, in Oran.

He had been a wanted man since he left the military and had gone underground.

LeClerc has denied all accusations linking him with terrorist activity in Munich or Algeria.

He faces trial and possible execution for crimes against the state.

LeClerc was brought to Paris under unusual circumstances reminiscent of the abduction in Munich last year of Col. Antoine Argoud, currently imprisoned for his OAS activities.

LeClerc was turned over to the police authorities by the three Germans, including a priest, who had driven him from Munich to Paris. The car they used had US Army license plates. They left the district station shortly after turning over LeClerc. Police are hoping they will return, as they promised they would do, to answer questions about their role in bringing their prisoner to France from Germany.

None of the three was identified. The officers who took LeClerc into custody said one of the three was an attractive blonde woman in her twenties who was called "Ilse" by the priest. The third man was only described as tall and thin. He was a bystander during the exchange.

Authorities in Paris hope to learn from LeClerc about other anti-government cells in Germany, France and elsewhere. Authorities say that he has, so far, not been forthcoming, insisting that he is innocent of all accusations presented to him.

He is currently being interrogated by national intelligence officers and ultimately will likely be arraigned within the next 72 hours.

"Jesus Christ," growled Howell. "Ilse! Our Ilse?

Bell nodded. "Probably."

"What the hell does she think she's doing?" He looked at the paper again. "Who the fuck is this priest? Where does she come up with these people? And the other guy. Hank?" He thought for a moment. "He's just smitten enough to follow her to hell." He smacked his palm against his head.

"No," he said, slapping his forehead. "It was Ted. It's got to be Ted. Her protector. What are they all thinking?"

He turned to Bell. "You're right. The locals will pick this up. Keep us out of it. And," he pounded his desk, "get that fucker Domjan in here. He's got some explaining to do. And we need to get the working group in. Let's have a shit show party," he said with disgust.

The news had not broken publically in Munich when Ilse drove to the military hospital to bring Hank home. Neither he nor she had any notion that Howell and others were already familiar with the LeClerc abduction, or that the *Abendzeitung, Süddeutsche Zeitung* or the international edition of the *Herald Tribune* would carry the French news the following day.

As per protocols, Hank was wheeled from his room to his car, happy to be out of the hospital, and thrilled to be with Ilse. Even more so when she suggested that they drive to her apartment where she would be his nurse and "help him recuperate." She made much of the fact that he had lost some strength and needed to take his medication promptly. Needless to say he was in full agreement and hoped to show her that he was not totally without strength. Or stamina for that matter.

She helped him up the stairs and had propped him in an overstuffed chair when the phone rang. It was Ted. She turned white when he told her that Howell wanted to see them both immediately. "I think he knows about our trip to Paris," he said. "To say the least, he is not pleased."

"I have to leave for a while," she stammered to Hank after hanging up. "Something's come up at the consulate. Howell wants to talk. It may be the Czech situation." She asked Hank if he would mind being alone for a while. He suggested she drop him off at his place where he could pick up some things, then pick him up on her way back from the consulate.

They spoke little on the short drive. "You're nervous about all this aren't you?" he asked.

"Very," she said. "Yes...I'm very nervous."

He refused when she offered to help him to his apartment. "I'm fine," he said. "I'll take my time. I want to save my strength." He winked, as he was leaving the car, hoping she got his message. She never saw it. Gunning the engine, she took off to the sound of screeching tires as soon as he was out of the car. In her rear view mirror, getting smaller and smaller, she could see a bewildered Hank Tollar watching her speed away.

He made his way to his apartment and began to gather some clothes and other items he would need for his stay at Ilse's apartment. He'd be ready when she returned.

He called Ted at the office to tell him he was out of the hospital. Ted answered on the first ring. "Glad to hear you're out," he said, sounding rushed. "I can't talk now. I've just been asked to a command performance in Charles Howell's office. I've got to get going right now." He hung up loudly. Hank stared at his phone, wondering what was going on? Ilse gets summoned to Howell's office and so does Ted. Ted works for me, he thought, Ilse works for RFE. Yet, they seem to be spending a lot of time lately with Charles Howell, ersatz Cultural Attaché, de facto CIA officer, at the American Consulate. What were they all up to? Why were Ilse and Ted so uptight?

Ted and Ilse had arrived at the consulate separately within a few moments of one another and had been asked to wait by Howell's secretary. They were both uneasy and sat in silence. They knew Howell and how he could intimidate. He could be especially intimidating if he thought secrets had been breached, lies had been promulgated or promises had been unkept. He was a crafty player in a dark world. His was a sometimes messy, occasionally violent, and always shady universe, but one whose values were sacrosanct. He was true to his professional code. Outside his professional, private world, he was very much the same. Those who knew him knew it.

There was a Star Chamber quality to the atmosphere in Charles Howell's office when Ilse and Ted were shown in. Members of the bombings working group were seated around a long conference table. All sat silently in glowering reflection. Howell scowled at the two as they sat in wooden chairs at the far end of the table. The two latecomers didn't have long to wait for specifics as to why they'd been summoned.

Howell hastily introduced the members of his group and explained their joint mission. Then, he exploded. "What the fuck were you two thinking," croaked Howell. "You jumped into the middle of our investigation and kidnapped a guy we very much wanted to talk to before turning him over to France." Dupuis from the French Consulate looked uncomfortable and played with the knot of his tie.

"It was amateur hour at a time when professionalism was called for."

Ilse interrupted. "I doesn't seem amateur to me when we were able to find LeClerc and you weren't."

"There are diplomatic channels and protocols for dealing with something like this...and with someone like LeClerc.

"France and Germany and the United States are walking on diplomatic egg shells at the moment on a number of fronts. Not following established procedures could affect negotiations on international agreements. Ilse, this action on your part could have a serious impact on our work on the issue in Czechoslovakia."

Realizing he had mentioned something the others would not be aware of, he turned slowly making eye contact with each member of the working group. "This is all off the record. Ilse and I have been working together on a matter concerning her father in Czechoslovakia and possible StB involvement. Enough said."

"I don't see that," she said. Who knows about the transfer of LeClerc? How did you find out for that matter?"

Howell pulled the two French newspapers from a pile of papers in front of him. He waved them like he was trying to hail a cab. "I'd guess half of France knows. And, tomorrow all of Munich will know, and five minutes after that, Prague will know and start putting two and two together. To them it will add up to 'our Ilse's an intelligence agent.' Bad timing don't you think?"

Ilse and Ted glanced at each other nervously. Howell dropped the newspapers. "Here's what *Le Parisien* is saying today." He read the transcribed article.

When he finished he said, "You can be pretty damn sure Munich papers will have the story tomorrow, not to mention the Trib. Its offices are in Paris."

Ilse turned to Ted and whispered, "I knew Gabriel's mentioning my name would be a problem. Damn!"

Lieutenant Erbach of the Munich Police Department was close enough to hear. "Who is Gabriel? Is he the priest?"

"Yeah, who the hell is the priest? asked Howell. "This'll likely piss off the Catholic Church as well." He turned to Ted.

"Ted, I specifically asked you to get back to me with any information you might come up with concerning French anti-government types operating in Germany. This publicity is only going to drive them deeper underground."

He paused, "And by the way, how do you think the German government's going to feel, number one, about German nationals independently working on behalf of the French government by tracking down anti-Gaullist leaders here and sneaking them back to France? If you remember there were some snippy exchanges when Argoud was snatched."

Howell's face was red with exasperation. The other members of the working group were exchanging side glances. Ted and Ilse's eyes were examining their feet.

Howell went on. "And, using a car with US military plates. Jesus, that makes it look like the US Army was involved. Hank's car I assume." Neither Ilse nor Ted responded.

"Ted, you haven't told me why you didn't keep me in the loop on this. Why did you go off like the Lone Ranger and Tonto? You of all people should have been smarter than that."

Before Ted could answer, Ilse shouted, "He did it for me because of our very deep friendship over many years. He's always vowed to protect me. That's why he went. He knew how much it meant to me to avenge Lucky's and the girl's murder."

"Ted?"

"That's it. I was uneasy about it. But," he looked at Ilse fondly, "I thought if I was with her, I could keep an eye on the situation knowing how emotional she was about LeClerc and the bombings." He looked closely at Howell. "We all have our priorities and Ilse happens to be one of mine."

"So," said Howell after noisily taking several deep breaths. "Who is the priest. He needs a talking to."

Ilse looked up. "None of your business," she said. "He's just someone like me...someone who was deeply affected with the murder of Lucky Manon and Kay Montgomery. He offered to drive, I accepted. That's it."

The two stared icily at each other. Others in the room shifted in their seats nervously. Ilse stood unexpectedly, her arms at her side, fists clenched like a boxer coming out of his corner. "And, by the way," she said angrily. "How dare you bring Ted and me into a room like this for a dressing down with all your friends sitting here like Inquisition judges. What's next? Thumbs up or thumbs down? What are you trying to do, cover your own failure to find and deal with LeClerc?"

She pointed around the room. "You should all be ashamed of yourselves for your incompetence...your inability to do what I...we...did.

"If you think you can humiliate me...and Ted...you're wrong. You all are the ones who should feel humiliated."

"That's enough," shouted Howell. "Ilse, here's what else you have done. You've put yourself in a tough position. LeClerc's allies, however few they may be, will undoubtedly be looking for you. You did them wrong and they won't like it. Not one bit.

"And, our friends in Czechoslovakia are not going to be happy with you. They will see you now as someone who can't be trusted. Someone who's working for the wrong side as far as they're concerned. You know how they deal with people like that?"

Not waiting for her answer, he turned to Ted. "So you, Mr. Protector, may...no, not *may*...will...have your work cut out for yourself. Good luck.

"One final question for you both. Does Hank Tollar know any of this? Ilse and Ted looked at each other but said nothing. Ilse turned back to Howell. Her eyes narrowed.

"No, he doesn't." She looked coldly at the men sitting at the table. "Not yet at least. But when he does gentlemen, I hope he spells your names correctly." Once again the group members shifted uneasily in their chairs, exchanging nervous glances.

"Come on Ted," she said standing. "Let's

get out of here."

When they got outside, Ted said, "Whew Ilse. That was quite a performance. But there's one other thing you now have to think about."

She turned to him, her eyebrows raised.

"He may be right about the Czechs and the OAS. But now there's something else. Now, some of the organizations those folks at the table represent may also have you in their sights. And that includes Charles Howell. They may feel compromised somehow."

Back in Howell's office, the Cultural Attaché waited until the two were well out of earshot. "So that's what we're dealing with gentlemen. As fiery as the lovely Ilse can be, she can also miss the big picture. I don't think she realizes what kind of a position she's put herself in. Or, what kind of a position she's put all of us in. The French nut jobs in Germany are going to get very nervous when they learn about LeClerc, whether they liked him or not. If they learn it was 'our' Ilse that turned him in...God help her. And," he added, "I can't go into detail, but the thugs in Czechoslovakia will be pissed too. She's working with us on something that could make the La Bouche bombing look like a church social. Tell your troops to keep their eyes and ears open."

He gestured to J. Harding Bell who had been sitting quietly throughout, taking notes in a corner of the room. "Bell, we've got to make sure the press doesn't jump on the car angle of the story. That could raise a lot of questions we don't want to answer. Play it down. Say it must have been stolen or some-thing...that the military is trying to track that down. And," he said as an afterthought, "if Tollar comes nosing around, handle him with kid gloves. We don't know what he knows but we don't want him to know any more than the basics from us." Bell looked up from his notes."

"Will do Charlie."

Howell grunted as he stood as if to go. "Thank you gentlemen. I guess that's all we can do for now. You're all as up to speed as we are. Stay alert everyone." The group got up and began to file out. "Dupuis," he said quietly to his French counterpart, "give me a minute will you."

CHAPTER 22

They drove in frosty silence to the Stars and Stripes office where Ilse barely stopped the car to let Ted out. "I'll call you," she said quickly. "I've got to pick up Hank." She noisily put the car into first gear, and for the second time that afternoon drove off leaving a bewildered passenger behind.

She pulled up in front of Hank's place, hesitated, then walked slowly to the door. Her hand shook as she pressed the doorbell. He answered smiling, carrying a little satchel with his things. She looked at it uneasily. Hank's smile faded. He knew immediately something was wrong. She had no color in her cheeks and didn't make eye contact with him. I'm the one who's supposed to be sick, he thought.

"What's wrong?" he asked. "You don't look very good. Howell get you down."

"I guess you could say that," she said flatly,

turning toward the car and handing him the keys. He stood for a moment puzzled. "We need to talk," she said moving toward the car. "I'll tell you right now you're not going to like it."

They were each lost in their own thoughts as they made the short drive to Ilse's apartment. It was a trip that Hank had longed for. He had foreseen a new start to the relationship, but worried during the drive that that was in jeopardy...that something was going terribly wrong. Ilse's eyes never left the road as she sat rigidly in the passenger seat. His concern intensified when they had parked and, as he started to retrieve his satchel, she said, "You might as well leave that here. I don't think you're going to want to stay."

Her comment took his breath away. It was over, he thought. Clearly it was over. That comment seemed to say it all.

When they entered her apartment, he took her by both shoulders. "Look, let's get right on with it. What is it that you want to say? You're driving me nuts with some of your comments. What is it I don't want to hear?"

"Hank, it's not something I want to say. It's just something that I have to say. Please sit down."

He did, fully apprehensive. He watched her as she paced, kneading her hands. She seemed to be struggling to find the words that, no matter what, she realized would be as painful for her to say as she knew they would be for him to hear.

"I have been very dishonest with you," she said. "You don't deserve it and it's shameful." His heart sank.

He listened, stunned at the realization of what she was saying, as Ilse spent the next half hour detailing the story of her feverish desire for revenge against those responsible for the murder of Lucky and Kay Montgomery, and how she had managed to find the man responsible.

She admitted she had fabricated the story about the trip to Hamburg to see the Beatles. She told him about Father Gabriel and how he and Ted had helped turn LeClerc over to the French police. She took a deep breath when detailing how the priest had mentioned her name and how it had made its way into influential French newspapers.

"I'm told it will all very likely be in the Munich papers tomorrow. I wanted you to hear it from me first." She wiped away a tear. She stung him with an admission that she had intentionally manipulated him to get him to lend her his car.

"I'm so afraid that could get you in trouble. The French policeman who remembered my name also remembered that the car we'd driven to Paris had US military license plates." Disconsolate, she sighed as if in pain. "Charlie Howell's furious because that could pull the Army, or even the American government into it. And that, he says, could have serious international diplomatic consequences."

"Did the French cop get the license number?" asked Hank. "There are thousands of cars with military plates in Europe. They can't do much to me without a number."

"I don't think they have it. But it may have been recorded in the border crossings. I don't know."

"Shit," said Hank. If they do, I can kiss my job goodbye."

"I'm sorry Hank," said Ilse as she began to sob. "The last thing I want to do is hurt you."

"Yeah, sure. Lie to me, use me, but don't want to hurt me. That's a laugh. Want to hear how much I hurt," he asked, his words spilling out angrily. "More than you'll ever know. Or care, I suspect. I thought we might have a future together, but that was before I find out that I'm just someone to be manipulated...just a chess piece to you." He felt slightly lightheaded and unsteady on his feet. "I had hoped for a lot more than that," he said sadly.

"I had hoped for more too," she said. "But..."

"Yeah...but...first things first. Revenge first," he said bitterly. "You got the revenge. Does it feel all better now? Think Lucky's resting more easily now? Think the girl's coming back? As long as the dead are taken care of, forget about the living." He shook his head sadly. His reaction made her gasp between inconsolable sobs.

"Anything else you want to tell me? he asked hotly. "I've got to go. I've got a story to write. Hah, that's a good one. I'll be writing a story that I'm involved in. But I can't disclose that. My journalism professors would love that."

She wiped her cheeks with both hands. "Charlie's not going to want you to write about it."

"I don't give a crap about what Charlie wants."

She stood and walked to the door. "I want you to stay," she said, "but I can see that's not something you'd want right now."

"It's something I want, but also don't want. It's definitely something I'm not going to do. Maybe I have to ask Howell about that too," he said sarcastically. "I get the impression my role is pretty much to do what other people want me to do." He stood with his hand on the doorknob. "Anything else I ought to know."

No, she thought, shaking her head. There was no point telling him about her situation with the Czechs and drawing him into that quagmire. And, in a strange way, she was happy he was leaving. If the Czechs or so called French "patriots" were out to get her, she wouldn't want him around where physical pain would be a lot worse that his current emotional distress.

"Hank, I'm sorry," she said as he was about to step outside.

"Yeah, me too," he answered, slamming the

door behind him.

Hank was feeling shaky after his emotional outburst with Ilse. Rather than face his thoughts and pain in the solitude of his apartment, he decided to go to the office before returning home. He wasn't sure Ted would be there and was happy when he found the office door unlocked. Ted was at his desk. "Well, I'm surprised to find you here," said Hank. "I thought you might be out brushing up on your French," he said with more than a touch of sarcasm.

Ted seemed to ignore the tone and gave him a lazy smile. "Well I'm not surprised to see you. I just talked to Ilse."

"Ah, the lady with the forked tongue and the lust for revenge. What did she want? Another trip to Paris."

"Okay Hank. I get it," said Ted irritably. "It was not a smart thing to do. But when she got her mind up to do it, I couldn't just let her go. I made promises long ago to keep her under my wing. To do that I had to go along. Sorry about the deception."

Hank sat down and took a deep breath. "You know, I've got to give her credit. She's ballsy. Not many people...much less a woman...would have taken that all on. Stupid but ballsy."

"That may have been the easy part," said Ted. "When that story gets out, a number of very turned off Frenchmen in Germany are going to be looking for a Munich blonde by the name of Ilse. Probably not more than a few thousand of them around here, but I'm guessing they have their contacts. I've told her she should find a deep hole and crawl into it."

"Seriously, they wouldn't waste their time on someone like her, would they?"

"Well, these guys are criminals. A lot of them face the firing squad if de Gaulle gets to them. My guess is this guy LeClerc will sing like Edith Piaf when they threaten to take off his other arm. When he does, if he does, and some of the boys over here begin to disappear, she'll be in trouble."

"Is she worried?"

"She won't admit it, but sure she's worried. Almost as much as she is sorry that she used you the way she did."

"Well, she sure did that. If she can man-handle them the way she did me, they don't have a chance." He folded his arms and looked closely at Ted. "Well, you're her protector. What are you going to do to protect her?"

"We'll see how the story breaks here. My guess is I'll move in with her after it does and stay pretty close until further notice."

"Howell, I guess, is pretty pissed off. Do you think he'll talk with me?"

"Yeah, probably to chew you out, and to tell

you to lay off."

"I can't."

"I'm guessing you'll have a chance to tell him why."

Howell agreed to see him the following day. Hank knew he was walking into the lion's den. He carried with him the Munich newspaper, the *Abendzeitung,* and the *International Herald Tribune*, published in Paris, both of which carried the LeClerc story, including mention of the woman, Ilse, and the fact that LeClerc had been delivered in a car with US Army plates. The Tribune made that the story with the headline asking, "US Involvement in Abduction of French Terrorist?"

"Well, your girlfriend really stepped in it this time," said Howell. "This Trib story has got the embassy in Bonn in a fucking frenzy. Queries from all over. V Corps getting it in Frankfurt, and I'm told that even McNamara's holding onto both cheeks at the Pentagon." He looked suspiciously at Hank while shifting his considerable bulk. "Your car is the star of the show, with Ilse up for best supporting Oscar."

Hank ignored both statements without confirming Howell's comment about the car. "I've got to put something out on this. I've already got my call into V Corps and I'm about to have a chat with Bell. The editors will pull together the story from our guys in Bonn and Washington. Just letting you know." He waited a moment. "You got anything I can quote?"

Howell produced a wry smile. "Sure. You can say", he said acerbically, "the Cultural Attaché at the American Consulate in Munich is 'following events closely.' Close quote."

"Very funny," said Hank.

"What did you expect?" asked Howell showing a derisive smirk and a disdainful glare.

"Just what I got," answered Hank.

Turning more disciplined, Howell said, "I've talked to the editor, Marcus, in Frankfurt. Just to make sure nobody goes off on a wild tangent. The official word on this one comes from V Corps, the State Department and the Pentagon."

"What about Ilse?"

"What about Ilse? There are probably ten thousand Ilse's in Munich and a hundred times that In Germany. Throw in all the Ilses in Austria, Holland and even Czechoslovakia or France," he noted sarcastically again, "and see how long it takes to find out which one was in Paris."

"And Ted?"

"I didn't see anybody named Ted mentioned in the story."

"You had them both in here yesterday for a little ass chewing."

"About other things," he responded.

"You should know I've talked to both Ilse and Ted. I know the story."

"Well I'd give a lot of thought as to how much you decide to report. I'll tell you this...if what you know goes public, some lives will be in danger.

"Ilse? Ted?"

"Draw your own conclusions."

The wheels were turning in Hank's head. He knew so much more than he could ever report. How was he going to handle it?

The next step, after a chat with Bell was to call Marcus in Frankfurt and get his input. Bell referred him to the military whose spokesman told him that the matter was being investigated "upstairs."

His call to his old friend, the editor Marcus Marcus, provided Hank with an interesting insight into how the government "system" works in a crisis.

"There's a story going around about the car that took the Frenchman to Paris." were the first words Hank heard from Marcus's familiar voice when he called him. "Was it your car?" he asked directly.

"I was in the hospital flat on my back when the whole thing went down in Paris. I certainly wasn't driving around Europe. I left my car at home when I was taken to the hospital by ambulance. It was my car that brought me home. All I was doing for three days was sleeping and having my arm riddled with hypodermic needles." Hank was grateful Marcus didn't ask who was driving when he was picked up. Everything he said was true, he thought, but with some significant omissions. He wondered if he'd have lied about Ilse if he'd been asked.

"Okay," said Marcus. "I'm putting together the story now. What are the folks there saying?"

"Consulate and military saying the same thing. It's all under investigation. Probably take days."

"Okay. That's all I need from you. I'll work it in."

Hank hung up relieved and upset. He was relieved because he didn't have to write a story that would have been impossible to tell completely or accurately, and therefore, he felt, would have been egregiously unethical.

Marcus had asked him questions that he could answer honestly while still misleading his old friend. He felt he was off the hook. For the moment. Had Marcus pressed, it would have been a much different situation. As it turned it, he told the truth without having really said anything at all. How much did Marcus know, he wondered, after that phone call that Charles Howell had mentioned? He may have felt he was off the hook, but Hank was bothered knowing also that while he had told the truth…he had not been honest. Not even close.

CHAPTER 23

In the days that followed, Hank felt like he was swimming against a riptide trying to get back to a stable shore. He was conflicted over how he had folded on the LeClerc abduction story. It had been to protect Ilse first and foremost, but also because important national interests were at stake. The pressure on him had been less than subtle, but there was an intensity in the result that gnawed at him. There was always the difficult-to-forget threat from Howell about selling pencils on a Baltimore street corner. Hank knew Howell could make that happen. Or worse. Nonetheless it wore away at him, even as the story faded, as all stories do, replaced by others, then others.

He was reminded of it a few weeks later, however, during a tobacco delivery for Gene Talbot. He dreaded the daily visits to RFE, fearing he'd run into Ilse. He knew that if he did, it would be emotional and he doubted he could hold it together without some attempt at reconciliation. He knew intellectually that it couldn't happen and probably shouldn't happen. Emotionally, however, he couldn't guarantee himself that he wouldn't try to make it happen. For him, trust had been broken creating what he felt to be a painful and unnavigable gap. Ted had told him that her guilt was consuming her. One day, thought Hank. One day...perhaps.

"The Frenchies haven't wasted any time, have they?" Talbot asked as he gratefully accepted another pound of Prince Albert.

"What do you mean?" asked Hank.

"Haven't you been hearing about it?" said the older man, adding, "I guess it has been kind of quiet. Seems the Germans have been rather methodically picking up a number of suspected French goons around the country. Not a lot of press, but some of our people here have been getting the word. My guess is that that whacko LeClerc is naming names as if he were reading the phone book. So, de Gaulle's won. One by one here and in France the opposition is being rolled up.

"That will leave him free to make mischief with Britain and continue to worry about the Americanization of France. And free to continue his plans for the restoration of yesterday's grandeur. That is the yesterday before the yesterday that the Germans rolled in, and over France practically overnight. Wasn't much grandeur to that," he mused.

"How many arrested? Any idea?"

"No. Just that it's happening. If some of the ones they take in talk, the days of the embedded French terrorists will be over, period!"

That should put Ilse at ease thought Hank. And, it should put her in a new light with the Charles Howells of the world.

This thought was on his mind as he returned to the office. Ted was waiting, grim-faced when Hank returned.

"Ilse's missing," he said.

"What?" said Hank. "Missing. How could she be missing"

"That's what has me so worried. How? That and the why? Because the why has me worried the most."

"The French?" asked Hank. "Do you think some of those nutballs found her?"

"That's what has me worried. She basically kicked me out the other day. She said there wasn't enough room for the two of us at her place. She wanted her privacy and said she felt safe. So, I left. I'd stop by from time to time. She wasn't there yesterday or today. I went inside. All her stuff is there. I called her office. They say she hasn't showed up for three days. No messages. Nothing."

"Have you called the police?"

"Yeah, and Howell."

"Howell. Why Howell?"

"Well, she's done some work for him. I thought he might have had an assignment for her."

"I thought they were on the outs."

"Personally yes. Professionally no. He has a lot of contacts. He's working on tracking her down."

"My god," said Hank. "I can't believe it. She has to be in trouble. She just wouldn't take off."

"No, she wouldn't." said Ted sliding into his chair. "I'm damn worried."

There was no sign and no word the next day or the next. The Germans had a full scale all points bulletin out on her. The French were questioning the people they'd been picking up since the LeClerc abduction. Nothing! She was simply gone. Vanished. No trace.

After two weeks of futility, authorities could do no more than wait and hope she would find them. Or, as everyone had come to fear, they would find her body. Few who knew of her involvement with l'affaire LeClerc felt there could be a good outcome. Hank was heartbroken. Ted was disconsolate enough to take some time off to grieve.

The weeks turned into months. The world as Hank knew it was changing. Charles Howell had been transferred to Berlin. Tom Morrow quit AFN to return to the United States. "Not to sell pencils," he joked with Hank at a going away party. He had taken a job with a television station in Florida. Ted came back from his grieving, but announced that he could only continue on a part-time basis. Even Gene Talbot had announced his retirement. "Time to get my tobacco on my own," he told Hank.

With all the changes around him, Hank began to wonder if it was time for him to move on. It was in the spring of the following year that he decided that he would make a decision after what he considered the most important assignment ever in his young career.

President John Kennedy was going to be visiting Germany in June, part of a visit that would also take him to England, Italy and Ireland. It was going to be a full court press by the media, including his paper, and Hank was assigned to be part of the coverage in Berlin. Kennedy was going to be on the move in Germany, and the paper wanted reporters to be there at every stop. Hank was thrilled to be a part of the coverage. A decision on "what next" could wait until that assignment was over. And, he reckoned, his involvement would not hurt his résumé.

As the excitement over the assignment intensified, his heartache over Ilse had lessened little by little. A grain of sand at a time. Time was a balm. But the the pain would be revived in an instant when he passed places where they had shared good times. Or if he was reminded of her by someone's laugh, or by someone who resembled her.

It had been six months since she'd last been seen or heard from. There was little hope that she was still alive. Ted was Hank's barometer on that. Certainly if she were alive she would have contacted Ted. He was probably the most important person in her life. She would not have voluntarily just taken off and left him to worry and to wonder. No, thought Hank sadly, the Ilse chapter is over. Time to move on. After Berlin.

The Kennedy visit was what the media called "a cluster-fuck." The American networks were following the president along with media from all over the world. Scores of reporters, producers and technicians were on the assignment following him every step of the way to several German cities before Berlin, then on to Ireland, England, and Rome where a new Pope waited to greet him. He put them all through their paces during the extensive trip.

Hank had a piece of the action, but it was a disappointingly small piece. In Berlin, the president spent a short time at Checkpoint Charlie, and it was Hank's assignment to cover him there. Other Stars and Stripes reporters were stationed elsewhere. As he waited for the President's arrival, Hank couldn't help but remember when he and Tom Morrow were challenged to return to the Western Sector after their visit to East Berlin.

Hank missed out on the President's headline-making event in Berlin. JFK announced to the world, and thousands of cheering Berliners at the Schoeneberg town hall near The Wall, "*Ich bin ein Berliner,*" that he too was a Berliner. Hank heard it later on AFN.

When his part of the workday assignment was over, Hank went to the officer's club to have a drink with his colleagues who had finished their day covering the President. The first person he saw when he entered the chrome, imitation wood, plastic-seat-covered American-style-restaurant-bar that mimicked thousands at home, was Charles Howell. He was sitting with a colleague at a small table near the door. He was nursing a seltzer and lemon and looked as surprised as Hank when their eyes met. He immediately raised his hand and beckoned him with a sweeping wave.

"Of all the gin joints, in all the world" said Howell, "he walks into mine."

"You do a terrible Bogey, said Hank extending his hand. "I was hoping we'd have a chance to say hello."

Howell nodded and introduced Hank to his companion identified only as "a State Department type," who immediately excused himself and left the table, offering his chair to Hank.

"I thought they might send you up for the big visit. Did you see the speech? I never saw such a crowd. He really turned them on."

"No, I got to see him do a walk-by at Checkpoint Charlie. Then, poof, he was gone. My big moment."

The two chit-chatted about the day and made some small talk about what each had been up to during the past months. Not surprisingly, Hank thought, he did most of the talking. They reached that awkward point, as conversations between people who don't know each other well sometimes do, when both men seemed to run out of things to talk about. There were those moments when they just listened to the chatter all around them that was too loud, and to music that was even louder. The noisy ambiance did not encourage conversation.

Hank got it going again when he asked, "I guess you never heard any more about Ilse? Still missing? Still presumed dead?"

Howell's fleshy face hardened. "Yup. Nothing. A great mystery. A pretty girl. Lots going on in her life. Who knows?"

"I'd like to know," said Hank."

"I know. Me too."

Howell looked closely at Hank and changing the subject asked, "How long are you going to stick it out with the Stars and Stripes? I would think you'd be looking around by now."

Hank marveled at how Howell seemed to be one jump ahead most of the time.

"You're something else," he said. "As a matter of fact I've been thinking about just that. I kinda wanted to get this one under my belt before starting with the help wanted pages. But I think it's about time. I want to sign on where there's less..."

"Pressure from the top," interrupted Howell. "Interference."

"This is you saying it, not me," said Hank.

"No, I've heard you say it, suggest it, imply it in the past. I think I told you a while back that this is a difficult time in a difficult place. Reporting here is a challenge because a lot of information has to be kept below sea level. The wrong phrase, the wrong nuance...sharing information that should not be shared can have dramatic consequences. Dangerous consequences even."

"I try to be attentive to that," said Hank. "I don't think I've ever come close to starting a World War."

"You never know," said Howell. "What reporters here learn from contacts can have consequence they couldn't conceive of. A good undercover agent passing as a "trusted" source can have tanks moving and diplomats scrambling."

"Again, we all try to get it right."

Once more Howell took the conversation in a different direction. "Talking to anyone yet about moving on?"

"I have some feelers out to the Baltimore Sun. Hometown paper. We'll see what happens."

"Good paper. But let me give you some advice. If you think there won't be downward pressure from the Sun, or the Times or the Post or any paper you'd be wrong. They don't have Uncle Sam looking over their shoulder worrying about national interests, but they do have advertisers, stockholders, boards and other interested entities who have their own interests. Even readers do. Uncle Sam has the First Amendment to contend with. Ford or Phillip Morris could care less. Just so you know Hank. Just so you know."

"Thanks for the pep talk," said Hank, joking.

"If you like, I'll write you a letter of recommendation."

"Hah," laughed Hank. "I'll bet you'd write it in invisible ink or whatever you guys use."

Howell laughed so hard his entire body shook. "That's a good one. That's very good. But the offer still stands."

"Thanks. I just might take you up on that."

Hank's last story with the Stars and Stripes in Germany was just a few months after the Kennedy visit. Germany, still basking in the afterglow of JFK's short but dramatic stay in June, was stunned, as was the world, with the assassination of the American president in November. Hank wrote about the reaction among the German people who almost universally thought they had not only lost a powerful person committed to supporting their national interest, but also lost a friend.

Hank was personally overwhelmed, and also touched, when he began getting phone calls, and later letters, from Germans he did not know, expressing their condolences over *his* loss. To him it suggested they believed all Americans were treating the loss very personally.

"Remarkable," he wrote, *"that a woman in Freiberg whom I had never met, would take the time to seek out me and my address in order to express her deep sadness not only over the president's death, but for my personal loss. It was the same kind of sentiment one might make expressing condolence over another's loss of a father or mother...husband or wife. That says many things about the late president and his legacy, and about that woman in Freiberg whose tears are the same as mine and yours."*

Less than six months later, Hank Tollar had put Germany and many of its memories behind him, as he signed in at the Baltimore Sun, his hometown paper. He knew he was richer in so many ways for the experience of the past four years, but, he realized with a recurring sadness he could not shake, so much poorer in others.

The Baltimore he returned to was not much different in most ways from the Baltimore he remembered. Its waterfront was dingy and downtown damp with summertime heat and humidity and storms off the Bay. It was steeped in celebrated history with monuments and streets named after famous people. It gave the impression that Baltimore took more pleasure, and placed more significance, in looking back rather than looking ahead.

Downtown was saved by good restaurants that drew people in, and a baseball team that inspired frenzied fans although it had yet to realize the promise that was to come.

The politics was Democratic, the political corruption non-partisan.

The city suffered from de-facto segregation. If one lifted the lid and looked closely, one could see simmering poverty and injustice that seemed just ready to be brought to a boil.

Nonetheless, Hank loved it, loved reporting it, and got better and better at it.

Over the two years after his arrival, Hank's byline was a page one fixture.

His best 1966 stories focused on the rise of a little known politician, Spiro Agnew. He won awards detailing how Agnew, a Republican, had the audacity to file for governor in a state where Democrats were deeply entrenched. A crowded Democratic primary helped change history. Eight men competed, only to split the vote so completely that a rich white racist emerged with a plurality victory, in spite of a dog whistle campaign slogan: A Man's Castle Is His Home – Protect It. It was effective. No one would have heard of Agnew without that candidate or that slogan. He won the general against the racist Democrat, beating the pre-primary odds.

He presided over the riots that followed the assassination of Martin Luther King. The rioting lasted for more than a week, the National Guard sent in troops. Federal troops followed. Six people died. Thousands were arrested. Property damage was enormous.

Agnew responded by berating exhausted black leaders for not doing enough to quell the disturbance. His stance caught the attention of Richard Nixon who tapped Agnew as his 1968 running mate.

Nixon apparently didn't know that Agnew throughout his tenure as governor was taking kickback money from contractors which led to his humiliating resignation as vice president four years later.

CHAPTER 24

"Remind you of Munich?" The familiar voice came from behind him as Hank sat at a bar on the western edge of town, far from the downtown rioting. It was a gathering place for people who worked late, or for those who got up early. With the downtown troubles it had become a hangout for journalists who did both. It was gritty, noisy and beer was inexpensive. Hank recognized the voice before he turned around to face on old friend from the Munich days...Tom Morrow.

"I don't believe it. Tom Morrow." He stood and shook hands. "I don't remember armed military, heavy equipment and dead people in Munich. Just horses and one sorry ass radio reporter who'd had the crap kicked out of him. How the hell are you?"

"Hanging in there. I knew you were in Baltimore but I didn't think I'd find you here."

"The beer was better in Munich. But, all roads lead to Quigley's these days," said Hank. "Sit down and fill me in. You still with that TV station in Florida?"

"Nah, they gave up on me. Or maybe it was the other way around. I'm with ABC now. Field producer. Here for obvious reasons."

"It's a bitch isn't it?"

"Yeah."

"So what's a field producer?"

"The glue that holds the network together," laughed Tom. "No, we set things up for the reporter or the anchor so they can get all the glory. And, I might add, make all the money."

"You sound bitter."

"No, I'll get back on air one of these days."

"Still want to say 'listen tomorrow to Morrow.'"

"No, I want to say 'listen to Morrow today.'"
They both laughed.

"And you?"

"I'm with the Sun...Baltimore Sun. Still trying to learn how to write. Maybe not for long though."

"Oh?"

"I may be going to Vietnam. Paper wants some new blood over there."

"Wow, as if there isn't enough blood already. It's pretty intense over there. Tet, Hue, Da Nang, My Lai. Cronkite crawls up LBJ's ass and he's out. Nothing but victims."

"Yeah, sounds like a vacation doesn't it?"

"Looking forward to it?"

"Like going to the dentist. You don't want to go, but you don't want the teeth to fall out. It's hard to say no. After this week downtown," he joked, "It might not be all that bad."

"Good luck on that."

In between beers, they shared some jokes and memories from their days in Munich and their "close call" in Berlin.

"I still don't know if that VoPo would have shot us," said Tom. "He sure sounded serious."

"I'm glad we didn't find out."

More banter among two old friends, when Tom asked, "Ever learn what happened to that girlfriend of yours?"

"Nope," said Hank, feeling that familiar twinge whenever discussion turned to Ilse. "Puff...like that she was gone."

"Shame. Sorry. What about Ted? What's he up to?"

"Don't know. He came in one day and said something about wanting to smell the roses. He called them posies," laughed Hank. Turning serious, he said, "I think when Ilse disappeared, he just felt a little lost. He, in a way, disappeared too. Smelling those roses somewhere. I hope he's alive and well. I keep hoping to hear from him. He was a good guy. He helped me a lot. I guess he's disappeared into the shadows...his own world."

Tom looked at his watch. "I've got to disappear too. My 'precious' is probably getting his beauty sleep. We've got an early morning spot on Good Morning America." He pulled out his notebook and wrote something.

"Let's stay in touch. Here's my number." He handed it to Hank. Hank grabbed a napkin. "Sorry, my notebook's in the car." He jotted down his number. "Yeah, let's keep in touch."

The day after Richard Nixon and Spiro Agnew were elected, Hank Tollar was on a plane heading for Vietnam.

He arrived in Saigon in the middle of a sweltering morning. He was carrying his sport coat but within ten minutes after arrival, his shirt was sticking to his back. From his own cab he watched other ancient cabs dodging bicycles and pedestrians crowding the dirty streets. The paper's office was in the hotel he'd be calling home. He was grateful for the cool shower even though the water was gray.

He went to the office and introduced himself to a homely Vietnamese secretary, or assistant, or both, who called herself "Your Girl Friday," in a squeaky, heavily accented voice. She was wearing shorts as was a Vietnamese photographer whose name was unpronounceable. He said he answered to the name of Sam. He smiled when he said it, revealing tiny teeth with a distracting gap between the two in front. Remarkably, neither she nor he was sweating. Hank wondered if it were genetic, or whether he could become acclimatized.

He asked about the other reporter assigned to the "bureau." His name was Ross Thomas. Hank was told he was "in the field." He learned later that "in the field" was hyperbole for "in the bar." For while Vietnam was a major story, much of it was written from military handouts that included jargon-filled accounts of distant battles, that more often than not were quick but deadly firefights. They produced the one other staple of the day's news...the daily body count. Actually getting "into the field" with troops could be problematic, requiring an okay from commanders, innumerable forms and a full reservoir of intestinal fortitude.

Thomas proved an amiable and capable sort who was clearly burned out in his assignment. He'd been in Vietnam for almost two years and for the last six months had begged to be relieved. He had hoped that Hank was, in fact, his replacement, but was quickly disabused of that notion by the bosses back in Charm City before Hank's arrival, and confirmed by Hank after he'd arrived.

Thomas took Hank by the hand during the first days, introducing him to military and civilian contacts who all told him how committed they were to getting the "truth" out to the folks back home about what was going on "in country."

"In fact," said Thomas, "they're all skittish as hell since Cronkite came over and gave his version of what's happening here. He burned the commander in chief. When that happens, the President chews out the Defense Secretary, who chews out the Joint Chiefs, who come down on the area commanders. Before you know it, the guy in the foxhole is bleeding because some sergeant is chewing him out. It's an equal opportunity gang bang. Everybody gets a piece.

"The embassy's not much help because the Secretary of State has also gotten chewed out and that same 'shit-flows-down, not-up'-thing happens."

The discussion took place at the American Club, a building that was more like a shack, where an entrepreneurial Vietnamese, who liked to be called Jack, presided. Thomas explained that the Vietnamese who fraternized with Americans took American sounding names. Jack had established a flourishing bar catering to Americans, mostly journalists. It was a fraternal group that, when together, complained a lot and drank even more.

Hank settled in, disappointed that what he expected to be an action-packed war story was, in fact, pretty much a rewrite job. Sometimes during the evenings, he would go to the roof of the hotel and listen to the sound of planes and helicopters. Occasionally, he would hear a distant explosion or see smoke drift toward the sky on the far horizon. It was the soundtrack of war, but for him, not actual war. More like a movie.

That changed abruptly for Hank several weeks after he arrived in Saigon. An up-and-coming singer from Baltimore was in Vietnam to entertain troops. She was performing at several large and small military installations. Her name was Sunny Day and although she was supposed to be quite talented, primed for stardom and the top 40, neither Hank nor Ross had ever heard of her.

Nonetheless Ross, who considered himself the paper's bureau chief in Saigon, told Hank that if he wanted to get out of Saigon so badly and "find the war," he could "do a profile on Miss Day for her fans back home," where she was known in Dundalk as Sylvia Terranova. Better than rewriting handouts thought Hank.

"Sam's going to stay here," said Ross. "Westmoreland's having a news conference to fudge some more body count numbers. An Army photographer will help you up north."

The next day, he was airborne by helicopter to link up with Sunny Day at Nha Trang, an old French base repopulated by Americans. It was located on the South China Sea coast about two hundred and fifty miles from Saigon. The Army brass was happy to provide the helicopter for a story that would be positive and hastily processed the necessary paperwork highlighting indemnification rules in case they stumbled upon the war.

About halfway to Nha Trang, the helicopter began to sputter and cough as the engine was giving all the hallmark signs of acute distress. The worried pilot, a young lieutenant, looked at his crewmate, a sergeant, and then at Hank. "I'm not sure we've got what it takes to get there," he said. His voice was tinny through the old earphones. "This is a sick bird." Hank grabbed his armrests until his knuckles turned white.

The chopper's engine continued to make unwelcome noises as the pilot fought the stick, which, in the resulting vibration, seemed like it wanted to jump from his hand. The crewman frantically pulled a leather case from beneath is seat and yanked a map from it. "We're not in a good place," he said. "The VC likely have some folks on the ground around here."

"I'm going to call for some help, fly her as long as I can, and look for a place to land. Keep that map handy."

Five minutes later, he said, "We're about seventy miles from Nha Trang. We'll never make it. I'm putting her down. Hang on." The helicopter swayed as if it were on a string as the pilot directed it to a clearing that had miraculously appeared. It was a godsend in the heavily forested jungle. The chopper hit the ground hard and bounced. The rotors slowly stopped spinning. Huge trees with thick vines and broad green leaves loomed.

"Okay, they're going to send someone to find us. It'll take a while. Let's just sit tight and hope for the best." He turned to Hank. "You okay Hank?"

"Scared shitless," he answered, shaking visibly. "This was not part of the package." He was sweating profusely.

"Never is," said the pilot. "He turned to his crewman. "Hey Nipsy, make sure that machine gun of yours is ready to go. Just in case someone comes calling."

Hank's fear was elevating. He wanted to cover a war, but he didn't want to be in it. Yet, here he was, in the middle of nowhere, with enemy soldiers possibly in the neighborhood. He took stock. There was a mounted machine gun in the doorway. The pilot and crewmate each had a pistol. He had a ball point pen and a reporter's notebook.

"We're about seventy miles out," said the pilot. "It should take them forty or forty-five minutes or so to reach us."

Hank looked at his watch. Then at the pilot. "Is there enough room for another chopper to land here?" he asked.

"Not much, but doable," said the pilot

lighting a cigarette.

"Lieutenant, I wouldn't smoke if I were you," said the sergeant. "If there are any gooks around here, they might smell it. They've got noses like dogs. It'd draw them right to us."

"You're right. Shit, can't a person relax?" He was smiling at his own joke, but Hank wasn't finding anything humorous in the situation.

Time passed slowly as the three anxiously awaited the sound of a rescue helicopter. All they were hearing so far were unseen insects singing shrill songs as if protesting the presence of intruders. Finally, they could hear the sound of a healthy chopper in the distance. The Lieutenant nodded, and said, "They sent two of them. Hot damn."

"You can hear two?" asked Hank. "Sounds like one to me."

"Ah, you're getting old," said the pilot. "There are two. One's bigger than the other. Trust me."

As they got closer, Hank could hear that he was right. The pitch between the two was different.

As if he could read Hank's thoughts, the lieutenant said, "One's a taxi, the other's a gunship. Just in case."

Just as he finished, static rattled on the radio, and a scratchy voice broke through. "Be there in a minute boys. Looks like you've got some playmates about a hundred yards north. I can see five or six headed your way. Better be ready to move quickly. I'll see if my shotgun can take them out."

"Nipsy, grab the big boy off the mount," barked the lieutenant. "We might need it. And give the Colt to Hank."

As the sergeant reached for his pistol, the pilot asked Hank, "Ever use one of these before?"

"Nope," said Hank, more fearful than ever. "Never."

"Well, just point it at the bad guy and pull the trigger. Nothing to it."

The sound of the approaching helicopters was much louder now, and the downwash from the rotors was making the leaves on the trees dance.

"The VC are just a few yards from you," said the incoming pilot. "I'm going to have my partner up here lay a few rounds on 'em. Be ready to hit the ground running as soon as I'm on the deck."

The sound of gunfire thundered, startling everyone. The men in the helicopter couldn't tell if the firing was on the ground or air-to-ground. Nipsy went immediately to the big machine gun and scanned the wall of growth in front of him. The jungle had gone silent. He saw nothing.

Suddenly the roar of the "taxi" overcame them as they watched the big rescue chopper land, blades flashing, dust and debris flying. "Go," yelled the lieutenant. "Go, go, go!"

More gunfire cut him short. This time it seemed to be at ground level. It was hard to tell as the gunfire competed with the noisy helicopter just a few yards away. The gunship wouldn't be firing so close thought Hank. Too much of a risk they'd hit their own. No, this, he was sure, was coming from the ground. The VC were that close. How many? Had the gunship gotten any of them.

The thoughts flashed through his mind as he jumped from the chopper. There was more gunfire and he could it hear it pinging as it ripped into the fuselage of the aircraft he had just abandoned. He looked back. Nipsy had let loose with a barrage of rounds from the big gun. The pilot hadn't left the helicopter. Hank was the only one on the ground and on the move.

There was another burst of gunfire from the jungle. A scream came from the helicopter behind him. He turned and saw Nipsy drop to a knee. He'd been hit. No sign of the pilot yet. Was he still on the aircraft? He must be thought Hank. There was more gunfire. Hank could sense that the VC were moving in, moving in for the kill.

Suddenly, Hank was on automatic-pilot. He turned back toward the chopper he had just left. He saw Nipsy writhing in pain, one hand on the big gun, the other clutching his side. Hank could see blood seeping through his fingers.

He was at the big door in a few steps. A glance to the right showed the worst. The pilot was still at the controls. His bloody head looked as if it were split in half. Nipsy was groaning in pain. Hank reached up and pulled hard. Nipsy tumbled to the ground yelping in pain. Hank grabbed him by the collar and pulled him hard toward the rescue ship which was parked noisily twenty yards away. It was positioned across twenty yards of open territory where its wheels bounced on the turf as if the chopper were impatient to take off. The spinning rotors churned dirt and loose debris into thick clouds blurring the entire landscape, and stinging Hank's eyes.

Nipsy was a big man and not able to cooperate in moving toward the helicopter. Hank dropped to the ground as more gunfire sounded. This time it seemed to be coming from the nearby helicopter. He saw one of the crewman from that craft jump to the ground and run, crouching, toward him. Nipsy was getting heavy, dead weight, and hard to drag.

Hank felt the impact of the bullet before he heard the single shot. It smashed into his hip...a hard hammer blow that sent him spinning to the ground. "I'm hit," he yelled, holding on to Nipsy's collar. The young sergeant was trying to propel himself by pushing the heels of his boots into the soft ground.

More gunfire. This time it sounded as if it

had come from above. The gunship was back in the fray now that he and Nipsy were far enough away from their helicopter that the one above felt it could engage. And then the shooting stopped.

He felt a heavy hand grab his shirt and pull hard. He looked up to see a huge black Marine pulling him and Nipsy toward the big helicopter. The Marine was sweating hard. As they neared the helicopter, the rotor wash from its broad blades whipped the droplets of sweat from the Marine's face at Hank and Nipsy. The downwash energy, like a gale-force wind, seemed as if it might push the three men backwards.

Another Marine jumped from the aircraft. The black Marine lifted Nipsy like a limp sack toward the open door. The second Marine hoisted Hank to his feet. He howled with pain and felt himself lifted into the shuddering aircraft. He was shoved roughly across its floor. The pain was at its most intense. Nipsy was moaning loudly off to his left. The gunship was firing more rounds into the jungle.

In that near chaotic state, just before he blacked out, Hank heard the pilot holler, "Up, up and away".

If he had been asked how long it had taken from the time he first left his helicopter, he would have said ten minutes. He was told later it had all happened in less than ninety seconds.

He woke up bouncing on a gurney as he was being rolled into the Nha Trang base medical station. His hip was on fire and throbbed with intense pain. He was biting his lip and fighting another wave of unconsciousness. To keep from tearing, he was trying to recall exactly what had happened. He could still taste the dirt and dust circulated by the downwash from the rescue chopper's blades, and could hear men's voices as they wheeled him inside. Then it all went dark again.

He awoke in a clean bed with crisp sheets and could hear voices mumbling out of his sight. He could not make out any of the words, until a man dressed in scrubs and wearing a surgical mask strode to the side of his bed. He nodded at Hank, then studied a row of monitors off to the side of the bed. He turned back to Hank.

"Welcome back," he said. "You've been out for a while."

Hank tried to speak, but his mouth was dry. He pointed to it. The doctor said something he couldn't understand and a moment later a nurse, also masked, brought him a large glass of water. Hank sucked on the glass straw until the water was gone. He raised the glass, gesturing for more.

"You've been out for a couple of hours," said the doctor. "Everything's fine. We had to operate to remove the bullet and repair some bone damage. Everything's okay," he said matter-of-factly. "You'll have trouble walking for a while, but that'll work itself out."

The nurse handed hank a second glass of water and he drank eagerly once again. "What about the sergeant who came in with me?" he finally said.

"He's still in surgery. He took a big hit. We're doing our best with him. He's got a decent chance. Sorry to say, the pilot's still out there from what I've been told. Meantime," he added, "we've got to get you back to Saigon. We just do the emergency patching up here. The fancy stuff's all done in the big facility there. So, we'll get you out of here in a bit. Nurse will sedate you in a few minutes and then you'll be on your way in an hour or two."

As he awaited the nurse, Hank was fighting a tendency to doze off as he had often since he was brought in. He heard a knock on the door, and grunted something that sounded close to "come in." A pretty brunette in a nicely fitted Army jump suit glided into the room. She looked to be in a mild state of shock and nervous uncertainty as she moved toward the bed.

"Hello," she whispered. "I'm Sunny Day." It took a moment for it to register on Hank that Miss Day was the reason he was in this predicament.

"I don't mean to bother you after all you've been through. I just wanted to thank you. I know you were coming here to see me. I just feel awful that this happened to you because of me."

"A man died," he said weakly. "Another's on the operating table right now."

She looked stunned, cupped her face in her hand, and burst into tears. "Oh my God," she gasped. "I feel terrible."

"So do I," said Hank. "Thanks for coming," he added dismissively. She wiped the tears from her cheeks. She looked as if she were going to say something when the nurse came into the room holding a hypodermic needle as if it were a first-place ribbon.

"Time to go nighty night," she said cheerfully. Sunny looked at the nurse, then at Hank, and without saying a word turned and left.

As the nurse rubbed alcohol on his arm before giving him the shot, he wondered why he had been so shitty to the singer, and regretted it. She was nice, and nice looking, he remembered. It wasn't really her fault he and the others had gotten shot up in the jungle.

The best thing about the hospital in Saigon was the availability of books. He was in his bed three days after being flown back from Nha Trang, reading an old favorite, Moby Dick. A shadow wiped across the bed as he read. He looked up and saw a familiar face looking back at him.

"Hello Hank," he said with an uncharacteristic grin.

"Well, I'll be damned. Charles Howell," said Hank, totally taken by surprise at the appearance of the former Munich consular officer. "You're about the last person I expected to see in Saigon. What brings you here?"

"You," said Howell.

"Me?"

"Yeah. Indirectly anyway. I've been attending a...a diplomatic conference in Bangkok."

"So you decided just to drop in?"

"Nipsy Delgado is my nephew."

"Well, I'll be damned," said Hank. "It is a small world after all."

"I flew in to see him and to report back to my sister as to how banged up he is. She's worried."

"Don't blame her. He damn near didn't make it. I haven't seen him yet, but I understand he's here now and out of the woods pretty much."

"A little infection, and a lot of hurt, but he's enjoying the drugs and apparently he's going to be okay." He studied Hank in what he hoped was an expression of gratitude. "He told me what a good guy you were for going back to the helicopter to get him. 'Heroic' he said. Said he would have bought it if you hadn't. The VC would've gotten him if you'd of left him."

"I couldn't do that," said Hank. "I want to go down to see him, but they won't let me move out of this bed. I'm not sure I could if they would."

"We'll I'm grateful. His mother will be too. She was frantic when she heard he'd been wounded. He's an only child. Her husband's dead and she lives in fear of being alone."

"Well, she'll have him back soon. I don't think even the Marines would want to keep him bad as he's been hurt."

Howell nodded. "Thanks again Hank. I owe you one."

The two men stared at each other cagily as if each was trying to read the other's mind.

"Want to pay up now?" asked Hank carefully.

"With?..."

"You know. Ilse."

CHAPTER 25

Howell spoke softly. "I guess it's time," he said. "I'll tell you what I know."

"Ilse?"

"Ilse," nodded Howell. "But here's where it stays. There's so much of this in a locked file, we'd both be done for if it ever got out. No newspaper story, no book, no movie, no barroom chit chat. You'll hear it and forget it. Right?"

"Well, I'll hear it, but I doubt I'll forget it." He held up his hand showing three extended fingers. "Boy Scout's honor on the rest of it."

Howell pulled over a chair, took a deep breath and cleared his throat. "Here's what I know. I'm pretty sure Ilse's alive. In fact, knowing her I'd bet on it. I don't know where she is, and it's been quite a while since I last heard about her. But she was alive when I did."

"Whew. That's a lot better than I'd ever dreamed possible," said Hank. He was almost dizzy with relief. "Why did she disappear?"

"She was in serious danger," continued Howell. "She was targeted for elimination. She didn't want to go. I ordered her out."

"Because?"

"They were closing in on her."

"Who? Those French crazies?" asked Hank. "They were being rounded up right and left thanks to LeClerc. They were running. I can't believe they'd stop long enough to be a threat or hurt her."

"Not the French," said Howell, pausing dramatically. "The Czechs." Howell let that sink in.

Hank was bewildered, trying to comprehend. Eventually, he responded. "Now I am confused. The Czechs?"

"She was working for me," said Howell, "and she was in deep on a secret project.

"She came to me at one point to tell me that Czech agents...apparently the StB...who else...contacted her in Munich out of the blue and 'reminded' her that her father was still in Czechoslovakia. Ultimately, the father contacted her begging her to help, no doubt at their direction. He told her he was threatened with prison and hard labor unless she provided what they wanted. That was for Ilse to provide the names of Czech RFE employees with families still in Czechoslovakia. Apparently they wanted to use them...coerce them...by threatening harm to their families back home."

"So they could apply the same kind of pressure on them they were using against her."

"Right."

"How would they use them? What could the Czech workers in Munich do that would be useful to the StB?"

"It's a powerful tool to have assets in the other fellow's camp.

"Think about it. Sabotage. Deadly mischief...like putting poison in the salt shakers. That's already been tried, and failed, a few years ago. They're obsessed with undermining the RFE mission. I'm sure there's no shortage of ideas. Prague and other East Bloc governments hate and fear RFE. It exposes everything they do. Truth is a powerful message against the bullshit thrown around in the authoritarian world. They want to stop it. As I say, the StB crowd is very tough, violent, dedicated, and would have no qualms...no moral sense at all...about doing anything to silence the broadcasts, or about coercing Czech refugees to serve any of their interests.

"We had Ilse provide a few names. We wanted to get some idea of what they had in mind. At first, they were able to strong-arm a few journalists to bend some of the news they were broadcasting in a more favorable way either by omission or commission. Eventually they hoped to do the same thing with exiles on the other desks. At least that was the story."

"That's kind of fruitless, isn't it?" asked Hank. "They have editors and overseers and other colleagues who would catch on. How much could they actually slant the news? And, to what effect in the big picture? Seems like a lot of work for limited results to me."

"Correct. That was just a preliminary round. Minor stuff. They wanted to find out who would be susceptible to pressure. Who could be manipulated most easily? These are clever and patient puppeteers. Everyone knows the Kremlin most certainly already has some of their own firmly entrenched inside the operation from countries RFE broadcasts to. They wanted to keep them in place, and recruit just the Czechs on the priority mission...most likely a suicide mission."

"And, what is that mission?"

"To blow the fucking place up. The whole place."

"Holy crap," blurted Hank. "Jesus H. Christ. A little more effective than writing slanted news stories."

"I'm pretty sure that part of it was bogus. They were just trolling for the most vulnerable employees. Ones they could use on a big, big project."

"But, if they already had people on the inside, couldn't they just use them? Why so much emphasis on the Czechs and new blood?" asked

Hank, perplexed.

"Because they had Ilse's father. And that meant they had Ilse. She was the conduit. Work with what you have, right? They're not dumb. Half the job was done. And, nobody over there much likes the Czechs very much anyway for reasons going back to the war. Also, the folks already in the fold...those on the inside...are fifth column types they can ultimately use elsewhere. When RFE was nothing but a smoking hole in the ground, they'd no doubt be given other positions in other agencies where they could be useful. Why waste them? Some of them could wind up in the State Department for instance. Or even the Pentagon. Anywhere. They'd already been vetted. As far anyone would be concerned, they were loyal...proven converts to democracy, supposedly eager to turn on their homelands and the forces that now ruled them."

"No wonder they're so good at chess," said Hank.

"So Ilse was in the middle of the whole show for us. Everything from them came through her. Everything to them came from her...and us. We fed them a lot of bullshit."

"Why was she targeted. Did they find out about her role? If so, how?"

"It was all ready to go, when suddenly she decided to freelance and go off the range to Paris on the LeClerc thing. I don't know what the hell got into her with all that. It just about blew the whole thing. She got back just in time to give the StB the green light for the attack on RFE. They were going to do it at night when the building was empty.

"She got the go sign the day she got back, and the big show was on. She waved them in. We moved on the team they sent over. A dozen of them with enough explosives to blow RFE into oblivion along with half of Munich."

"And then?"

"We knew the other side would put two and two together and figure out that Ilse had played them, and was wearing our jersey. That was like a death sentence. No question."

"I don't get it. She was born in Sudeten-land...German Czechoslovakia...lived in Germany...was a Francophile and didn't give a damn about her father."

"Ilse, as I came to know her," said Howell, "was a young woman of intense passion and principle.

"She had great loyalty to people and things she felt strongly about. I think that at some level she did worry about her father and wanted to protect him, or at least felt she should.

"She was outraged over the bombing that killed Manon and the girl, and felt an obligation to avenge their deaths. Remember, she was brilliant in finding LeClerc. That tells you how effective she could be.

"And, she was loyal to RFE and all her friends there. And, that meant she was loyal to us because of...what shall I call it...our stewardship and guidance?"

"Hah, best kept secret in town, right?" They both chuckled.

"But," said Hank, "I'm not so sure about the loyalty...for personal reasons."

"Hank, let me tell you something. The reason she brushed you off at the end was because of her loyalty...feelings...for you. She knew she was in a compromised position with the Czechs. She wanted as much distance between them and you as she could muster. For your safety. She didn't want to put you in danger. I think that's a very important indication of loyalty. Even love maybe."

Hank shifted in his bed and winced with pain, physical and emotional. He asked himself, was that the answer to the big question...to Ilse's backing off? Had there been feelings there, languishing in the shadows of the life she had chosen in which she had conflicting, heartrending priorities?

"You got her out, you said. How?"

"Do you remember Dupuis with the French Consulate? He was part of those meetings...that working group...trying to pin down who was behind the bombings."

"I vaguely do...yes."

"He was my counterpart on the French side. They were very happy with the gift basket she, Ted and that priest brought to Paris. The day after we rounded up the Czech hit team, a car with two men in it showed up outside Ilse's place. She was with us at the time, but we'd had her place under surveillance just in case something like that happened. We picked up the two guys after they'd sat there for a full day. They didn't admit anything, but they were killers and were armed to the teeth with the tools of an assassin's trade.

"When I explained her predicament, to Dupuis, he agreed to get her out of Munich. Safe passage through France. Where that led, I have no idea. Anyway, true to his word he got her out quickly through France."

"Did she resist the idea?"

"Yes. And no."

"Details?"

"I think she was thinking of you. And of Ted, and how much danger she could put you both in. But, I'm guessing. When we told her we were going to pull her out, she almost collapsed. She asked to be left alone and took an hour to decide.

"Let me remind you, she's still in danger. Even now. The StB has a good memory. They'd snuff her out in a heartbeat. They know she's disappeared, but they also know they didn't make that happen. I doubt they think the French whackos got to her. If she popped up on their radar, she'd be a goner. They've probably been watching you to see if one day you might lead them to her.

"You might remember I was suggesting to you after she disappeared," he said using air quotes, "that that it might be time to take the next step in your career, move on from the Stars and Stripes. I didn't want you around looking for Ilse. For her sake, and yours."

"You're a devious son-of-a-bitch," said Hank, remembering that conversation. "What about Ted. Where does he fit in?"

"Ted's was always a loner except when it comes to Ilse. He was committed to her, partly because of a promise he'd made to her mother years ago to help her daughter and protect her. Ted lives in the shade. He's caught in the shade between the darkness of his own past...and Ilse's light."

"Is he with her?"

"I have no idea."

Hank leaned back as far as he could and stared at the ceiling. "Would you tell me if you knew where she is?"

"No. You'd run right to her if I did, wouldn't you?"

"Hah, you bet. In a New York minute."

"For all I know, she's married with a bunch of kids."

"Where is Dupuis? Maybe he'll tell me."

"Not likely. He's dead."

Hank winced.

"He was assassinated here two years ago. You know the Vietnamese don't have a whole lot of love for the French. He was stabbed to death in a bar by some fanatic who had lost a brother at Dien Bien Phu."

"Sad. Lots of darkness to this story.

"What about the people at RFE? The infiltrators from the East? Were you able to identify them?" asked Hank.

"It's a constant worry. We have some. Maybe missed some others. We're very alert to the threat they represent.

"We did learn from one of the group on the bombing mission that Ilse's father is long gone. He died years ago. So whoever contacted Ilse saying he was the daddy was bogus. She couldn't know. She barely knew him and their contact was mainly by letter.

"Some of the agents in the East had eyes inside RFE when Ilse was there. They knew she was being worked and kept tabs on her. We didn't know that, of course, but that shows how much danger she was in...and how good she was. I'm guessing her relationship with you made them nervous. She played it perfectly. They never caught on she was working for us until the very end."

"What a gal," said Hank. "Tough. Fearless. Damn, I wish I could tell her how much I admire her for what she's done." He sat silently reflecting on the woman he had come to more than admire.

Finally, resigned, he said, "Looks like that's the end of the story as far as Ilse is concerned," he said sadly. "Too bad. I really fell hard for her."

"And, my guess is she did for you."

"But gave me up to save me."

"Something like that."

"It's like the GI here who said they had to burn down the village to save it."

"Right."

"But the village was still destroyed."

They both thought about that for a minute. Hank gave Howell a pallid smile. "Thanks Charles for telling me. It may help me sleep a little better. Or, maybe not. She's still out there."

"I hope you can sleep better. She made a choice. If I were you I'd respect it for what it is."

"I hear you Charles, but it hurts. It still hurts. Time doesn't always heal"

"I get it. And, I hope you're on the mend and feeling better soon. What's the plan now?"

"Back to Baltimore to recuperate. Rehab and all of that. Then, we'll see. They tell me I'll have a little hitch to my giddy-up in the walking department, but I can deal with that."

Howell stood. "I wish you the best. You get a gold star in my book for pulling Nipsy out of that chopper. He's got a lovely lady waiting. Get down to see him when you can. He wants to thank you personally."

"I will," promised Hank. "I definitely will."

It was four days before Hank could get to Nipsy. They had a short but emotional conversation, saying all the things that might be expected of two men who had survived a dangerous situation and in which one felt he owed his life to the other.

Nipsy fought back tears when he discussed the lieutenant, the pilot, his friend who had been shot dead before he even had a chance to get out of his crippled helicopter.

The conversation included promises of a life-long friendship and frequent get-togethers, but they were promises they both knew probably would not be kept.

"I had a nice visit the other day," said Nipsy toward the end of their conversation. "Sunny Day dropped by. She was all teary about the whole thing in the jungle being because of her. She promised to take me out to dinner back in the states. She's a babe. I'm all for that."

"So, maybe some good comes out of a bad day," laughed Hank. "Good luck with that."

A nurse was checking her watch and approached Nipsy's bed, politely asking Hank to leave. "He needs his rest. You'd best be moving on," she said in a musical southern accent. But to Hank, it felt like she might have been saying to him, "It's time to get on with the rest of your life."

EPILOGUE

In November of 1970, Hank had been back in Baltimore for six months, and back at the paper for three. His rehab had not gone the way he had hoped. He walked with a more pronounced limp than he had bargained for and as a result felt he had been put on the shelf by the paper. He had been relegated to desk duty while therapies continued, having been designated not ready "for the street" until he was able to maneuver more easily. He was not happy as a copy editor and was impatient to get back to what he loved most, reporting.

He had been thrust back into a previous life three days earlier when the news broke that French President Charles de Gaulle had died peacefully at his country home at Colombey-les-Deux-Églises. It triggered memories of those days in the early sixties when the Secret Army Organization and affiliated fascist organizations were attempting to bring down de Gaulle's Fifth Republic and restore French rule over Algeria. He had died peacefully in his bed years after the anti-

Gaullist movement had all but splintered into non-existence.

De Gaulle's death, and his spectacular funeral on the following November Thursday brought those days in Munich, and of course Ilse, into sharp focus for Hank as he watched television coverage of the event. The world's political and diplomatic glitterati were there, along with tens of thousands of mourners from every walk of life, all crowded into the tiny French village.

The memories depressed him. Hank broke away from watching to clear the wires filled with detailed accounts of the event, the day's biggest news story. The AP and UPI wirephoto machines were cranking out dozens of images of the funeral activities at Colombey.

Because he had nothing else to do, and because everyone else seemed to be transfixed by the television images from France, Hank took it upon himself to clear the wirephoto machines. He peeled several yards of the streaming ribbon of images and cut them into single photographs.

Their quality was not high. Images transmitted by wire tended to be grainy. One photo, however, caught Hank's eye. It was a crowd of mourners jammed ten deep along the funeral procession route. Hank was startled by one photo. It gave him a sudden surge of excitement and curiosity. He abandoned his effort to clear the wire machines, took the single photo to his desk and stared at it until his eyes burned.

There, emerging from the throng, was what seemed to be a familiar face. It was of a young woman grieving the late president. Could it be? He went to a colleague's desk and borrowed a magnifying glass. It was not much help. It only made the photo more grainy.

The woman bore what to him was a re-markable and unmistakable resemblance to Il-se...his Ilse. Or was it? The closer he looked the more uncertain he was. Then, a moment later, certainty. Back and forth it went. His pulse leap in his chest as he studied the indistinct image.

Almost unnoticed, until it was, was the partial profile of a man standing next to the woman. Not all of his face was visible, but what he could see reminded him of Ted. Ilse's protector. The same nose and jawline. And, the man's size relative to the woman next to him would be the same as the tall Hungarian. And, thought Hank, if he were alive and anywhere, Ted would be close to Ilse. Were his eyes playing tricks trying to get him to see what he wanted to see rather than what was actually there?

Hank had to turn away from scrutinizing the photo from time to time, then turn back to see if the image might magically have come into sharper focus. Of course, it did not. But he re-mained fixed on the woman. It could be Ilse. It could also not be. He could not be sure if it was

Ilse, nor be sure it wasn't.

If only she were smiling he thought, then he would know for certain. If only he could see that woman in the photo smile. That would decide it. For what did remain in sharp focus, even after nearly a decade, was the clearest memory of all. No one had a smile like Ilse's. No one.

But, people don't smile at funerals.

It is written that there are none so
blind as those who will not see.
It is also written that love is blind.
What does that mean then when one is in love?

ABOUT THE AUTHOR

Don Marsh

Don Marsh is recently retired from an a 60 year, award winning career in broadcast journalism. After publishing three non-fiction titles earlier in his career, he turned to fiction at the age of 80 and now has four published titles.

He holds an honorary degree from the University of Missouri-St. Louis and resides in St. Louis with his wife, Julie.

Also by Don Marsh

Secrets
The Damned and the Doomed
A Wink and a Nod
(Non-Fiction)
Coming of Age: Liver Spots & All

How to be Rude Politely
Flash Frames: Journey of a Journeyman Journalist

Made in the USA
Monee, IL
31 January 2022